DANA'S VALLEY

Books by Janette Oke

Another Homecoming* / Tomorrow's Dream*
Celebrating the Inner Beauty of Woman
Dana's Valley†
Janette Oke's Reflections on the Christmas Story
The Matchmakers
Nana's Gift
The Red Geranium
Return to Harmony*

CANADIAN WEST

When Calls the Heart   When Breaks the Dawn
When Comes the Spring   When Hope Springs New
Beyond the Gathering Storm

LOVE COMES SOFTLY

Love Comes Softly   Love's Unending Legacy
Love's Enduring Promise   Love's Unfolding Dream
Love's Long Journey   Love Takes Wing
Love's Abiding Joy   Love Finds a Home

A PRAIRIE LEGACY

The Tender Years   A Quiet Strength
A Searching Heart   Like Gold Refined

SEASONS OF THE HEART

Once Upon a Summer   Winter Is Not Forever
The Winds of Autumn   Spring's Gentle Promise

SONG OF ACADIA

The Meeting Place*   The Sacred Shore*
The Birthright*

WOMEN OF THE WEST

The Calling of Emily Evans   A Bride for Donnigan
Julia's Last Hope   Heart of the Wilderness
Roses for Mama   Too Long a Stranger
A Woman Named Damaris   The Bluebird and the Sparrow
They Called Her Mrs. Doc   A Gown of Spanish Lace
The Measure of a Heart   Drums of Change

Janette Oke: A Heart for the Prairie
Biography of Janette Oke by Laurel Oke Logan

*with T. Davis Bunn   †with Laurel Oke Logan   01B

JANETTE OKE
LAUREL OKE LOGAN

DANA'S VALLEY

BETHANYHOUSE
MINNEAPOLIS, MINNESOTA

Dana's Valley
Copyright © 2001
Janette Oke & Laurel Oke Logan

Cover design by Lookout Design Group, Inc.

Published by Bethany House Publishers
A Ministry of Bethany Fellowship International
11400 Hampshire Avenue South
Bloomington, Minnesota 55438
www.bethanyhouse.com

Printed in the United States of America by
Bethany Press International, Bloomington, Minnesota 55438

ISBN 0-7642-2451-4 (Paperback)
ISBN 0-7642-2514-6 (Hard cover)
ISBN 0-7642-2516-2 (Large Print)
ISBN 0-7642-2515-4 (Audio Book)

Library of Congress Cataloging-in-Publication Data

Oke, Janette, 1935-
  Dana's valley / by Janette Oke & Laurel Oke Logan.
    p. cm.
  ISBN 0-7642-2514-6 (alk. paper) — ISBN 0-7642-2451-4
(pbk.)
    1. Sick—Family relationships—Fiction. 2. Teenage girls—Fiction.
I. Logan, Laurel Oke. II. Title.
PR9199.3.038 D36   2001
813'.43—dc21   00-013253

Dedicated
with love
to Edward and Marvin,
who have been both supportive and encouraging,
not only in regard to our writing
but in every area of our lives.
We love you both.

JANETTE OKE was born in Champion, Alberta, during the depression years, to a Canadian prairie farmer and his wife. She is a graduate of Mountain View Bible College in Didsbury, Alberta, where she met her husband, Edward. They were married in May of 1957 and went on to pastor churches in Indiana as well as Calgary and Edmonton, Canada.

The Okes have three sons and one daughter and are enjoying the addition of grandchildren to the family. Edward and Janette have both been active in their local church, serving in various capacities as Sunday school teachers and board members. They make their home near Calgary, Alberta.

LAUREL OKE LOGAN, daughter of Janette and Edward Oke, is the author of the bestselling *Janette Oke: A Heart for the Prairie* and *In the Quiet of This Moment*. Laurel, her husband, Marvin, and their four children live in Carmel, Indiana.

PROLOGUE

I SLIPPED THE BUTTERFLY BOOKMARK between the pages of the journal and gazed out the window of my bedroom. I had been determined to keep any tears in check, but the familiar handwriting and the long-ago memories filled up my heart and tugged at my emotions, and I wiped at my damp cheek. It was more nostalgia than pain, though, that evoked my deep feelings. I guess I was rather surprised when I realized that fact. Then came sweet relief, and I felt myself smile as I picked up the book to continue my perusal. But I didn't resume reading immediately. I sat staring at the small volume in my hands, musing silently. The journal's story was not mine—but it was so intricately involved with my own personal journey that the words on the page seemed like my own.

Perhaps it is only when we are deemed adults that we really begin to understand, to appreciate, to evaluate our formative years. I think it has certainly been so for me. Looking back, I feel I am beginning to put some events from those years into a broader context. I am discovering the roots of the values I hold dear. Those mental images of childhood I have now been able to frame and arrange in some kind of order so I can step back and look at how

I have been shaped into who I am. My understanding of life, of its joys and struggles, of family and of relationships, of how they mold and stretch us beyond who we might have been on our own, takes on new significance.

I know no family is perfect. But I also know that my average midwestern Christian family tackled the changes and trials we faced remarkably well, all things considered. Our parents must have started us out with a pretty solid base—or our story might have had an entirely different ending. We are closer to one another now than we have ever been.

My understanding of my heavenly Father—who He is, how He loves us—has been changed as well. This fuller view of God can only happen when one has faced challenges and trials, when one has been stretched beyond what is secure and comfortable. God is now more real, more present, more involved, in every part of my life. As my grandmother shared recently with me over a cup of tea, that is indeed the goal of our journey here on earth.

But perhaps you will understand more fully what I am attempting to say if I tell our family's story. To do that, I must take you back some years. . . .

CHAPTER ONE

BY OUTWARD APPEARANCE you could have thought that the small stuccoed Cape Cod tucked in among the still-barren trees at 129 Maple Street was empty and silent. You would have been wrong. And only in the dusk of the early morning hours could such a mistaken impression have been possible. We were a family of six, with kids ranging in ages from four to fourteen, and our home was seldom quiet. Even this early, there had been stirrings for a couple of hours—more or less—and my mother, who hummed as she moved about the kitchen preparing another in an endless procession of meals, was soon to make sure the activity would increase.

"Brett. Girls. Time to be up."

The call drifted up the stairs along with the aroma of freshly brewed coffee and frying bacon. Newly awakened from slumber, I sniffed to sort out the beckoning smells. Even coffee smelled good when it wafted in on the morning air. I'd tasted it once and found that the fragrance was deceiving. No wonder ten-year-olds were normally denied the privilege. To my thinking, it didn't taste nearly as good as it smelled. But bacon—that was something else. It also was an unexpected treat on a school morning.

"Dana and Erin." This time the volume was turned up a notch.

I opened an eye and sneaked a peek at my sister to see if she was stirring. Light was beginning to filter through the blinds, and I could just distinguish her face above the motionless lump of pink comforter on her bed. We had always engaged in a contest of wills to see who would move first.

Dana still had not opened her eyes, but she did mumble, "It's your turn to practice first."

"I practiced first last time," I argued. I was now awake and, with the vigor of the younger sister, ready to fight for my rights.

"No, you didn't."

"Did too."

"No, you didn't—just ask Mom." Dana's eyes were open now. Wide open and looking directly at me.

Even though her expression held no malice, I knew she had no intention of backing down. She tossed back the faded Barbie quilt and reached her foot to the cranberry-and-mint rug beside her bed, feeling around for her slippers and catching the edge with her bare toes. We'd chosen the matching bedroom set three years back when Dana was eight and I was seven. Now we both looked forward to the promised decorating updates somewhere in the near future.

I was about to launch another objection when I remembered. Dana was right. She had taken her turn first at the family's secondhand upright piano the day before. I let the matter drop. There would be no point in asking

Mom. She remembered such things only too well. She would side with Dana.

I tossed back my own Barbie quilt, jumped out, and spent a moment scrambling around under my bed for my own slippers. I still didn't want to admit that Dana had been right all along—but I knew better than to continue an argument I could only lose.

The school bus would be coming in just over an hour and a half. Our morning chores and piano practice had to be done before bus time. If things ran a little behind— for one reason or another—the second person to sit at the piano for a romp through the scales and exercises would be lucky enough to have a shortened practice time. We had made that discovery on our own during the first year we were both taking lessons, and each of us had tried to use it to her own advantage. But Mom hadn't missed our discovery either. She quickly put an end to the manipulations by declaring we would take turns being first. And that meant the first person to practice had to put in her full half hour.

Dana was already pulling out dresser drawers, deciding what she was going to wear for the day, when I turned from making my bed. "You're full of lumps," she said after glancing my way.

I looked down. My pj's were rumpled a bit but hardly "full of lumps."

"Not you, silly—your bed," Dana responded in answer to my frown.

I looked from Dana to my bed, then could see for myself what Dana was talking about. The bed did have some lumps. I looked down at my pj's again, and then we both started to giggle. I shrugged, quite willing to leave the offending spread as it was. I had obeyed the rule of our home that beds must be made before we left our rooms. And mine was made. That was good enough.

But Dana came over and threw back the covers. Beginning with the sheet, she straightened it carefully, smoothing it with her hand as she pulled it up. Then she flipped up the quilt, tugging here and tucking there, and the bed was done. Now it was as smooth as though no one had slept in it. A perfect match for Dana's own on the other side of the room.

I shrugged again and made some mental excuses for myself. After all, Dana was older. She should know how to make a bed better. But I knew that wasn't a very good excuse. There was only fourteen months' difference in our ages. Fourteen months. I was used to people making remarks about our "closeness." Though I still couldn't really understand why this fact should be of importance to anyone else. I liked the way our family was. It seemed just right and not at all something to be considered unusual or even special.

I had heard Mom tell the story over the years, always with a bit of a twinkle in her eye, that this was one time when Daddy's plans hadn't quite worked out as he'd expected. At his prompting, they—"they" being my father, David Walsh, or Dave as he was usually called, and my mom, Angela—had mapped everything out carefully, thinking that once they decided they could begin their family, two to three years was a good spread between siblings.

Brett had followed their plan. He had arrived at precisely the designated time, which was a couple of years after Daddy had finished his training in accounting and investments and settled into his first real job. Mom had turned in her notice at the local phone company office a few months before Brett was due and hadn't gone back to work since. I've gotten the impression in hearing her talk about those days that she wasn't crazy about filing and typing anyway.

Just as predetermined, Dana arrived three years later—almost to the day. Mom and Dad's plans were working out just fine. A boy—then a girl—three years apart.

Apparently, they still hadn't made up their minds about adding to the family. Mom was busy with a baby and an active three-year-old, and Daddy was building up a list of clients at work. Besides, the family already seemed just right. That's when they got their little surprise. Another baby was on the way. And this one would arrive far short of the two- or three-year spread that previously had worked out well.

However, by the time I made my appearance, it seems they had pretty much accepted the reality. Mom always looked happy when she told this part of the story. She would shrug matter-of-factly, smile serenely, and admit that God knew far better than they what the family had needed. Dana had a little sister to mother, and being close together in age, we quickly became good buds as well. Mom maintained that, looking back, she wouldn't have had it any other way. That sounded fine to me.

For several years they felt the family was complete. And certainly there was not the slightest feeling among Brett, Dana, and I that there was any need for change. But God had another surprise. At least that's the way Mom described it. They named this next surprise Corey. He tagged along, six years younger than I. And Mom never missed a beat. If you hadn't known her well, you almost might have suspected she'd planned things that way all along.

The first time she laid eyes on Corey from her pros-
trate position in the delivery room, Dad said her face
fairly glowed with joy, with a sense of completeness that
accompanied the arrival of this baby boy. And I think her
attitude was infectious. I'll never forget the moment I
peeked into the little bassinet where he was sleeping next
to Mom's hospital bed. His face was awfully red and wrinkled, but his hands—his darling, tiny hands—opened and
closed even in his sleep. And when I reached down to
gently touch the soft fingers, they closed around my own.
I think I've been captivated by the wonder of Corey ever
since.

I had begun kindergarten before anyone knew of
Corey's coming, and I think Mom had been somewhat at
loose ends and lonely at home. Now she claimed Corey
was her "bonus baby." She often said she was so blessed
to have another little person to treasure and discover.
And none of us had felt any the less loved. After all, he
was our baby too. If Mom wanted to spend her days de-
lighting in the baby's warmth and smell and love, we were
glad simply to share as much of the experience as our
school schedules would allow.

I've heard people say that Mom is a bubbly, upbeat
person by nature. I never really thought about it much—
but even I was aware that the new baby seemed to bring
out a renewed enthusiasm in her. She laughed a lot,
teased more, and even drew Daddy, with his more
serious-minded nature, into the silliness that we all
shared as we enjoyed Corey. He soon became our little
playmate, and with his energy and wide-eyed wonder at
the world, he made a good one. In fact, Corey added new
life and enjoyment to the entire household. I guess we all
adored him. And, of course, he knew nearly from the

start that he was the center of attention.

Dana and I were still dressing when Mom's voice called again, in singsong fashion, "Breakfast. Everyone up?"

Dana answered for us. "Coming" was all she said as she pulled on some new cream-colored pants and a matching sweater. I had settled for my favorite jeans with a comfy knit top.

"Brett? Are you up?"

We heard a faint mumble from behind Brett's closed door across the hall. His words couldn't be understood, but it usually took him a little while to get his motor running. That was Mom's description of Brett in the morning.

We left our room just as Brett struggled out of his door, still tucking in his shirt. It was easy to tell he hadn't been up for long. I thought for one zany moment that Dana might cross over and give him a hand with the tucking, but instead she just smiled and said good-morning. Brett mumbled again.

His hair was all rumpled, his eyes still looked half closed, and he was even yawning. He looked disheveled and funny, as though longing to turn around and bolt for his bed. I wanted to giggle again.

Corey was already downstairs. I could hear him chatting but didn't know if it was Mom or Daddy whom he was following around, spouting off about whatever it was that had captured his four-year-old curiosity and had him so excited this time. Corey always sounded excited. It was probably this general gusto that drew Corey out of bed before any of the rest of us on most mornings—even before Mom and Daddy. But he liked company, so he usually wasn't alone for long. He made sure of that.

He and Brett shared a room. But Brett, a teenager,

liked to sleep as long as possible and wasn't very good company in the mornings. Corey had long since accepted that fact, so he would leave their room and look for someone else. Sometimes, if our folks were unresponsive, he would come to our room. He'd beg for a story or try to talk us into a game. Dana was very patient. I wasn't much more excited than Brett about mornings. But I really didn't mind too much when Corey interrupted my sleep. He was still pretty cute, and he always made us laugh at the funny things he said.

When we were all assembled around the breakfast table and Brett, whose turn it was to pray, had wakened enough to say a sensible grace, the morning seemed to pick up speed. Mom sat for only a moment or two before popping up again to get something she'd forgotten. Daddy checked homework assignments, spending the usual extra time with Brett. I listened, feeling almost dizzy hearing the two of them talk about certain things that Brett was required to learn in school. It made me appreciate the fact that I was still in fifth grade. My teachers said I was a good student—and maybe I was. Anyway, most of the assignments were easy for me.

"Hey, Sissy, see what I can do." Corey was perfecting a balancing act with his spoon teetering on the edge of his orange juice glass. He tried every morning, but it usually ended with another wet spot on the table.

"Honey, just eat, please." Mom was amazingly patient. There wasn't even an edge to her voice. Corey put the spoon down beside his plate and grinned in response.

"Daddy, my music teacher says I'll need a new book soon," Dana was saying. "I can buy one from her, or we can go down to the music store ourselves. Can we go down to the store, please? I want to look at other books too." I was sure Dana already knew what the answer would be. Daddy always carefully budgeted for our music lessons, as with every family expenditure, and he wasn't likely to spend more on a whim of Dana's. But I waited for his response anyway. If he said yes, it might mean that this was an opportune moment to ask again about new tennis shoes.

He looked up, winked across the table at Mom, then smiled toward Dana. "You've almost finished another book? I'm proud of you. You're working very hard. But I think we'd better wait on shopping for extra books right now. You've got a birthday coming up, remember?"

Dana smiled back, not quite concealing her disappointment.

"And what about you, Erin?" Daddy went on. "Are you ready for a new book too?"

Suddenly I was sorry I had taken an interest in their conversation. I'd already finished eating and easily could have been excused from the table and seated at the piano by now if I hadn't hung back to see how Daddy would answer Dana.

"No, not yet." I dipped my head just a bit so he couldn't read my eyes. The fact was, I was only about halfway through my book, and I hadn't done too great a job on the first half either. I didn't care much for piano.

"Maybe if you didn't sit and read those mystery stories while you're practicing . . ." Brett let the sentence dangle accusingly and slid out from behind the table to head for the corner trash bin. It was his job to gather the garbage for the weekly collection.

Mom looked up at me and frowned. "Oh, Erin, you're not trying to read again while you're practicing, are you? I thought we agreed that you weren't going to do that anymore."

I would've liked to stick out my tongue at Brett, but he had his back to me. Anyway, there was a good chance I would be reprimanded for that too, and both parents were already frowning at me. Instead, I scowled in Brett's direction and turned back to face Mom. "I only did it once since you told me to stop—yesterday was the only time—and that was because I wanted to know how the chapter ended before school. It was only a couple pages, anyway. Marcy always asks me how far I got, and I never get as much time to read as she does. I hate it when she's always ahead."

Daddy didn't seem impressed. "Well, Erin, don't let it happen again—no matter how far ahead Marcy gets. We're paying for those lessons, and we want you to be serious about practicing. If I see you doing it again, there *will* be consequences. And I'll be checking up on you. Understand?"

"Yes, Daddy."

I dragged myself to the piano stool and managed to make my fingers stumble through the scales and simple songs. My hands always felt stiff and resisting, much better suited to holding a basketball or swinging a bat. Dana, though having taken piano only one year longer than I, could already play complicated pieces that truly sounded like music. I wasn't convinced I would ever be able to achieve that kind of skill. But if Daddy said to practice, I would practice. I adored my father. I hated to disappoint him, even if at times I did feel his discipline was a bit rigid and he hadn't taken quite enough time to let me properly explain my point of view about a situation.

Once all of the morning routine was complete, the

walk to the corner to catch the school bus was almost pleasant. Brett always dashed on ahead. I guess by the time we were sent out the door, Brett had finally gotten his motor running—or something—for he was able to sprint down the street, his gangly long legs making fast work of the concrete sidewalk. If he got to the bus stop a little early, he had time to shoot a few baskets in Sanders' driveway while he waited.

Dana and I followed more slowly. We always joined up with Marcy and her sister Carli two doors down from our house. We'd been walking to catch the bus together ever since we'd moved to our cozy little house on Maple Street back when I was in first grade.

Everyone said our community was a jumping-off spot for families on the way up. "Starter Homes" was how the real estate companies had described the area, so there seemed to be ample reason for families to move in and then to move on, to a fancier, upscale suburb. I was glad my own family had chosen to settle. I liked the way the town kind of tucked itself in between the hills. It was small enough to feel cozy and friendly, but large enough so we could go to a movie once in a while and out to McDonald's afterward. I liked our neighborhood. Our friends. Our church. Even our school, though I didn't often admit that fact publicly. I saw no reason to move on—anywhere—and felt relieved when Daddy seemed quick to agree. He would quote the Bible verse about how it was better to eat a bowl of vegetables where there was peace than a fatted calf with strife. According to his way of thinking, it was more important to work on building a happy home than a particularly prosperous or impressive-looking one. I knew from overhearing a few conversations that he'd had opportunities to relocate for a better job, but he'd chosen to stay put, even though neighbors, coming and going, often boasted about the advances and promotions they were receiving.

As I grew older, on more than one occasion I had been struck by how difficult Daddy's approach to life seemed to be for our grandpa Walsh to understand. I enjoyed eavesdropping on adults' conversations and tried to gather as much information as I could. It seemed to me that Grandpa, who owned a business or two of his own, placed a great deal of value on "getting ahead." That explained why he often pressed Daddy to be more like him, like a Walsh—independent, self-motivated, and successful. Every time they would visit, Grandpa Walsh seemed to have some new business opportunity for Daddy. But Daddy would just smile and say "no, thank you" in a variety of ways until Grandpa finally had to give up again.

Over the years I had managed to piece together bits of the Walsh family history. They had come from Ireland many years ago, poor and needy, yet with a great deal of independence and family pride. Grandpa Walsh always stressed *that* fact when he talked of the family roots, as though independence and pride were two very important characteristics. He never let the story stop there but always went on to tell how, since then, most Walshes had owned their own businesses and through hard work and smart planning had managed to attain success.

Daddy's older brother, my uncle Patrick, had opened his own law office and was very successful, by our grandfather's standard. He lived in Chicago with Auntie Lynn and their three boys. But we didn't see them much.

There had been another brother too. Uncle Eric had died on a military training exercise. Since Grandpa Walsh had not wanted him to join the military in the first place, this had been particularly difficult for the family. I felt I could understand how much Grandma still missed their son, and I shared with her a special affection for the picture of Uncle Eric that she kept on a little shelf beside her kitchen sink. A variety of individual and family pictures was scattered through the house, but this was the only one in which Uncle Eric was proudly poised in full uniform. For some reason, as I studied his face, I became convinced that he was thinking about Grandma at just the time the picture was taken. I'm not sure why I was so certain, but I was, just the same. I tried to ask Grandma about it one time, and I think she was pretty sure too.

Though I could never quite understand why, that picture also brought some discord to the family. Grandpa seemed to hate it. I had seen him scowl at it over Grandma's shoulder when he thought no one else was around. And I had heard him mutter under his breath in a conversation with a neighbor, "Not even in combat, but by a stupid error on someone's part." That was the only time I had heard Grandpa speak of it. But it was not the only time I'd seen anger flare in his eyes at the mention of the loss of his middle son.

Apparently, though, as much as he resented the reminder of Uncle Eric in uniform, he had not demanded that Grandma remove the picture. Or if he had, she had not complied. For each time we visited their home, I stole back to the kitchen to see if Uncle Eric was still there, and every time he was right where he belonged on the little shelf. Uncle Eric—still young. Still looking proud.

For my part, I thought Uncle Eric very handsome and wished with all my heart I could have known him. When I was younger, I even secretly dreamed that the man I would someday marry would look just like him. Maybe he would wear a sharp-looking uniform and have his hair clipped just so. He might even have a dimple like Uncle Eric's. His dimple hardly showed in the uniformed picture because of the formal pose, yet his green eyes had not been able to hide their twinkle in a mischievous little-boy fashion.

I liked the fact that Uncle Eric's eyes were like Daddy's. I often wished it had been me, instead of Dana, who had taken after his side of the family. Dana had been blessed with the musical talent, the thick russet hair, and the beautiful hazely green eyes from the Walsh side. Instead, I had gotten the plain, straight blond hair from Mother's family. And dark eyes. Dark eyes were not as . . . as alive and riveting as Daddy's greenish ones. Though I admit I was always a little bit pleased when folks pointed out that I was going to be tall like my mother. Tall and willowy. That was what I had heard Daddy say. He made it sound as though being tall and willowy was something to be desired. The thought always made me stand just a little bit straighter.

Dana was on the short side for her age. A little skinny too, I guess. Though Mom always called it petite. I had already passed her in height. Green eyes aside, I took some consolation in that fact.

CHAPTER
TWO

THE SCHOOL DAY HAD INCLUDED the usual flurry of hallway action while students scrambled to classes, calling frantic short-term good-byes to friends whom they would meet again within hours over lunchroom tables. Then the comparative calm of the classroom, students bent over assignments or listening to their teacher. And finally, after what seemed a long and tedious day, we grabbed jackets and backpacks to rush out into the crisp early spring air where all our pent-up energy could be released.

Since it was Wednesday, we knew we would need to hurry home and complete homework assignments before church club activities began. But even so, Dana and I rather dallied as we walked home from the bus stop together, chatting about the nonevents of the day. Then our talk switched to the evening's activities and our steps picked up some. Club night was always exciting.

Well, at least it had been. Brett, in his first year of senior-high youth group, had a renewed enthusiasm for Wednesday night church ever since the school year had begun. A new youth pastor seemed to be able to invent fun things to do, and he managed to attach some type of significance to them so they passed for sanctioned youth activities. Brett often returned home talking about scavenger hunts or music videos, making Dana and me long for the day when we would be a part of all of the teenage fun. It was difficult not to gripe about the fact that we were still dutifully memorizing Bible verses for modest prizes and playing the now-familiar games. We would have quite willingly admitted that we enjoyed our club activities had it not been for Brett's boasting. But how could we claim to be having fun with a Bible drill when he was talking about finding the mystery man in a game of Clue at the mall?

In no time we'd done our assignments, eaten supper, and scrambled into the family van for the drive to church. When Daddy pulled up to the curb in front, we tumbled out and scattered—Brett to the youth room to see what adventure awaited him that evening, Corey and Mom to the basement, where they would share the preschool experience together, and Dana and I to our individual classes. Daddy was left to search for a parking spot on his own.

"Hey, Erin, how many sections did you finish in your book this week?" Marcy had spotted me walking down the long hall to our classroom. She seemed to think it was her duty to keep track of everyone's progress.

"Three." I slowed my step to match Marcy's.

"I did two. And a half—almost. But Jenna beat you again. She did five. I don't think Jenna does anything else. How could she and still finish five sections of her book in one week?"

I didn't really care, so I didn't bother to respond. Instead, I tried to divert Marcy's attention. "Are you coming swimming this weekend? My dad said we could go. Dana hasn't decided if she wants to yet, but I'm going for sure."

"What's the matter with Dana? She loves to swim."

"I think it's homework or something. She's got extra reading to do because her regular teacher is back, and Mrs. Ryan wants them to catch up on what the substitute teacher didn't make them do."

"That's not fair," Marcy asserted.

"I guess. But Dana's going to catch up anyway. She likes Mrs. Ryan."

"Has your mom decided what you're doing for Dana's birthday yet? I hope you have a sleepover again. Your mom throws the best sleepovers. I'm invited, right?"

"I don't know. I don't have any idea *what* she's planning. We have two family birthdays right close together, remember? And we had a big celebration when Brett turned thirteen. Mom might wait for Dana to turn thirteen before she puts on another big party."

Marcy nodded. "But a sleepover, that doesn't really cost anything."

"I suppose." Marcy never really understood how our system of checks and balances worked. I'm not sure I fully understood it either, though I'd asked Daddy to explain it to me once. At any rate, I wasn't going to count on a big party for Dana this year, and it annoyed me a little to hear Marcy expect it. It was a familiar frustration to me to hear about the plans at all, since I had a summer birthday and usually had trouble scheduling a time when my friends were all available and could do something special.

By then our class had started, and games were about to begin. Marcy and I dropped our backpacks in a corner and hurried to the crowd of kids, trying to position ourselves in the lineup in such a way that we'd be placed on the same team.

Once club time was over, there were always a few more minutes to talk before our parents gathered us back together. Marcy and I slipped into a private corner to chat some more about our swim outing. Then I noticed Daddy out of the corner of my eye. "Gotta go. See ya, Marcy."

Marcy cast one glance toward my dad and didn't argue. "See ya," she responded, her tone matter-of-fact. It was well-known that Daddy didn't care to be kept waiting by loitering offspring. But as I walked toward him, he continued talking with three men who had just come out of the board meeting room with him. I probably could have allowed myself a few more minutes.

Daddy had been on the church board for as long as I could remember. I couldn't recall ever hearing him complain about the fact. I guess he naturally liked to manage things—projects and money and people. I'd heard our pastor say it was his "gift." I wasn't too sure about what that meant, but even I noticed that he was quite good at taking charge, which was how Mom described it. All I knew was that whenever there was a hint of disagreement about some issue in the church, my dad was usually called upon to help settle it. He was good at finding some way to fix things up again, whether at home or at church. Probably at work too. I didn't know much about it except that he was an accountant and had his own company.

I stood nearby to wait for him, trying to look patient and yet letting him know I was ready to head for home. Club was over, and I knew it was getting close to our bedtime. Not that I worried too much about that, but if we got home early enough, Dana and I could still catch the very end of the TV show we currently liked.

Corey came scampering up, pushing a paper into my hands and insisting that I see what he had done. There were scribbles across the page in several colors, but it didn't seem to me he had really tried to draw anything in particular.

"Tell me about your picture." Mom had taught us not to ask, "What is it?" because it might hurt Corey's feelings.

"I drawed it on the table, but Miss Laura didn't like it that way so she gived me a paper to draw on."

"Corey, you're not supposed to draw on the table. You know that."

"I didn't mean to. My crayon was in a hurry."

His eyes were so big and his expression so earnest that I couldn't scold him any further. I was sure his teacher must have felt the same. "Next time, wait for the paper before you start to draw," I said. Corey just nodded, his eyes intensely green.

"I will." He nodded again, then quickly hurried on. "See, Sissy. See. I drawed our house. There's my room, and there's Brett. He's doing his homework." And sure enough—with Corey's help I managed to pick out the scattered parts of a crude stickman. He was even wearing a baseball cap. "And there's your room, but I didn't draw you and Dana 'cause your door is shut. And Momma is sewing and Daddy is at work."

"Why didn't you draw *you* in the picture?"

He paused for a moment to ponder. Suddenly his eyes lit up, and he lifted his face with a smile. "I am in the closet playing hide 'n' seek with Brett."

"Of course you are." I just grinned and tousled his

red-blond curls. He grinned right back at me. "Let's go
see Daddy," I said as I watched the group of men disband
and go their separate ways. At first I reached for Corey's
hand. Then I changed my mind and scooped him up,
struggling to carry him over to Daddy. He was getting
much too big for me to tote around. We both knew it,
but I still liked to try. He always wrapped his arms firmly
around my neck and sort of hugged while we walked. It
made me feel rather grown-up and protective. He was,
after all, my little brother.

※　※　※

When Saturday rolled around and it was time for
swimming, Dana was still unenthused. I knew she'd already finished her reading assignment. The truth was, she
had spent Thursday and Friday after school lounging in
the bedroom with her books.

When I tried to talk her into going, she said she had
to work on the first stage of a school report. But she just
lay on her bed and stared up at the ceiling. This was so
unlike Dana. It caught Mom's attention at once.

"Aren't you feeling well, honey?" I myself could almost feel the quick brush of Mom's cool hand across
Dana's forehead.

"I think I'm all right. I just don't feel like doing anything."

"Well, maybe you're beginning to come down with
something. I think you're right. You'd better stay home
today. Swimming isn't what you need right now. You can
always go next time."

"Okay."

I was disappointed that Dana would be absent, but Marcy was already waiting at the door, so I hurried down to meet her. I certainly had energy to burn.

❧ ❧ ❧

With Sunday came Sunday school and church. Our family had been invited to an evening potluck meal with Marcy's family, but Dana was still dragging around. It was decided that Brett would stay home with her, since there were no boys in Marcy's family anyway. He cheerfully agreed—he would command sole possession of the TV remote control, a rare privilege in our home, even though he often complained that there was nearly nothing that we were allowed to watch.

Marcy's parents, Rick and Deb Ward, were avid gamers, and we always looked forward to an evening at their house. Mom, too, had grown up playing games often, and she was always ready to gather for a time of fun and fellowship. At least, that was how she described it.

Mom toted the Crockpot filled with our favorite chili recipe on the short walk to Marcy's house, and Daddy followed with the big Tupperware container filled with tossed salad. Both Marcy and I were disappointed that Dana hadn't come along, but we quickly fell into our usual chatter and started a craft project that Marcy had purchased the night before at the mall. Soon we were knotting special string to make bracelets, chokers, and key chains. Then the Wards challenged our family to a Dutch Blitz session—which we won as usual. All too soon it was time to leave.

When we got home Dana had tucked herself into bed

and was sleeping peacefully. And Corey was ready to collapse himself. Daddy toted him up the stairs, and everybody was soon asleep.

Dana was back to her old self in the morning. I was awfully glad but sorry for all she'd missed. Here she had been sick all weekend and didn't even get to skip a day of school. I was really happy she was up and around again. It had seemed odd not to have her there wherever I went.

CHAPTER
THREE

COREY DIDN'T MEAN TO spill the beans about the birthday plans. It had happened when he'd wandered into our bedroom just after supper one night when Dana was browsing through a department store catalog.

"Whatcha doin'?" he wanted to know.

"She's dreaming. Dana hopes Grandma and Grandpa will send enough birthday money so she can get a new spread for her bed—even if we wouldn't match anymore." There had never been a birthday gift even close to being that lavish. But Dana had refused to listen to my opinion on the matter.

Corey hopped up beside Dana and peered at the book. He glanced over the pages with her, then shrugged. "I like the blue ones best."

"Which blue ones?" Dana flipped another page.

"The ones Mommy put in the garage. She gots the paint out there too."

"What do you mean, Corey?" Dana turned toward him intently. I knew she was hardly able to suppress the hope that what he was saying might be true. "Did Mommy *hide* them in the garage? When did you see them? Did she buy two?"

"I forgot. I am *not* supposed to tell."

I could hardly keep from laughing at the play of expressions across his face. He had important information, but he had been instructed to keep it secret.

Dana was about to ply Corey with more questions, but I interfered. "It's all right, Corey. Dana isn't going to ask you anything more—and that way you won't tell any secrets. Okay?"

"Okay." One affectionate hand moved out to pat Dana's knee. "Okay, Sissy?"

Dana cast a crosswise look up at me, but she nodded in agreement to Corey.

"How 'bout we play hide 'n' seek? I'm the counter, and you guys are hiders," Corey explained.

"No. Dana and I have homework to do. And we've got to finish, so you'd better scoot."

Corey frowned. "Okay." He looked back over his shoulder as he padded out the door. "Anyway, I didn't tell. 'Least, not everything."

"That's right. You didn't." I closed the door quietly behind him and then spun around to grin at Dana.

She didn't give me a chance to speak. "What did you do *that* for? I wanted to know whether there are any comforters out there or not. Since when are you above a little snooping?"

"You don't get it. If Corey understood that he'd already spoiled the secret, he'd go straight to Mom. This way, he thinks he's still keeping the secret. Now we can look in the garage and find the presents ourselves. It's perfect. Mom won't suspect a thing."

Dana hesitated. "That's not very nice, Erin. Mom

really likes to surprise us. I wanted to know if I was *getting* one. I don't necessarily want to *see* it right now."

"Fine, but I'm going to look in the garage. You don't have to come if you don't want to." Dana was right on my heels as I left the room.

"Girls? Is your homework done already?" Mom was at the kitchen table putting last-minute touches on a church mission project, all the while chatting with a friend on the telephone. Somehow she still managed to notice our attempt at an exploratory excursion to the garage.

"Not quite," we admitted. "We were just going out for a few minutes. We'll be right back."

"Any particular reason?" she asked, covering the mouthpiece of the phone.

Mom, who was as trusting and pleasant a person as you'd ever meet, always seemed to have a sixth sense whenever her children were about to step out of line.

We decided, after a silent conversation of meaningful glances back and forth, it was best to retreat. "No reason. Never mind."

There was an inquisitive look in our direction. But Mom let the matter drop as we turned and plodded back up the stairs, hoping there would be a moment after school the next day to slip undetected into the garage for a look around.

But by the next afternoon, there was no hidden parcel. Not in the garage. Not in the large closet under the stairs. Not in any of the usual hiding places. The only thing Dana and I could conclude was that Mom had figured out where we'd been heading and had moved her surprises to a neighbor's garage. She'd been known to do so in the past. Now there was nothing to do but wait.

Dana decided to continue perusing the catalog just in

case she would still need to fall back on her original hopes—that enough money would somehow materialize when the mail arrived carrying the usual birthday check from Grandma and Grandpa Walsh. These were some very slim hopes, we both realized.

Brett's birthday came first, falling this year on a Tuesday night and heralded with his favorite supper followed by his favorite cake—German chocolate with coconut pecan icing. Brett easily blew out all fifteen candles in one breath and still had enough air to exclaim excitedly, "Wow—now I can get my driver's permit." We all laughed.

Mom had allowed Brett to invite one friend over for dinner to celebrate with us. He had chosen Travis, the pastor's son. I liked Travis, though he rarely spoke to me. But I always felt if he ever did address me, he was friendly enough. I couldn't say the same about all the buddies that Brett brought home. In fact, Travis was a favorite of Mom and Dad's too. And I think they did what they could to encourage the friendship.

Not that the boys didn't naturally share common interests. They had both played on the school basketball team for the last two years. And both planned to make the varsity team in high school. Travis was somewhat taller than Brett, but Brett was quicker. So far he'd been able to make significant contributions to the team despite his size disadvantage.

"All right," Daddy began after the cake had been devoured. "Why don't you start, Corey? You tell Brett one thing you like about him, and then you keep count so we end up with fifteen—one for each of Brett's years. Okay?" This was a favorite family birthday tradition.

Corey nodded and bit his lip in serious concentration.

"Wow, fifteen! It's going to be hard to think of that many!" Every birthday somebody said it. This time it was Dana. Brett laughed it off and tried to pretend he had outgrown the ritual.

"I like Brett because he lets me play with the toy cars he builds." The truth was, Brett only let Corey have a selected few of his model collection, some of his first attempts. The rest he kept on a very high and guarded shelf above his desk.

"My turn," Mom was quick to chime in. "I appreciate what a kind older brother you are, Brett. There are lots of benefits of a larger family, but it's not always easy. And, Brett, you are consistently kind and polite to your siblings."

"That's two," I noted.

We all waited for Daddy to speak next. "I'm proud that you take responsibility and that you are a conscientious worker."

Corey cut in. "Daddy, is that one or two?"

"We'll count it as just one."

Brett was looking a little red and tried to avoid eye contact with anyone. Dana was ready to add her comment next, a teasing smile playing across her face. "I like you because kids in school like you—and when they hear that you're my brother they expect to like me too."

Brett laughed. "Yeah, until they get to know you." Immediately he caught himself and squirmed in embarrassment. "Not really, Dana," he mumbled. But she hadn't been bothered by his joking.

It seemed that my turn had rolled around and I hadn't really thought about what to say. "I like you because . . ." I began the sentence in hopes that something would pop into my head—and it did—"because you teach me some of your basketball moves. Most brothers wouldn't do that. I'm glad you do."

Mom looked as though she was just about to speak again when Travis cleared his throat. "I like you because you're the only other guy on the basketball team who believes in God. And it makes me feel better knowing that . . . that we can kind of look out for each other."

Mom waited a moment and then continued the countdown. I'm not sure Brett heard any more of it, though. I guess there's only so much praise a fifteen-year-old boy can handle.

Now Brett was ready to dive into the gifts.

"Open mine, Brett, open mine." Corey was electric with energy at any type of gathering. And birthday parties—anyone's birthday party—seemed to make him more excited than anything else.

"All right, Corey, let's see." Brett picked up the wrinkled little package and shook it. "Is it a watch?"

Corey giggled. "No."

"Is it . . . a diamond?" This time the laughter was louder.

"It's not an elephant, is it?"

By now Corey was jumping and clapping. "Open it! Open it, Brett."

Brett tore the wrapping off to reveal an odd little blue plastic bag. With a curious glance at Corey, he opened it and out fell two little white cylinders.

Corey was delighted. "They're for your ears. They're ear bugs." We all chuckled, but Corey hurried on. "So you can stay asleep in our room even if I sleep there too. Momma helped me get them."

This time Brett's gaze searched Mom's face. She was thoroughly enjoying the surprise.

"You're goofy, Corey." But Brett's words were softened when he reached out and touched Corey's shoulder lightly, and Corey grabbed his hand long enough to give it a little squeeze.

The next gift Brett opened was from Mom and Dad. It was a large, awkward-looking package and was obviously a mystery to Brett. He peeled back a corner and made an odd face. It was a skateboard. It was not what Brett had hinted for. Brett had always been too into basketball to be interested in any other sport.

Travis jumped right in. "Hey, Brett. That's great. That's a super make. Mine's not nearly as good."

Brett cocked his head toward Travis, still looking reluctant to show enthusiasm. "You've got one? I never knew that."

"Sure. There's a park in the city. A bunch of us guys go whenever we can. It's great. But you've got to have a lot of nerve to do it. The ramps are really high."

"How high?" I could tell Brett was warming up to the idea. I wondered if it was the thought of needing nerve that appealed to him.

The next gift from Mom and Daddy was a helmet and a set of pads. Brett flipped them over and over. I was pretty sure he was trying to picture what he'd look like in them.

Travis laughed and slapped him on the shoulder. "Don't worry about what you'll look like. All the guys wear them—and you'll need them. Believe me."

Brett's next gift was from Dana and me, a new model car because we weren't quite sure what else he'd like. Dana had wanted to try to be more original, but I talked her into staying with the sure thing. Brett could always use a new model kit.

"Thanks. *This* I know what to do with."

There were a few more gifts, and then Mom bundled up the torn gift wrap while Brett handled each of his gifts again.

※　※　※

The next morning Dana's gaze was a little preoccupied while we were walking to school. I knew that look. She was dreaming of the gifts she might get. And she had never stopped thinking about the possibility of the new bedroom accessories.

At last Monday night and Dana's birthday celebration arrived. Both Marcy and Carli had been invited for the birthday dinner. They entered with giggles and chatter, sliding onto the bench on the far side of the table between Corey and me. Dana was allowed to sit in Daddy's seat at the head of the table, and Mom stood nearby, her camera in hand. The supper that Dana had chosen was Chinese food. She loved sweet-and-sour chicken and fried rice. Since none of the rest of us were crazy about it, this was a rare treat for her, and she savored it thoroughly.

Dana had made another odd choice for dessert. A cheesecake, topped with cherries. Mom had already positioned and lit the candles on this nontraditional birthday treat, and we sang "Happy Birthday" as we watched the tiny lights flicker against the shiny red fruit.

We did the usual counting-of-family-compliments thing, but I wondered as I watched Dana if she was really hearing the nice things we were saying about her. Her smile was looking more and more forced, and she was fidgeting on her seat.

Once the presents were gathered and set before her, she seemed rather ill at ease. I was pretty sure I knew what the problem was, but I wasn't about to explain. Even unwrapping the gift from me, the new music book, just what she had wanted, brought only a wistful smile.

Finally there were no presents left, even though Mom and Dad's was conspicuous by its absence. Just as Mom was about to begin a little speech, Dana raised her tense face and whispered, "Mom, can I talk to you for a minute? Please?"

Mom looked surprised but led Dana into the laundry room, where their conversation was just barely audible. I knew what was going on, even though no one could make out their words. Dana was confessing. But to my way of thinking, there had been no crime. Not even a slight transgression. What kid wouldn't, if given opportunity, want to snoop out a birthday surprise before the actual day arrived? That was just common sense to me. And I was certain that when I became a parent, I would just expect my children to be tempted. I'd simply choose my hiding places well.

But Dana, who lived by "What would Jesus do?" could not rest until she had confessed to Mom that she had attempted to discover the hidden surprise. Mom had described Dana as having a "tender conscience." I felt she was just a bit too goody-goody.

When Dana returned, she was smiling again. And Mom made her special presentation of the mystery packages. A lovely pair of blue comforters with delicate white pinstripes on one side and a print of darker blue rosebuds on the other were revealed to squeals of delight from both of us. The comforters were reversible. We could change the look anytime we liked.

In addition there were cans of soft blue paint to coordinate the walls with the new spreads, and also a beautiful wallpaper border as an accent. Last, but not least, Mom had sewn a pair of white lace balloon curtains. Together the gifts really would transform our room. Dana's eyes shone. And I was grateful for my share of this extravagance. Though I was pretty sure that when my birthday arrived in two months' time, I too could expect a gift that would be shared equally between us.

That was all right. Dana and I were used to sharing.

We used our new comforters that very night. Then Daddy took a day off on Thursday to help Mom do the painting. By Friday evening, all the accents had been added and the bedroom was complete.

Dana and I would have simply thrown the old comforters into the trash, but Mom washed them carefully and wrapped them in plastic. She and Corey would make a trip to the inner-city mission. She went fairly often and knew she could find someone who could make use of the faded but warm Barbie quilts.

❧ ❧ ❧

Before my birthday actually arrived every year, the greatest gift of all had presented itself—freedom. School was over, and summer vacation beckoned with its invitation to outdoor fun. No more assigned reading. No more worksheets and reports. And definitely no more math problems!

My birthday celebration turned out to be a family

dinner and a birthday cake of my choosing—heavy-duty chocolate with thick chocolate icing. We didn't have any guests, and I didn't really care. Marcy was away, as usual. I knew my special turn would come when I hit that magical age of thirteen. Marcy had already promised that even the temptation of visiting her grandparents at the lake would not keep her from celebrating that birthday with me. Besides, I admitted as I snuggled under my new blue comforter each night, I had sort of muscled in on Dana's birthday anyway.

I was pleased with my gifts, especially the used computer that I was to share with Dana. Daddy's office had been upgrading, and he had gotten a good deal on what we deemed to be an exciting machine. Now we wouldn't have to vie for time to play video games or surf the 'net in between Brett or Corey. But with the freedom from classes and schedules, even the computer sat unused.

I intended to make the most of the all-too-short summer months. Dana and I were allowed to stay up later, to watch more television, and to visit with neighborhood friends almost as often as we wanted. Even Mom got into the summertime spirit with extra flare. This would be the last summer before Corey would begin kindergarten, and we knew she would savor every moment with her youngest.

At least once a week she loaded us all into the van, and we took a picnic lunch down near the shady creek-side park to sit, eat, and relax. Sometimes on a quiet back road she even let Brett take the wheel, though she insisted that he go painfully slow. Normally it was only Daddy who took Brett on his practice runs.

At the park Corey splashed in knee-deep water, caught minnows and tadpoles, and soaked himself to the skin. Dana curled her legs up under her on her favorite rock and read blissfully, soaking in the sunshine. I chatted with Mom, stretched out on the cool grass, or wandered alternately between Corey and Dana. Brett had taken to bringing a fishing rod, and on rare days he actually hooked a fish that was large enough to take home and cook, which was always Daddy's job. Mom would not cook anything she'd seen moving and alive. She had a pretty hard and fast rule about that.

On other days we were allowed to walk to the strip mall that sat on the highway near our neighborhood. It wasn't much. Just a gas station, a mini mart, and a bookstore, but we always felt it was worth the trip anyway. The chance for an outing was really our main interest. Mom wouldn't allow us to ride our bikes because she said the sidewalks were safer and we'd be more careful if we weren't racing.

In August Grandma and Grandpa Walsh arrived in their motor home for a visit. They parked their rig in the driveway, hooked our hose up to supply their makeshift kitchen, and placed their lawn chairs directly in front of the basketball hoop—no more playing in the sprinkler or shooting baskets.

"Now, Angela, we don't want to be any trouble. Just pretend we're not here at all." I knew Mom wasn't quite sure what the expected response should be. But she never tested the concept to see if they were serious either. She cooked extra at every meal and canceled all of the unnecessary engagements for the duration of their visit. Daddy said she didn't have to, but Mom did it anyway.

I enjoyed visits with my grandparents. Grandma taught us to do things like crochet and knit. Dana took to these lessons much quicker than I did—but then I could always hang around Grandpa and whatever he was tinkering with, whether in or around the motor home.

When the visit was measured in weeks, though, the whole thing began to lose its appeal. By then Grandpa had begun to get restless and had started to make work for himself around the house. It was true that he was better at general household repairs than Daddy, but we had managed to keep things quite well maintained in spite of our limitations. Even Mom was pretty handy for most odd jobs. So I always sensed a bit of tension when he took on projects that no one had asked him to do. Our house was old, and there was always something that could be improved, though I thought Mom looked rather askance at the missing banister rung he replaced with one that didn't quite match. But at least I got to ride along on the frequent trips to the hardware store.

Grandma was pleasant and generous with treats for us—especially for Corey. But she tended to need to be talking most of the time, so Dana and I often abandoned Mom to their somewhat one-sided conversations and struck out on our own.

Unfortunately for us, the visit also meant that Mom had less time to drive us where we wanted to go. And, sure enough, it fell exactly on the two weeks when Marcy and Carli were at summer camp. So we were often left to fill time by walking with Corey to the mini mart or by taking a few laps around the neighborhood on our bikes. If we hadn't had each other, I'm not sure how Dana and I would have made it through the summer.

By the time Grandma and Grandpa's motor home pulled out of the driveway and Marcy and Carli had returned, bursting with camp stories, school was about to begin. At this point, it was a welcome relief. At least there'd be plenty of friends around again.

CHAPTER
FOUR

THE END OF SUMMER when we began shopping for school supplies was one of my favorite times of year. The anticipation of beginning something was always attractive to me, and I loved to have new things. Even if it was just notebooks and pencils and paper. And this year it was especially fun to watch Corey browsing for his own school needs. He was entering kindergarten and was anticipating learning to read. He seemed to be expecting to do so immediately. We hoped he wouldn't be too disappointed when he realized that we'd been right—they'd start with the alphabet and colors. Those he already knew.

Brett didn't bother shopping for himself. He sent the list with Mom, including specific instructions that she not get anything fancy. Apparently he wished to make no statement whatsoever with his notebooks and accessories.

Dana, on the other hand, chose quite carefully. For the first time she brushed past the cutesy folder covers with kittens and puppies and dolphins, choosing instead the plain dark colors that no doubt were intended for the high school crowd. To me it only served as a reminder of the most disturbing aspect of the upcoming school year.

Dana would be attending George Washington High School with Brett now, and I would be remaining behind. Somehow the new school and all seemed to have affected her whole outlook.

I suppose much of it was due to some chats between her and Carli. Marcy's sister was a year older than Dana and had become quite conscious of her advancing maturity. It looked to me as if she was attempting to draw Dana up to her level, into her crowd. I had asked Mom about it, but her answers didn't really satisfy me.

"Well, Carli is at a difficult stage in life. She's searching for a new identity because she feels that she's not a child anymore. On the other hand, she's not quite sure what growing up means. She's experimenting, really." Mom seemed to be going back—to somewhere—in her thinking.

"Will Dana act like that too? I don't want her to become like Carli."

"Dana is not Carli. And I think we have to remember that your sister has developed enough as a person to make her own decisions. She's never been one to follow the crowd before, and I don't expect her to do so now. But, Erin, she *will* begin to change. There's no question about that. And so will you. Maybe next year. Maybe even before. And it's a very good thing. You wouldn't want to be a little girl forever, would you?"

"No. But I sure don't want to be like Carli."

Mom reached out to pat my arm. Her voice softened, and her eyes had a bit of a proud shine to them, as if the thought of us growing up brought both sadness and pleasure. "The thing to remember about maturing, Erin, is that it usually comes with starts and stops. This is a big moment for Dana because she's entering a new school.

Just give her a little extra space, and she'll probably seem like herself in no time."

I hoped so.

With Dana and Carli off and busy together, Marcy and I were left to find amusement for ourselves, but we quickly decided not to let it bother us. I explained to her what my mother had said. That next year we'd be back in step with them. And I had figured out on my own that we'd have the added advantage of watching them go through everything first. Maybe it would be easier for us when our turn came.

Marcy and I were lucky enough to share a homeroom class for the upcoming year. Many of our old friends were there too. Marcy had her eye on one in particular. Stephen Bryant had somehow managed to shoot up at least six inches over the summer. Now he was even taller than I was. And for some unknown reason, he really appealed to Marcy.

Strangely, she could not recall that this was the same Stephen who had purposely tripped her in fourth-grade gym class and not even bothered to apologize. At the time she had vowed never to speak to him again. This was also the same Stephen who had used some very foul language in the lunchroom near the end of the last year. So bad that the teacher who happened to be nearby had walked him down to the principal's office, and he had been given a detention.

I was amazed that Marcy's memory could be so short. But she wasn't listening to me at all. So I just tried not to roll my eyes too much while she talked on and on about *Stephen*.

Brett was playing basketball again, so that fall he often allowed me to play one-on-one with him in the driveway.

He didn't admit it, but I was pretty sure I had improved a lot since last year. The problem for me was that he had improved too.

As November arrived we were back into "wear-your-coat" weather. Mom seemed a little too concerned that being outside without proper attire would send a person into a fit of flu, and I just couldn't help but think that she overdid the warnings a bit.

Lately there'd been so many reasons to trot back and forth to the Wards' house. Carli and Marcy's mom had agreed to let them plan a party. They had decided on a costume party and had enthusiastically included Dana and me in the planning. The party was still two weeks away. Mrs. Ward observed that it was amazing how much work we could come up with that could be categorized as *necessary* for a party's success. We wrote and mailed invitations, made decorations, and worked tirelessly on our own costumes and food planning. Dana was perfectly suited for organizing it all. I just followed along and did whatever seemed fun at the time.

❧ ❧ ❧

One morning before school Dad got up from the breakfast table to answer the phone. We weren't paying much attention, assuming it was merely something to do with his work.

In fact we'd all been listening to Corey announce his latest plans.

"When I get up on the moon, I'll wave to you," he promised solemnly, his eyes gleaming with the thought of being way up there above earth.

"No one can wave from the moon," I said. But I grinned and rumpled his hair. I didn't inform him that no one was bothering to go to the moon anymore. Mars was more the ticket—but I didn't want to spoil Corey's astronaut dreams.

"Sure I can." He stood up by his chair and demonstrated with big sweeping gestures. "You'd just have to go outside and look when it's nighttime."

"We'd never see you from so far away." I might not know much about astronauts and space walks, having never really taken any interest in something that had been going on since long before I was born, but at least I knew that much.

"Then I'd put my shirt on a long, long pole and wave that."

We'd just seen a Saturday cartoon where a marooned rabbit had waved a white flag of some sort on a pole as his sign of surrender to his enemy, a hulking big turtle in a pith helmet.

We all chuckled. "We wouldn't see that either," I persisted.

"Then get glasses."

We all started to laugh again when Mom pushed back her chair and said, "Shh." She must have caught a bit of Dad's conversation that had immediately gotten her attention.

I looked up then. Dad was still on the phone, but his face held an expression I'd never seen before. The whole table fell silent. I guess we all sensed at once that something was wrong.

"I see," Dad was saying, which sure didn't tell us anything. Then, "How's Mother?"

The answer to the simple question seemed to take an

awfully long time. Now and then Dad mumbled, "I see," or "Yes," but he looked agitated. Worried. He paced back and forth, the long cord trailing along after him. He rubbed his forehead and ran his fingers through his hair. I'd never seen him like that before.

Mom had gone very white. She looked as if she wanted to get up and go to Dad but couldn't find the strength to do it. She just sat, very still, her brown eyes looking round and even darker in her pale face. As soon as Dad replaced the receiver and turned, she asked with a shaky voice, "What is it, Dave?"

Dad didn't answer right away. He took a few steps toward the table but stopped behind Mom's chair and put his hand on her shoulder. He seemed to take a big breath as though to gather his wits—or his emotions. He had everyone's attention by this time. "It's Dad," he said at last. "He's had a heart attack."

"Grandpa?" Brett's disbelief was evident in his voice.

Mom grew even paler. She reached up and curled her fingers around Dad's hand. "How bad?" she asked, her voice shaky.

Dad swallowed. His hand started up to his brow again, then stopped midway and returned to hold on to Mom. "He's gone," he said, his voice low.

A little shock wave traveled all the way around the table. How could that possibly be? We'd seen Grandpa Walsh such a short time ago, and he was just fine. How could he be *gone*?

"Oh, David," Mom said. She hardly ever called him that. Tears started to fill her eyes and then spill down her cheeks.

Things were a blur from then on. I don't really remember all that happened. I do know we completely ignored the school bus. I guess no one was even thinking of it. I also remember being assigned the task of looking after Corey. I was to read to him to get his mind off what had just occurred and keep him busy while Mom and Dad made phone calls. It didn't work. He kept wanting to talk about it. Asking all sorts of questions that I couldn't answer.

"How did he get dead?"

"His heart stopped working."

"Why?"

"I don't know. Maybe it was sick. Or tired. Maybe it had worked too long."

"Did it hurt?"

"I don't know." I didn't want to admit that I suspected it had been very painful.

"Why couldn't the doctor fix it?"

"I don't know. Maybe there wasn't a doctor in time. Maybe there wasn't anything he could do."

"When can he come see us again?"

"He won't be coming again, honey," I said as gently as I could.

"Never? Why?"

"Because when people are dead they aren't here with us anymore."

"Where do they go?"

That was a tough one. I knew that if people loved God and had asked Him to forgive their sins, they could go to heaven when they died. I didn't know—for sure—if Grandpa Walsh had ever done that. I did know that my folks had taught us to pray for him—and Grandma. Corey's question troubled me. What if—? What if Grandpa Walsh had not taken care of this very important matter before he died?

"Do you want to hear the rest of the story or not?" I asked a bit sharply. I don't think Corey really wanted to continue, but I started to read again anyway.

Mom came to rescue me before too long. "I'm sorry, Erin. But Daddy and I had things we had to take care of. I'll look after Corey now." As she spoke the words she lowered herself to the sofa beside Corey and scooped him into her arms. I could see that her eyes were still puffy from crying, though she tried to force out a smile.

"Maybe you should go see Dana. I think she needs some company."

I didn't even ask where. Dana would be in our bedroom. I headed there, sort of in need of company myself.

I found Dana stretched out on her bed. She'd been crying, but now she just looked sad and lonely—and maybe a little bit scared. I wondered if she too was thinking about whether Grandpa Walsh had asked God to forgive him. When I walked in the door, we looked at each other and then we both started crying again. I crossed to Dana's bed and flopped down beside her. We entangled our arms around one another and sobbed rather noisily.

We didn't cry for long. I guess we both knew we had to talk. We sniffed and snuffled and reached for the tissues. We still didn't know much about what had happened. We only knew that we'd just lost a grandpa whom we loved. We were going to miss him.

"Poor Grandma," said Dana. "She'll be so lonely."

I nodded and blew my nose.

"I didn't know he was sick," I said.

"I don't think anyone did."

We both thought about that for a little while.

Dana spoke again. "I didn't know you could die like that—so fast. I thought you had to be sick first. I thought . . ." But she didn't finish.

"I'm gonna miss him," I said and almost started to cry again. Dana nodded silently.

We were still in our room trying to comfort each other and sharing our thoughts and our grief when Dad knocked on our door. First he just held out his arms to us, and we scrambled off the bed and went to meet him. He hugged us both. I felt him kiss me on the top of the head. "How about coming down to the kitchen," he said at last when we had stopped crying again. "Mom made some hot chocolate. We need to talk."

By the time we entered the kitchen, Mom and Brett and Corey were already there. We all took our regular seats at the table while Mom poured the hot chocolate, adding lots of cool milk to Corey's cup. She had sandwiches and cookies on a plate, and in spite of feeling so sad we all were glad for the snack. Somehow we had missed out on lunch.

I was on my third cookie when Daddy said, "I've been on the phone with Uncle Patrick. He and Aunt Lynn have already gone over to be with Grandma."

Dana and I exchanged glances. Both of us knew that Grandma Walsh and Auntie Lynn often had differences of opinion. It wasn't discussed at our house, but Grandma often made little remarks during our visits, and when we were with Aunt Lynn we heard the other side of the stories. Mom refused to speak about it when we kids were around, but I once overheard her and Dad talking about what a shame it was that family members couldn't get along.

"Your mother and I want to leave as quickly as possible," Dad was continuing. "We've asked Mrs. Joyce to come and stay with you."

"Can I come?" Corey put in quickly. "I want to see Grandpa too."

Poor Corey. He still didn't seem to have things figured out.

"We will only be seeing Grandma now," Mom said patiently. "Remember. I explained about Grandpa."

Corey wrinkled up his face in concentration. "Oh yeah," he said and leaned up against Mom. She put an arm around him, and her fingers reached up to brush the reddish hair back from his forehead.

"I think you need to know how it happened," Dad went on. "Grandpa and Grandma had gone to bed, and for some reason she awoke in the night. She couldn't hear Grandpa breathing, so she turned on the light. That was when she discovered that he was gone."

"Where'd he go?" piped up Corey. "I thought you couldn't walk when you got dead."

In spite of the sadness we all felt, I saw Dad smile just a little bit. "That's right," he said, reaching out his hand to Corey's knee. "He was still there, but he was dead. Grandma didn't know he was dead—for sure—so she called an ambulance. They took Grandpa to the hospital, and the doctors there said it was too late. Grandpa had already died."

I was about to start crying all over again. I looked over at Dana. She was already in tears. For some reason that made me determined to hold my tears at bay. I had done enough crying. I fought back the lump in my throat and blew my nose hard on the tissue I was holding.

"Your mom and I will be back home tonight. We need to meet with Grandma and Uncle Patrick to arrange the funeral service. But we will be back tonight. It may be rather late because of the three-hour drive. We want you all to mind Mrs. Joyce. Go to bed at your proper time. There will be school for you tomorrow."

That last remark did not come as a surprise to me. Daddy had commented before, when other families had gone through similar sorrows, that he thought it was best to keep as much of the familiar routine as possible. So it seemed reasonable to me that we wouldn't miss another day of school tomorrow. In fact, I decided that I didn't want to sit at home the next day crying every time I looked at another family member's teary eyes. But by the way Dana's face twisted, I gathered she would have preferred to stay home one more day.

I looked around the table. Everybody looked very sad—though I was sure Corey still didn't have too clear an idea what death was all about. Dana certainly did. She looked ready to burst into tears at any moment.

Then my eyes moved on to Brett. I didn't see any tears on his cheeks. He didn't even have puffy eyes. He just looked—strange. Angry—or frustrated. I knew he'd been counting on the fishing trip that he and Grandpa had been planning for almost two years. Now there wouldn't be one. I wondered if Brett was thinking about it while he sat there staring hard at his empty hot chocolate cup. His fist was curled up into a hard knot, almost as if he were hiding something in it. But when he opened his hand to push his way up from the table, there was nothing there.

He looked in a big hurry to leave, and when we all went our separate ways Brett just went to his room, closing his door behind him firmly. It wasn't long before Corey was peeking in our door. "Will you play with me?" he asked, looking from Dana to me and then back at Dana again to see which one of us might respond favorably. Neither of us felt much like playing a game. Dad and Mom had already left to go see Grandma, and Mrs. Joyce was down in the kitchen opening and closing cupboard doors, probably searching for dinner fixings.

"Brett won't play," said Corey, spreading a favorite game out on the edge of my bed. "He just turned on loud music and buried his head with his arms when I asked."

I looked across at Dana. She didn't seem up to entertaining Corey either. In fact she looked pale and tired. I picked the red game piece and handed Corey his favorite yellow. Neither my heart nor my mind was in it, but Corey likely wouldn't notice.

❧ ❧ ❧

We all went to the funeral. Even Corey. Mom had talked with him to let him know what would be happening. By then I think he had a general idea about the finality of death, but every once in a while he'd say something that didn't quite fit the reality.

The funeral was not held in a church. The funeral home had a large room with rows of seats filled with important-looking dark-suited business people and ladies in smart clothes and huge hats, some of them even veiled. Grandpa and Grandma Walsh moved in social circles to which our family was not accustomed.

Dana and I nudged each other when one particularly fashionable woman was ushered down the aisle. Her hat was black, with a swept-up sea-wave type of brim and a huge bow. The whole affair was perched on a fancy red hairdo. The lady wore the highest heels I had ever seen in my life, and over her shoulders was draped some kind of animal skin that still had a nose and mouth and eyes that looked rather beady. I don't think they were real. Her husband, who may have been as tall as she was if he'd been wearing equally high heels, wore a dark suit with a white scarf hanging loosely from around his neck. A hankie with a fancy fold stuck just so in his breast pocket. I didn't dare look at Dana or I'm sure we both would have giggled—but you don't do that at a funeral.

The organ played some mournful tunes. We didn't sing much. A woman with a high trembly voice sang a song I hadn't heard before about a beautiful isle of somewhere. It was kind of a pretty song, but I didn't really understand it. Was Grandpa supposed to be on an island someplace?

A minister—I guess he was a minister, though he seemed far different from our pastor—spoke words about life's journey being over for Grandpa and that he could now take his well-earned rest. I couldn't feature Grandpa Walsh being much enthused about resting. The whole thing made me feel sadder than ever.

When it was finally over, we drove together in the van to a big hall where we had a lunch. By then we kids were ready to eat. But we finished long before the grown-ups, who lingered over their coffee cups, chatting. We didn't know what to do. So we just sat and occasionally talked in hushed voices. It was quite boring, really—especially for Corey, who had been continuously fidgeting. Finally Brett took him outside. I think they were both glad for a break. Dana and I endured as long as we could and eventually dared to follow.

At last Dad came out to speak to us. "We're going to take Grandma home with us for a few days," he told us.

"She's not ready to go back to her empty house yet. That means you'll all need to remember that she is with us and is still adjusting to Grandpa being gone. We'll need to be extra thoughtful and considerate."

Brett looked alarmed. I wondered if he was afraid he wouldn't be able to play his music. Or maybe he just wondered how it would work with an older person in the house.

"It will mean someone will need to give up their bed," Dad was saying.

We all looked at one another. Dana was the first to speak. "She can have mine."

Dad nodded his thanks and put his hand on Dana's shoulder. "I think she should be in a room of her own," he said. "We haven't worked out how we'll do that yet."

We all knew there were no extra rooms in our little house.

"Why doesn't she go to Uncle Patrick's?" asked Brett. "He's got lots of room."

That was true and we all knew it. Dad didn't even answer the question. I'm sure he knew we were aware of the reason.

"We'll work it out when we get home," he said instead and turned to go back to Mom. I thought he looked tired. Sort of like he often did in March and April when he came home after an especially long day of work. Then Mom would explain to us that it was Tax Season again, and we would know not to bother Daddy.

It took a while for Grandma to pack a couple of suitcases. I wondered if she'd pack her special picture of Uncle Eric, but I knew better than to pry. Dad made arrangements with the neighbor lady to care for the plants and take in the newspaper and mail. And then we all crowded into the van and headed for home.

I wondered just what was going to happen when we got there. If Dana gave up her bed and Grandma needed her own room, that would mean that I'd have to move out too. But where? There weren't very many empty spots in our house.

In the end it was Brett who moved. After he and Daddy talked in the backyard for a while, they apparently agreed on a solution. They moved his bed down to a corner in the basement. I think Brett rather liked it that way. He took his boom box too, but Mom made sure he remembered his headphones. Corey was moved into our room on a borrowed cot. It sure made things crowded. Dana and I could hardly get our closet door open. But I figured this arrangement was much better than having to give up our room entirely.

It was sort of hard at first, but I guess we all adjusted— or something—for things gradually slid into some kind of routine again.

Still, whenever I thought about it, I felt sad. It seemed so strange not to have a Grandpa Walsh anymore.

CHAPTER FIVE

COREY HAD BEEN TRYING unsuccessfully to tie his shoe. Normally I would stop to help, but at the moment I just wanted him to move over so I could get into the closet.

"Corey, can you just . . . can you move over to your bed? I've got to get my clothes for school." I pushed against him a little for emphasis.

"I got school too."

"Come here, buddy," Dana called to him. "I'll help."

I didn't look at her, but I could feel her disapproval anyway.

Brett poked his nose into the room. "Mom wants us for breakfast. Don't forget to wash, Corey," he mumbled.

Ever since Grandma had arrived, Mom no longer called up the stairs from the kitchen. She didn't want to disturb Grandma, so she generally had Brett walk up and summon anyone who hadn't appeared yet. He didn't seem to enjoy his new assignment.

I closed the closet door and grabbed up my robe. I'd have to come back upstairs and dress after breakfast. At least Dana would practice piano first.

"Good morning." Mom kissed each of us on the cheek as we entered the kitchen. "I made your favorite, Dana. Cheesy scrambled eggs."

Dana smiled her thanks, but it looked kind of forced. "I'm not very hungry," she said. "I think I'll just have some toast." She must have been concerned that Mom might be hurt, for she quickly added, a bit brighter, "But thanks. Brett can have my share."

Mom studied Dana's face for a moment. "All right, but be sure to take your vitamin."

Corey hopped up onto his chair. "Mommy, I'm hungry."

"That's good, honey. I made plenty." She lifted the steaming frying pan and scooped eggs liberally onto Corey's plate before turning to serve Dad.

"How are the plans coming for Carli and Marcy's party?" she asked. "It's only two days away, isn't it? Is everything ready?"

"Yup. All that's left is to blow up the balloons. But they won't do that until Friday so they don't shrivel up," I noted.

Brett stopped gulping eggs long enough to ask, "Who did you invite?"

Dana answered, "Just kids from our church group and a few from our school classes. Carli invited some older kids, but none of them have said they're coming."

"What about Travis and his brother Graham? Did you invite them?"

Dana looked puzzled. "I guess we didn't think about them. Would Travis come? He's your age. And Graham seems . . . I don't know . . . kind of bookish."

"He is. But he's a decent guy," Brett said. "And Travis says that Graham's trying to get out with the youth group more. So I think he might like to be invited."

I marveled at this much information from the morning stoic. Not wanting to be left out of the conversation, I asked, "We still have time to call, don't we, Dana?"

"I suppose. But I feel funny about it. Will you call him for us, Brett?"

Brett stood, collected his dishes, and headed toward the kitchen counter. "Nope. 'Cause you never invited *me* to your big fancy party either."

I looked at Dana and she stared back, her eyes round and surprised. We hadn't suspected that Brett would be remotely interested in our party. There was a moment or two of silence. We could hear the back door close as Brett left with the trash bags.

Dana was the first to speak. "Oops. We never even thought to invite Brett." I watched her as she looked from Mom to Daddy, probably hoping they would tell her how to fix our mistake.

"Well, Dana. It's probably not too late to invite your brother either." Mom's tone was a little terse.

"Excuse me," Dana said as she gathered her own dishes and rose to place them beside the sink. In a moment we could hear the same door close softly behind her. I sat awkwardly, not knowing whether to follow.

Daddy spoke. "Erin, I think you should start your piano practice."

"But, Daddy, it's Dana's turn to . . ." I left the sentence unfinished. The look on his face made me certain it would be best if I just obeyed.

By the time we were headed toward the school bus, it looked as though Dana had corrected the problem. I'm not certain what she said to Brett, but she seemed to have smoothed his ruffled feathers. It was probably a good thing I hadn't been involved. Conversations between Brett and me had not been going smoothly lately. I probably would have just fouled up the process.

❅ ❅ ❅

The party was the only topic Marcy could converse about on Friday. She was so excited she hadn't even bothered to read the science assignment the previous night, and now she was worried that she might be called upon to answer a question about it. That would be particularly troublesome for her because Stephen happened to attend this class too. Fortunately for her, she was overlooked in the discussion time.

At lunch she was fairly bursting with enthusiasm.

"Okay, I think we're almost ready. Carli and I got up early and blew up balloons. It nearly made me sick. But we had to hurry so we wouldn't miss the bus. And Mom said she would tape them around the basement so we don't have to do it when we get home."

"What about the streamers?"

"We did those last night."

"How many kids said they'd come?"

"Twenty-one. That's counting Brett and Travis and his brother Graham." Marcy stuffed the last of her sandwich into her mouth, now having to talk around it. "I haven't heard back from Stephen yet. But Chris told Michael Kelly that he heard Stephen say he *might* come."

"That's good," I answered lamely. Secretly I hoped Stephen wouldn't be there. If he showed up, Marcy wouldn't be good company at all.

After school Dana and I scurried home, dropped our

books inside the back door, grabbed up the bags that held our costumes, and sprinted back out the door. We changed at Marcy's house, crowding into their bathroom, laughing and giggling continuously.

Marcy had decided to be a rag doll. She liked the idea of wearing a big floppy-yarn wig and had made it herself—a bright red one. Always a bargain hunter, her mom had stopped at the local resale shop and been lucky enough to pick up a cast-off square-dance dress made of calico with loads of ruffles. It was perfect. With her painted cheeks, big black shoes, and tall white stockings, her costume looked fabulous. Marcy was thrilled. She even wore one stocking up and one down. She had a flare for fashion. We weren't surprised that she'd pushed for a costume party.

Carli had gone in an entirely different direction. She'd concentrated on some type of inanimate object. For a while she had wondered about being a rocket. But that seemed a little too boyish, so she had decided to dress as a lamp—a very feminine one. She had cut and bent a large piece of cardboard to make the shade, then covered it with pink ruffly cloth. Her father had even rigged up a battery-operated lantern so she could be "turned on," and she had draped an extension cord over one arm as if it were the lamp's plug. We laughed hysterically when we saw her in full costume.

Dana had chosen to turn herself into a butterfly, with large wings of sheer white fabric on which she had painted a kaleidoscope of colors. She had labored intensely to get them just right. Dana was always so fussy about details.

I had changed my mind several times before beginning my own costume. Finally settling on being a teddy bear,

Mom had helped me plan and assemble the fuzzy brown suit out of an old blanket. But I still needed all the girls to help me with my stuffing. No matter how much we tried to smooth it out, I was lumpy. By the time we emerged from the bathroom, we were giddy with laughter.

Guests began to arrive a little before the appointed time. We welcomed pirates and waitresses, princesses and several animals. It was such fun to guess who was who and discover what each of our friends had decided to be. We all made our way into Marcy's basement. I noticed Marcy watching closely for Stephen, but he didn't show up. I felt a mixture of relief on my own account and pity for her. She had really set her heart on his being there.

Then three little old ladies arrived. Stooped over and slow, wearing faded dresses, gray wigs, funny old hats, and wire-rimmed spectacles, they had even worn knee-high hose, complete with holes, drooping down around their ankles and sturdy shoes. Whoever they were, they played their parts to perfection. When we noticed that two of the pairs of legs were quite hairy, we all howled with laughter.

Dana recognized one set of legs and announced that they belonged to Brett, and this brought on another round of laughing. The second old lady was Travis, and the third turned out to be Graham. They all looked fantastic. Once they realized they'd been recognized, they each took off their hats, nodding and bowing for us in elderly fashion. The room applauded.

Dana and Marcy each had a camera, so flashes blinked as cameras clicked. We got used to the sudden flares throughout the evening as one or the other caught some incident on film.

Marcy's mom had been quite generous in allowing us to choose our own menu. She also had gone to a great deal of effort to prepare it all for us. We girls spent some time running up and down the stairs, bringing down ice and drinks and refilling platters. By the time the guests had finished eating, we were starting to feel tired. But we hadn't even gotten to the games yet.

After participating in two, which included a great deal of raucous laughter, I ducked out of the third and sat in a corner where I could see the fun. The floppy brown paws of my teddy costume had become stained with punch, so I took them off and put them on the seat beside me. I wondered how the thick paint that I'd used to make my big black nose was holding up.

"Hi."

Surprised, I looked up at Graham Dawson, Travis's brother.

"Hi."

He eyed the seat beside me and motioned toward it. "Mind if I sit down?"

"No, go ahead." I picked up my discarded paws and stuffed them under my chair. "I like your costume."

He grinned back. "It was Travis's idea. We got the clothes from my grandma. She keeps *everything*. I'll bet they're over fifty years old."

I laughed. "They suit you."

"Yeah, that's what my dad said. I'll take that as a compliment, by the way." He grinned. "Mom wasn't quite as enthusiastic, but we talked her into letting us use her makeup."

The party game was over. I rose to go.

"Hey, Erin, I'm sorry about your granddad." He clearly was feeling awkward about how to say the words, but I liked the sincerity in his voice. It was good to know that people around cared—even though I really didn't know Graham that well.

"Thanks."

All in all, we thought the party was a huge success, and we already were talking about the next one.

✿ ✿ ✿

I guess we all expected Grandma to stay with us for a while and then decide to go back to her own big house again. But it didn't turn out that way. She talked about it from time to time, making statements like "I should really be going home and letting you get on with your lives." Or, "I just hate to think of being all alone again." Or, "Brett, you must be getting anxious for your grandma to let you have your own room back." Each time she said something like that, either Mom or Dad would assure her she was welcome to stay in our home for as long as she liked. But I think we all were feeling a little bit crowded, in more ways than one.

The first clear indication that she was reluctant to carry on with her own life was when she told Uncle Patrick over the phone to go ahead and sell the motor home. I don't think any of us expected her to drive it. Still, I saw Brett look up with a funny expression. There went the fishing trip for sure. Maybe he'd been hoping that he and Dad would be able to take it.

Grandma did go back to her house once. She made it clear that she planned to be gone for just a short while. She stayed away for only three days, and then Dad got a call that she was at the bus station and he could come pick her up.

She had more suitcases this time. And she did bring Uncle Eric's picture. She had some other pictures too. Her favorite one of her and Grandpa, and some of the whole family. I think it was the pictures that made me realize she intended to stay for quite a while. Maybe forever.

If Mom and Dad were concerned about it, they certainly never let it show. Mom must have gotten tired at times of Grandma's chatter, but she smiled and added a few words of her own now and then. I had the feeling, though, that the necessary drives to take us places or the daily trip to pick up Corey after morning kindergarten were now welcome excursions for Mom. She'd sort of take a big breath as she crawled behind the wheel. It probably felt good to leave the house for even a short time.

Yet I was taken totally by surprise when Dad's voice took on the "family conference" tone one morning as we were gathered around the breakfast table. Grandma usually slept late and fixed her own toast or muffin to go with the leftover coffee in the pot. So it was just our family who sat around the table enjoying Mom's blueberry pancakes.

"Your mother and I have done a good deal of talking—and praying—and we think that it might be the right time to think of a bigger house," Dad said, looking around the table.

That sure got our attention in a hurry. I saw Brett jerk his head up as though in disbelief and Dana's eyes grow large. Corey was busy poking a fork into the yolk of his egg to make it "bleed," so he wasn't paying much atten-

tion. The yolk didn't run very well. Mom was too concerned about making sure it was thoroughly cooked.
Corey didn't like blueberry pancakes, though I never
could figure out the reason. And it was the only time that
I remember Mom allowing any of us special privileges
with the meal offerings. She seemed too baffled by it to
insist that he eat his pancakes.

"What kind of a bigger house?" Brett spoke first.

"Just a . . . a medium-big house," Dad went on.
"Nothing fancy—just more room. We've even thought of
something with a mother-in-law suite."

"What's a mother-in-law suite?" I could feel myself
frown as I asked the question. I knew enough about family relationships to know that Dad's mother-in-law was
Grandma Tyler, but I hadn't heard anything about
Grandma Tyler needing a place to stay.

My Tyler grandparents were missionaries. Except
through letters and cards, and now even more frequent
e-mails, I felt I hardly knew them. Mom had pictures of
us kids taken with them when they had been back in
America on one of their home assignments. But being
medical missionaries and desperately needed at the clinic
in Bolivia, they didn't come home as often as some missionaries—nor stay as long. But Dad was answering my
question, even as my mind whirled with more questions.

"That's just two or three rooms—sort of like an apartment—attached to a home. If we had something like that,
Grandma Walsh could be with us . . . yet have some space
of her own."

"She's not your mother-in-law," I heard Brett say, expressing my very thought.

"Well . . . it doesn't have to be for the wife's mother.

Not for any mother, in fact. But it often is—that's why the name."

"Isn't Grandma Walsh going back home?" Corey asked directly. There. The question we all wondered about was on the table. Corey had been listening after all.

Dad just shook his head. "I'm not sure," he answered honestly. "She still seems sort of lonely. We want her to know she can stay with us for as long as she wishes. But we don't want all of you crowded in together either. It isn't fair that you have to give up your rooms."

Mom hadn't been saying much, but I noticed she nodded every now and then as though to second everything Dad was saying.

Actually, it sounded rather exciting. Already my mind was beginning to think of a new room for Dana and me to share. One with bigger closets and room for another chest of drawers so we wouldn't have to be arguing over who had what space all the time. I could even envision a window seat like I'd seen in a magazine. I wondered if Mom would let us have one. They were great places to curl up with a book. You could even tuck your book under a cushion if you didn't feel like putting it back on the shelf when you were done.

"Can I have my own room?" Brett was asking. "Or do I still have to share with—?" He stopped before he'd actually uttered Corey's name, but even Corey got the point.

His head came up. "Uh-uh," he said, shaking his head emphatically, waving a bite of egg in the air. "I don't want to sleep alone. I get scared."

"You've gotta learn to sleep alone sometime," Brett argued. "Won't be long until I go off to college. Then what?"

"I'll go too," said Corey without a moment's hesitation.

Brett snorted.

On the other side of the table, Dana seemed to be deep in thought. "Where?" she asked, as if she hadn't even heard anyone else's comments.

Dad understood her question. "We don't know yet. We need to look around."

Until that moment I hadn't thought about the *where*. I had just assumed that the new house would be right where we were—or at least somewhere very close. Surely Dad wouldn't move us away from our community. Our friends.

"You mean we might have to move somewhere else?" My voice squeaked at the incredible notion.

"Most likely."

I think all of us just sat and stared. Dad had always said that what we had was just fine. That good homes were not fashioned out of wood and bricks—but love and respect. Now he was prepared to move? *Away?*

"I don't think I want to move," said Dana, shaking her head and echoing my feelings exactly.

"I do," piped up Corey.

"How do you know? You've never moved. You don't even know what it's like." I was a little short with him. I didn't want anyone reinforcing Dad's idea until we'd at least had some time to think about it.

"I know," said Corey, pushing a piece of toast into the egg yolk without too much success. "But after I move— then I *will* know."

I guess, somehow, that made sense. Anyway, there was little point in arguing with Corey. I turned my attention back to Dad, who was speaking again. "Mom and I have been doing a lot of praying and talking. It seems that now would be a good time to make a move. As you kids enter the teen years, you could use more space—each have your own room. And it seems . . ."

But he lost me right there. Was he thinking Dana and I would not be sharing a room anymore? We'd always shared a room. I couldn't imagine sleeping alone. It wasn't that I was scared—like Corey. It was just that I liked Dana's company. She must have felt the same way because before I could even speak, she asked, "Would we *have* to have separate rooms?"

She had interrupted Dad. Usually we were gently reminded that we were not to do that, but this time Dad stopped midsentence and looked at Dana. "You don't want to have your own room?" He sounded a little surprised.

"Not really," she answered, sounding less firm. Maybe she was wondering if that made her odd.

I spoke up quickly. "Me neither."

Dad just shrugged and looked over at Mom. She shrugged back—but she also smiled. "You won't be required to have your own rooms if that's the way you feel about it," she said. She looked rather pleased—as she sometimes did when we remembered our proper manners in public or were thoughtful about another person or something.

"Me too," said Corey, stuffing in more toast. "I'll sleep with them too."

I couldn't help but smile at his simple solution.

Dana was shaking her head. "Then why move?" The question seemed to be directed at Corey, but I don't think he was getting the message. Dana continued, "We would be just as squashed in the new room if we had to have three beds in it."

"Then we'll put in a big bed and we can all sleep together," said Corey around a bite of toast.

Dana rolled her eyes. "No, Corey. You need to be in a boy's room. Not with us girls."

"But Brett don't want to share."

"Doesn't," corrected Mom, but she gave him a little pat on the arm. I couldn't help feeling a little bit sorry for poor Corey.

Dad stirred. "We don't have any more time to discuss this right now. You need to get at your morning chores. It's something we'll all pray about and think about, and we'll talk about it again later. We might even take a few drives to look around. See what area looks good. What we can find. We want to be sure to have access to good schools."

Good schools. The very words frightened me. I liked my school. There was no way I wanted to move to another. I'd lose Marcy—and my other classmates. I was ready to shake my head and vow that I for one was staying put. But I bit my lip and said nothing. Dad was already standing up, and I knew he expected us to get right to those chores he had spoken of.

It wasn't until later that I started to sort it out. It was really Grandma Walsh's fault. If it wasn't for her, we'd be just fine. We'd had enough room in the past to all fit.

But I couldn't stay angry with Grandma. I'd seen her sad face over the months since Grandpa had died. I couldn't blame her for not wanting to be alone. I wouldn't want that either.

Suddenly I felt angry with Grandpa Walsh for dying. I'd always thought of him as old—but he really wasn't, not as grown-ups count age. I'd overheard several people say, "What a shame. At his age." Or, "He was so young to go so quickly." I hadn't really paid attention to them till now. I'd also heard remarks like "He worked too hard. Just wouldn't slow down." "It's a lesson for us. You just have to take care of your heart." "Exercise more." "Watch that cholesterol." Things like that. So if Grandpa had been doing wrong things—and not doing right things—it really *was* his fault. He should have taken better care of himself. Then Grandma would be in her own house—not looking so sad and hanging out in Brett and Corey's bedroom. Things could have stayed the same. We wouldn't have to be thinking about a move at all.

But I also felt increasingly guilty about being mad at Grandpa. I loved Grandpa, and it was such a mixed-up feeling to love and be angry all at the same time. One minute I chided myself and tears came to my eyes. I still missed him. Then an ugly feeling would go all through me, turning that love to thoughts like "He shouldn't have . . ." Or, "He should have . . ." and I'd be mad again. It was confusing—and painful—all at the same time.

But I didn't talk to anyone about it. In fact, I would have been very ashamed if anyone had suspected how I felt. I tried to hide it—and mostly I could. But once in a while something almost slipped out, and then I would say or do something to try to quickly cover it up. I'd never tried to deceive that way before and it was hard. Almost as if I was living a lie. I knew I couldn't hide my true thoughts and feelings from God. He knew my very soul. My deepest emotions. Mom and Dad had always taught us that. It was scary. Sometimes I found myself fearing that God might strike me down dead—or something. Once I even caught myself quickly looking down at my hands to see if I'd been smitten with leprosy. I'd heard in Sunday school class that leprosy was how He punished people in the old days—like in the Old Testament. I was relieved to see that my hands still looked okay, but I didn't really know what leprosy looked like anyway. White . . . I think. Something about white.

I didn't even dare to pray about it, because that would be admitting there was a problem. To myself. And to God. If He hadn't caught on yet, I sure didn't want to be the one to draw His attention to it.

I didn't talk to Dana about it either. I was used to sharing everything with Dana. But she had been somehow different lately. She didn't seem to talk about much of anything. And she didn't laugh as much as she used to either. Did growing up make so much difference? She often just lay on her bed. Sometimes reading. Sometimes just staring at the ceiling, with the book abandoned on the bed beside her. I couldn't understand it. She'd never been as excited about activity as I. But at least she'd been doing something. Now she didn't really seem to care that much about pursuing fun.

Then another thought struck me. Maybe that was Grandpa's fault too. Maybe Dana didn't want to move either. Maybe she was struggling along, trying to hide angry thoughts as well. Maybe I should talk to her.

But I couldn't. I didn't dare. What if I were all wrong? Then Dana would give me one of her disapproving looks—probably far more disdainful than any that she'd sent me recently. And, worse than that, she'd *know*.

CHAPTER
SIX

EVEN MOM AND DAD were looking disappointed as we filed back into our home after another long afternoon of searching for a place to build the new house. It was a cold and dreary February day, and our moods suited the weather well. The few lots scattered here and there in the established neighborhoods near our current house had been rejected as unsuitable for several years. It seemed that, if we were to build at all, we would be forced to extend our search to a much larger radius.

Actually, the choice of a floor plan was going much better. Mom and Dad had narrowed their original ideas down to three layouts. And, from then on, the final selection would be based upon the lot.

Brett was enthusiastically favoring the one with a walk-out basement. But Dana preferred the Cape Cod that more closely resembled our current home. I tried not to get involved in too many of the discussions about the house. But I sure was looking over the properties carefully. And I was watching the people too. I still hadn't seen any of the kids from my school around the lots where we'd been looking.

Corey was the only one who still had the energy to talk about the house. He followed Dad into the living room, chattering away. "Daddy, when we get the right place, can I have my own tree? 'Cause I'd like to be able to look outta my window and see the birds building nests in it. Then I could even leave some string and stuff around it so the birdies could get 'em in their beaks and fly way up to where they're building. My teacher says that birdies will use stuff like that if you leave it by their tree."

Dad dropped into his easy chair and pulled Corey onto his lap. "It would be nice of you to take care of the birds. And I'm sure they would use your string. I'll tell you what. Why don't you gather the kinds of string you want to use, and we'll cut it up and put it in a plastic bag. Then you'll be ready in the spring to put it out by a tree somewhere. I can't promise you that you'll have one by your window. But I'm sure we can find a nice tree nearby."

"That's a *good* idea! I'll go get my special scissors and ask Mommy for some of her strings. The ones with the bright colors. Mommy!" He had already bounced back off Dad's lap and trotted away.

I approached Dad quietly. His head was leaning back against the chair, and his eyes had closed. I wasn't sure whether to speak to him or not, but the floor squeaked under my feet and his eyes popped back open. Then he smiled at me warmly.

"Hi, honey. Are you as tired as I am?"

I drew closer to the chair. "I guess I am."

"Did you want to talk to me, Erin?"

I blushed a little. To be truthful, I wasn't quite sure what it was I wanted to say. I felt the need to express something of what I'd been feeling. But the words eluded me. "No, I just wanted to see how you're doing." My hesitation must have indicated otherwise.

"Come here, honey." Dad sat forward and reached out to hug me. I wrapped my arms around his neck and buried my face against him, trying hard not to cry. I wasn't even sure why I was fighting tears. But somehow the closeness seemed to be releasing some of the feelings I'd tried so hard to force down.

"It'll be okay, Erin. In a few months all this hard work will pay off, and we'll have a nice house to show for it. We'll probably even look back and laugh. They say it's always darkest before the dawn. So I'll bet we find just the right place really soon."

I couldn't speak. I didn't trust my voice.

"You know, pretty soon you'll probably be too old to cuddle. Would you like to just sit with me for a while?"

Dana and I had decided some time ago that we were too old to sit on Daddy's lap the way Corey still did. But tonight I just wanted to be close to him. Dana might not approve, but I didn't care. Maybe I'd wait and grow up next year. Instead, I snuggled up against his chest and tucked my feet between the cushion and the side of the chair. I didn't fit well anymore, but it felt wonderful. We sat in silence together.

After some time, Dad whispered, "Can you tell me what's bothering you?"

Maybe now I could speak without crying. I thought I'd better try or I might never find the courage. "Things are just . . . so different now," I whispered, trying to gather my thoughts. "So much has changed . . . and so fast. Grandpa's gone, and Grandma's here. And now it's hard to think about *more* change with the house. I don't want to complain. It's not really bad anyway. It's just so different. I guess." My words began to flow more quickly. "I guess I'm scared. That's probably dumb, because there's not really anything to be afraid of. It's not like being afraid of the dark. I guess I just thought I knew how things were supposed to feel . . . and it doesn't feel like that anymore. I liked it the way it was."

Dad sighed. Then I felt him press a kiss against the top of my head. "I know just what you mean. I feel like that too," he said.

I was shocked. Surely my dad never questioned the way his life was going.

"But, Erin, life doesn't ever stay easy and familiar. Life always changes. And we have to try to change with it." I could tell he was choosing his words carefully, trying not to lecture. But right now, I didn't mind at all. I just wanted some words of comfort, no matter what form they took. "It's like this house. Nobody wanted to move. We all wanted to stay. But life changed—and in the process pushed us out. Even if we dug in our heels and insisted on staying put, it isn't the same. Our family has changed. We have Grandma to take care of now—and you kids are growing up so quickly. We have to move on too."

I swallowed back my response. I wished I could tell Dad that I sometimes blamed Grandpa for all of the changes. But I could never say that out loud. Even if I had to keep that secret, though, I felt so much better just sitting with Dad right now, and feeling loved.

"Erin, I've been thinking about Psalm Twenty-three for some time now. You know it. It starts, 'The Lord is my shepherd, I shall not want.' This is a little bit of a 'valley of shadow' for us right now. It's so encouraging to remember that we never go through those valleys alone. That God always goes through with us." Then he smiled.

"And the truth is, we have to admit that this particular valley is not so deep. You and I in our lives will probably need to face much darker times than these. In fact, this is more like simple growing pains. I think we'd all be able to enjoy the idea of building a house if it hadn't followed so quickly on the heels of Grandpa's passing away. Your mom and I have dreamed about doing this for years."

"You have?" No one had ever mentioned that to me.

"Sure. That's one of the reasons we've been so careful with our money. We knew we couldn't live here forever."

My mind was working to absorb the thought. Maybe this wasn't Grandpa's fault after all. That would be a huge relief. I knew there was another question I needed to ask. It had plagued me, along with those other dark feelings about God.

"But, Daddy, why do we have to have those valleys at all? I mean, if God can heal blind people and make the winds stop and all that, why does He let bad things happen to us?"

He was quiet for a long time. "That's a good question, Erin. It's a question that lots of adults ask too. And I don't know how well I can answer it, but I'll tell you what I think.

"I think there are many reasons why God allows unpleasant things to happen—or maybe it's better to say there are lots of ways He uses the difficult things to bring good in our lives. Sometimes it's to make our faith stronger. So we'll believe that God can help us in the really hard times because we've already seen Him at work. It's one thing to read the Bible and learn that God calmed a storm; it's another thing to know that He's calmed a storm—that He's solved a serious problem—in our own lives.

"Then again, sometimes it's to call us back because we've begun to let other things be more important than God in our hearts.

"And I would have to say that sometimes it's just because that's the way our world works. Adam and Eve sinned. And we sin. And the guy living next door sins. And the lady on the other side of the city sins. Every one of us does things that displease God. And all that sin just makes life painful sometimes. God didn't plan our world to be painful. What we see are just the side effects of all that sin. Dying. Struggling to make ends meet. Feeling unloved. Even most of our own anger and frustration. If we really understood, we'd see that most of it comes from sin."

I could hear Corey's footsteps coming up from the basement, and I knew I didn't have much time left. "Do *you* think God still punishes people like He did the Israelites in the Bible?"

He paused, a puzzled expression in his eyes. "Yes . . . I guess I do. But I'm very sure that if and when He does, it's out of love. I know it would only be done to get our attention and save us from the disaster we'd face if we kept going the direction we were headed."

Daddy's arm tightened around my shoulders. "But, Erin—sometimes it isn't about us at all."

I frowned.

"It's because someone else needs to see God at work. In our lives. How He helps us to handle difficult things. That is one of the marks of a Christian and is often the reason that another person realizes God is who He claims to be. When we have a strength that isn't our own to draw on—a peace even in the bad times—it's a wonderful testimony to others of what God can do for those who love Him."

I thought I was beginning to see, but before I could even nod to agree with Daddy, Corey burst in upon us.

"I got 'em, Daddy. I got the strings. And just look at all the colors!"

I slipped off Dad's lap. "I think I'll go finish my homework."

"Erin." His eyes met mine and asked me to listen just a moment more. "The most important thing to remember is that God loves you. I know you've heard that all your life. But it's really an amazing thing, honey. And God never *tries* to hurt us. He always works for our good. That's a promise."

"Okay," I whispered, trying a wobbly smile before I turned away. It didn't all make sense. But I was willing to believe my dad knew what he was talking about.

❦ ❦ ❦

There was something mysterious in the air. Dana and I could feel it from the moment we walked into the house after school. There was something about the way Mom was acting. So we decided to hang around in the kitchen and see if we could pick up any clues. She wasn't telling, though. She just chatted as usual while she moved about, making fried chicken for supper. She did tell us that Grandma had gone out for supper with a friend.

When Daddy got home, she met him at the door and plunked a kiss on his cheek. He looked surprised but just grinned and said, his eyes twinkling, "I guess you missed me today."

They both laughed. Mom stood there smiling into his eyes.

"What's up? You look like the cat that just swallowed the canary."

"I thought we'd picnic tonight."

"Picnic? It's way too cold! I admit we've had a warm spell, but it's still officially winter, you know."

"We could eat in the van. I'm almost done packing it."

I looked at Dana and she looked back, but neither of us could offer a thing about what was going on. She whispered, "Do you think we'll be invited?"

I just shrugged. At least Mom had made plenty of chicken.

But when we all were immediately hustled into action, I knew we were in on it—whatever it was. Dana stayed with Mom to help finish with the picnic, I scooted Corey up to the bedroom to hurry him into playclothes, and Brett was sent to get the well-used picnic basket from the attic. None of it made sense, but we followed directions anyway and grabbed our jackets before heading to the garage.

"Where to?" Dad eyed Mom across the front seat. He was thoroughly enjoying the suspense.

Mom was too. "Just drive. I'll let you know."

Mom's fried chicken was making my mouth water even before we'd left the driveway. I sure hoped she'd let us dive in soon. Dana, who shared the middle bench seat with Corey, was put in charge of distributing our picnic from the basket at her feet. She served Mom and Dad first, then got Corey set up with a plate, and finally passed food back to Brett and me, who were seated in the back. We settled back with a favorite supper and a trip to—where?

Mom directed the car through town and then out into

the country. We shot past fields and little farmhouses for a while before coming over a hill and finding a few houses scattered around a little valley. It looked like a miniature town. Mom's instructions took us down a side street in the middle of it. Then the side street became an old lane that ended in a patch of woods just beyond the last cluster of houses. There was a "For Sale" sign tacked to an old fence post.

Dad's face lost some of its enthusiasm. But Mom just opened her door and called everyone to follow, reminding us to toss our paper plates and napkins into the trash bag as we climbed out. We lost no time jumping from the van and scurrying toward the sign. We all understood immediately what she was thinking. We had never explored properties outside a regular neighborhood before this.

"Why don't you kids take a walk down that path? See the clearing over there? Take a few minutes to look around, will you?" Mom instructed. Dad and Mom followed behind us at a distance. She had slipped her hand into his, and they were talking in low voices.

Corey, beside himself with excitement, scampered through the trees, exclaiming at each early bird he noticed. Apparently they had been studying birds at school, and he was setting out to become the expert. Dana dutifully followed him. I moved around with Brett more systematically, wanting an overview of the property.

The street side was thick with trees. A jumble of bare branches stretched up to form a tangled web above us, and the air smelled wet and woodsy. There were still mounds of snow in places where the sun hadn't been able to reach, but we tramped forward as if we were frontier explorers. It was wonderful.

Once we were through the trees, we could see we were

on a hill that sloped down from the road. We knew that somewhere behind us the property line stopped, because we could make out the stubbled stalks of a cornfield. A wonderful view stretched on to where there had to be a river. A line of trees meandered away to the west.

To the south, Brett pointed out, there was another cluster of trees and a big house tucked into it, looking as if it had been built recently and the grass hadn't been planted yet. To the north, there was a steeper slope that stretched downward to a sprawling assortment of farm buildings. We weren't quite sure what the shapes were that dotted the field, but they seemed like they might be cattle or sheep.

Brett looked back over his shoulder at me. "We could build a ramp. For skateboards. Out here we could build an awesome ramp. I could never build one in town. But I'll bet Dad'll let me build here. Just imagine how big we could make it."

I was still wondering how the conversation between Mom and Dad was going. I didn't want to make too many plans until I saw how that turned out. Actually, I didn't see Dad as a country dweller.

Just then Mom and Dad emerged from the wooded area and joined us on the hillside. It appeared she'd been able to talk him into walking around with her. They stood looking out over the valley together and talking quietly.

"I like the view so much," Dana enthused. "It's like a picture. Where would we build the house?"

Dad was the one who answered. "It *is* a nice property. There's no question about that. A person could clear a few of the trees up near the road for a lane and put the house back here where it looks down this hill." He seemed to be thinking things through as he spoke. "I suppose a well would be necessary. Or maybe the housing development has water out here. But there would be the added cost of bringing in the utilities. In a neighborhood, that would already be included in the lot price. I wonder how much that would run."

"We could ask John and Nancy Kelly," Mom pointed out. "They just built their home a few years ago. It might be unreasonable to pay that extra, but it does seem that you'd get a nice location for your effort." The two had gone back to talking only to each other.

"Well, there's no denying that the location is nice. But I think it's also more costly to build out here and harder to sell. I'll have to check around and see how other homes compare."

"But if the money from Dad's estate can cover the added expense of the land, it shouldn't cost us any more than what we'd planned." Mom was trying hard not to sound as if she were pressing him, but we could tell where her heart was.

I listened quietly, trying to decide if I liked the idea of country living.

"Possibly," I heard Dad say.

"I know that it's farther from school and friends, but—"

Dad interrupted. "That's another thing we'd have to check on, Angie. I'm not sure it would be the same school system."

Dana, Brett, and I froze. Mom looked thoughtful. They had mentioned once or twice that we might have to change schools if we couldn't find a lot close enough, but we had each held out hope that it wouldn't happen.

"Where would we go to school?" I knew Dana was working hard to keep her voice under control.

Mom and Dad suddenly seemed aware that we were listening. Dad sounded cautious as he answered, "I'm not sure. This little town is much too small to have its own school, so maybe there's a bus that comes out here to take you back to your school. I'm just not sure. It would be another thing we'd have to check."

"Well, anyway," Mom concluded the discussion brightly, "we've enjoyed our first picnic of the year and dreamed a little dream. Maybe that's all that will come of this, but I've enjoyed myself. Anybody else had a nice time?"

"It was great!" Corey's exuberance hadn't ebbed.

We wandered back through the trees and climbed into the van, avoiding the topic of the acreage. It wasn't until days later that we kids managed to overhear more as our parents gathered information. The land behind the neighboring house would soon be developed, and many new homes added. So the lane from the housing development would become a paved road. The field behind the land we'd looked at would stay as it was. Dad said it would help the resale of any house built on that land to have the subdivision near it. That was one point in favor of the land. On the other hand, it might be some time before construction there would begin, and we probably would have to watch it being developed over the next five to ten years. That might be unsightly.

The biggest drawback to the property came when it was confirmed that the school system would be different. Children in that area were bused in the opposite direction from our town. And in my mind, that was the most difficult obstacle to overcome. Dad said we'd need to pray about it for a while, but the real estate agent was saying we didn't have long to decide. I hoped God would speak quickly. My own feelings were torn. I had seen Corey nearly burst with excitement every time he described the acreage, and I could picture him living there. The vivid image drew me. Even Brett had become excited about the possibility of living "out," as he called it. Dana and I were the ones who hesitated.

I personally was surprised that Brett was so open to the idea. I think it helped him to remember that Dad was allowing him to try for his driver's license during the summer, and so the place seemed less isolated to him. I think he pictured bringing all his friends over and having room to roam—or build a skateboard ramp, or whatever. Brett was talking a lot about skateboards lately.

I hoped I wasn't expected to be excited about Brett's dreams of his own ramp. He'd likely bring all his new skateboarding friends to enjoy it. I couldn't imagine much peace or solitude with a gang of guys Brett's age occupying our yard. I could almost hear the clunk and whir of the skateboards against wood, and it seemed to me to be hopelessly out of place on that quiet hillside. And I was certain he wouldn't let me participate anyway. We didn't even play basketball together much anymore. He was much more anxious to be with his new friends. No, the ramp was not something I would look forward to.

One day passed, and then another. There were frequent calls from the real estate agent alerting Dad that someone else had been looking at the property. Even Mom had lost her conviction that it was "just right." Switching schools was not what she'd had in mind.

In the end, the land won out in all our hearts. For various reasons, we each came to believe that it was worth the sacrifices we'd have to make in the short term to have what we pictured as an idyllic setting in the long term. Dana and I agreed to it because, being best friends, we were sure we wouldn't really be lonely. And Corey's excitement was contagious. Also, Dad had promised that we'd still make the drive to our church so we weren't going to lose touch with our friends completely. The turning moment for the two of us was when Dana pointed out that she and I probably would be in different schools next year anway, and we might as well move to an area we liked so much.

Once we had finally decided for sure, Grandma went to meet with Uncle Patrick to make the arrangements for him to put her house on the market. We knew then that she was with us to stay.

So Mom and Dad left us watching Corey while they dashed about to numerous meetings with architects, contractors, and bankers. It was all happening so quickly now. And I found myself daydreaming about what it would all be like when it was finished. I guess, without realizing it, I was becoming as excited as Corey.

❧   ❧   ❧

Immediately after Brett's birthday, he tried for his driver's license. He failed and spent the rest of the day slamming around the house, muttering things about unfairness and biases against teenage guys. He and Dad took frequent trips to parking lots, where he practiced for next time. He was sure he'd be ready. I wondered if Dad felt Brett had been failed unjustly or if he too thought Brett needed a little more experience. But he kept encouraging and coaching.

I was beginning to think the whole driving issue was

tougher on Mom. Even though Brett had grown just as tall as Dad during the last school year, I could tell that Mom wasn't convinced he was ready for the responsibility of driving. And I noticed she was never the one to take Brett out for his practice sessions.

After a couple of weeks, Dad took Brett to the city to try again. I think this time they were both very excited. We watched them drive off down the street and wondered if the next time we saw Brett he'd be beside himself with joy—or glum again. I was certainly hoping for joy.

When the two returned, it was definitely joy we saw. That joy radiated out through the windshield from Brett's face, behind the steering wheel of Dad's car. Corey and I rushed to the front porch and cheered as they mounted the steps. Corey was twirling and bobbing in fits.

"He made it. Brett can drive by hisself! He can drive *me* around. Let's go. Come on."

Brett picked him up and tossed him into the air. Then he looked back at Dad. "Can we?"

Dad grinned and held the keys out to Brett again, saying, "You'd better take the van this time." With an air of excitement, everyone jumped at once to climb in. Only Grandma stayed behind.

We kept mostly to the less-traveled roads, Mom telling Brett to slow down a bit and Corey repeating, "Speed up. Speed up." Finally Dad insisted that he hush.

It was exhilarating to watch Brett. His face shone even though he tried not to let his excitement show. And on the way home, Mom suggested that we "hit the drive-through for ice cream cones." We all caught the pun and howled our response.

Dad said with a grin, "Don't bother to hit it. Just pull up at the window." That brought a rowdy whoop from the backseat where Corey and I were riding.

Mom patted Brett's shoulder, and Dana just smiled and looked content. I suppose each of us was anticipating the additional possibilities we'd experience with another driver in the family.

❧ ❧ ❧

When we celebrated Dana's thirteenth birthday in grand style, it had an underlying feeling of a "farewell party." All Dana's school pals were invited, and most of them managed to gather in our backyard for hot dogs and games. I wandered through the crowd of familiar kids and wondered if we'd ever fit in so well in the new school. Mom and I had spent much time together preparing for the party. I tried not to let my feelings spoil the day, but I'm not sure I succeeded very well. Looking at these friends and realizing that I would rarely see them anymore, I had a hard time getting myself up to celebrating anything. This was besides the fact that Dana was now a teenager and I was still just a preteen.

And, further, Dana had become increasingly distant. She seldom wanted to ride bikes or do anything with me. In fact, outside of school and church, Dana rarely went anyplace anymore. We were all a little baffled, but we had hopes she'd pull out of it shortly. Mom maintained that it was all part of growing up. I sure hoped I wouldn't become gloomy and introspective when it was my turn.

Shortly after the party, Dana fell ill. We assumed it was a simple cold with a mild fever, and that it might even explain her recent sullenness. Then she developed a strange rash on her face. So Mom took her into the doctor twice, and Dana was given antibiotics. It must have worked because the rash went away, though she still dragged around. And, try as I might, I couldn't talk her into joining me when I explored our emerging new house. She routinely waited in the car reading a book while Mom and Dad talked to the builders and Corey trotted along behind me.

❧   ❧   ❧

The end of the school year this time would mean saying good-bye to many of our classmates. The importance of being able to see so many of our best friends every Sunday at church, no matter where we lived, could not be overstated. But Marcy was dismal during most of our times together throughout the last weeks of classes.

She drove out with us as often as she could to visit "our land," as she had dubbed it. She stood with me as we watched the first trees being uprooted and cast aside. We paced off imaginary walls together on the grassy knoll and tried to imagine where each bedroom would be between the flags that had been stuck into the ground.

But Marcy missed the whole exciting ground breaking while her family was on vacation. By the time she got back, the basement had been poured and the first level had been framed over it. The rows of two-by-fours alluded to where the walls would be, though it was surprisingly difficult to make it seem right in our minds. The skeleton looked even smaller than the house we had now.

"They already put in the stairs to the basement. Can we go down?"

"Sure," I answered as if I personally were the homeowner. "Just be careful. There's all sorts of nails and things."

"Wow. It echoes down here." We walked a few steps farther, and Marcy squealed. "Wow," she said again, "I love a basement with big walkout glass doors. What room is this?"

"This is going to be the family room. There was supposed to be one on the main floor beside the kitchen, but Mom and Dad changed that to make a bedroom, a bathroom, and a little sitting room for Grandma. See, this is where the fireplace will go, and this is where we're going to build a bathroom. But we're not going to do that for a while. And, eventually, Brett gets a bedroom over here. For a while, he's still got to be with Corey."

"Bet he's not excited about that."

"I don't think he minds. I think he's tired of being in our basement. He'd like something besides cement walls around him for a while."

Marcy nodded. "Yeah. I would too."

We stepped out the glass door and walked far enough away to get a good view of the back of the house. Then we turned to look out over the cornfield, which was just beginning to show a hint of green. It was a wonderful thing to be moving to the country, where all around were signs of life and serenity. I was sure Marcy was feeling the same things. We breathed it all in deeply, and I felt contentment seep through me.

"I'm trying to talk my parents into moving to that new neighborhood you said they were going to build up here. Where is it?" Marcy asked.

"Over there, past that house and down toward the river just a little." We were both old enough to know that it was an irrational dream, but we allowed ourselves to embrace the notion just the same.

"Hmm. I think I'd like it here too. Can you ride your bike farther?"

"Mom says we can go on the neighborhood streets, but we have to stay off the main road." Then my emotions flopped back to the grim reality. "I don't know why we'd want to go, though. We don't know anybody."

"You will." Marcy tossed an arm over my shoulder and marched me back around to the front of the house. "It's a great house. And I expect to be invited to sleep over all the time."

I smiled. "Oh, you will. I told Mom we'd better just make another room for you." If only that could have been a serious offer. If only Marcy could have just come along with us.

❀ ❀ ❀

Summer was passing slowly. We registered at the new school and began to pack for our upcoming move. The building of our new house had progressed quickly at first. It had taken shape almost overnight, and then everything slowed to a crawl. By outward appearances, it was nearly done. But on the inside, improvements seemed minuscule, as I saw it. The builders fussed with the plumbing and wiring and such things much longer than I thought necessary. But they finally got around to finishing walls, and the rooms began to make sense. That was the most exciting part of all. Where there had only been a jungle of two-by-fours, there were now rooms and closets and hallways. I found the whole process both frustrating and fascinating.

There were plenty of trees in our new wooded front yard, but Corey's window was at the back of the house overlooking the hillside. One night he brought his little bag of colored yarn to Dad, reminding him of his need for a tree he could watch. Remaining true to his word, Dad took us all to the nursery to pick out one tree each. There was plenty of room in the big backyard to plant them. Brett went for a blue spruce, Corey picked a mountain ash so there'd be berries for his birds, and Dana, who loved things big and sweeping, selected a weeping willow, though it would be many years until it fulfilled its potential. I had a hard time making up my mind, but I finally chose a sugar maple. I looked forward to the day when I'd look out my window and see its array of fall colors.

The next task was to get them planted. We paced back and forth over the yard, lining up new bedroom windows to be sure that we'd each see our own trees. It was fun—but it was a lot of work. I think Dad was especially tired by the time the task was done. He had done almost all the digging. But now we all felt like the new house was really ours. We had planted trees and staked claim.

The day finally came when it was time to move in. Our little house had sold quickly, and the new owners were anxious to take possession. The country house wasn't quite finished yet. There were still moldings to add and a few cupboards in the kitchen and bathroom that had to be hung because the wrong ones arrived the first time and they'd had to be reordered. Most of the painting had been completed. All except the laundry room and Dad's office. But once the flooring had been put in, the whole place had finally begun to feel livable. It would be home.

Mom left a big sheet of thick gray paper by the front

door. The builders had used it to protect the new vinyl
and carpets from their dirty boots. Now Mom would keep
it there until Corey got used to taking his shoes off on
the front mat. Our yard was still solid mud whenever it
rained, with several planks thrown down for a makeshift
sidewalk.

We had tried to think of the best ceremony for moving
day. Brett wanted to shoot off some fireworks that were
left over from the Fourth of July. Dad thought that might
be a little too much commotion.

Dana suggested we could each write out our thoughts
and read them to one another before we went inside. But
since none of the rest of us spent time journaling the way
Dana did, we weren't convinced it would be a good experience. Dana's notebooks were already filled with
thoughts describing her feelings about the last few
months. She'd let me read a few pages here and there.
And I enjoyed it. But not enough to start writing in a
journal of my own—and it was the last thing I wanted to
do in the excitement of moving day.

In the end, our family and the friends who had come
to help gathered around Dad as he said a prayer of ded-
ication for the house while the moving van waited behind
us in the driveway. Then he picked up Mom, much to her
surprise, and carried her across the threshold. We'd all
been in and out so many times already, it seemed rather
strange. But I secretly liked the fact that Dad did it. He
didn't normally do things like that—unexpected things.
Things that surprised even Mom. I got the feeling she
liked it too.

Once those formalities were behind us, there was a
frenzy of activity. Furniture was carried in first, followed
by more boxes than I had ever imagined. Most of them

seemed to be labeled Kitchen, but my job was to watch for those that needed to go upstairs to bedrooms and lug them up if I could. Dad and the other men were unloading boxes onto the front porch; then Brett and two of his friends were bringing them inside and placing them into their assigned rooms. Dana was helping Mom unpack in the kitchen, and Corey was flying everywhere underfoot. I thought I'd better give him a job before someone inadvertently trampled him.

"Hey, Corey, how about putting your books on your shelves? Mommy would be so proud to see you're helping."

"Okay." I had a feeling he would start with a flourish but lose interest quickly. I turned out to be right.

By the end of the day, we were all exhausted. One of Mom's friends stopped by with a casserole, for which Mom just couldn't seem to say thank-you enough, and then we collapsed around our kitchen table. We were half starved—but almost too tired to eat.

Only Grandma seemed to be able to carry the conversation. She'd stayed with a friend until late in the afternoon. Upon arriving, she exclaimed over and over again about her rooms.

Right in the middle of the bustle of the day, Uncle Patrick had arrived to deliver some of the furnishings from her house. The pieces she'd decided to keep had been placed in storage when her home was put up for sale, and the rest had been auctioned off. Now she was delighted to see that the remaining furniture had been brought in and set up in her suite.

"Oh, David, the armoire fits so nicely between the windows, and—Brett, how about another serving of casserole?" She didn't skip a beat as she scooped out more noodles, chicken, and sauce onto Brett's plate. "And my spread and chair coordinate so well with the color of the walls. I have to admit, Angela, that I wasn't sure when you suggested I use that paint. I had always kept my bedroom yellow with that bedspread, but it certainly looks good against that shade of green. What did you call it again?"

"Moss," Mom sighed. We were all excited for Grandma, but we were just too tired to express it right then.

"Moss. I'll have to remember that when I write to my friends."

CHAPTER SEVEN

COREY HAD TAKEN a third helping of oatmeal, and no one seemed to notice. It was the first day of our new school, and attentions were diverted elsewhere. Dana had been late coming to breakfast, and even now she was complaining of aches and pains. Mom tried to question her, wondering if she might be coming down with another flu, but there seemed to be no symptoms other than the aches. We'd already nursed her through an episode of flu since we had moved into the new house, and now I was a little perturbed. Surely she wasn't doing this just to get out of school on the very first day. But in my heart I knew this wasn't in Dana's nature.

"How'd you sleep?" Dad inquired.

Everyone was so preoccupied with Dana that no one was paying any attention elsewhere. I decided since no one else had noticed the dribbles of oatmeal running across the table from the pot to Corey's bowl, I'd better step in. "Corey, I think you've had plenty."

He looked at me crosswise. "I'm big today. So I can eat more."

"Dana, I just can't figure it out," Mom was saying.

"You don't have a fever. Maybe it's just a growth spurt that's making your back and arms ache. Though it seems like I've heard more often about leg aches with growing pains. What do you think, Dave? Should she just stay home?"

By this time Dad was standing behind Dana and feeling along her spine. "When you say it aches, honey, what do you mean? Does it hurt in one place like a bruise, or does it feel more like you've strained a muscle or something?"

Corey began pouring his third serving of milk into his bowl, splashing freely.

"I don't know, Daddy. It just sort of aches. It's almost like the pain moves around. I can't explain it. Maybe I should just take some Tylenol. It'll probably go away once I get to school."

"Dave, I don't like it," Mom murmured. "It's too strange a thing to just let it go. I think I'll call Dr. Miller. I'd feel better if we got it checked out. Though I'm not sure what more he can tell us."

Dad nodded, and Mom headed for the phone in the office, where she could hear better.

"I know just how you feel, Dana." Grandma, who was now frequently joining us at the breakfast table, patted Dana's hand. "I get those aches and pains too. Lucky for you, you'll *outgrow* yours."

When Corey had dumped three large spoonfuls of brown sugar into his bowl, I couldn't keep silent any longer. "Doesn't anybody else see this?" Once I had their attention, I motioned at the mess around Corey's dish and its heaping contents.

"It's just sugar, dear." Grandma smiled at Corey. "It won't hurt him."

I wanted to argue with her but instead turned back to Dana as she spoke.

"I'll be okay, Daddy. But I'd like to go lie down. If I can just rest for a while, then I think I'll be okay. Maybe I could go to school after lunch."

That was as much as I could take. I had piano to practice, and I was glad for a chance to get away from the chaos around the table. Corey could eat all the oatmeal and sugar he wanted. I was just glad to wash my hands of it.

I would even have to admit that I banged on the piano slightly harder than was necessary, just so I wouldn't have to hear the jumble of conversation in the kitchen. Before I was quite finished, Mom popped her head into the living room and informed me that Dana wouldn't be going to school. Perhaps if Dana felt better by noon, she could be dropped off for the last part of the school day. Mom also asked that I watch out for Corey and make sure he got to his new classroom. He'd need help finding his way.

Mom had planned to take Corey herself but was now waiting for a call back from Dr. Miller hoping he could see Dana during the morning. I told her I would go with him and then cross the street to my own school. Dana had managed to spoil Corey's first day of first grade, and my own nervousness was now magnified by her absence. I left the piano bench to gather my backpack and trudged upstairs to see that Corey had his school supplies together. Just as we were tying his shoes, Mom appeared at the doorway to his room, camera in hand.

"I want to take a picture of your first day of grade school, honey. And, Erin, I need a picture of your first day of junior high. Junior high! You're growing up so fast I can hardly believe it. Stay just like you are, you two.

I'd like a picture of you helping Corey, Erin. Smile."

I smiled dutifully and followed behind Corey while Mom escorted him to the front door to take the traditional first-day photos. Dad and Brett followed too.

After the camera clicked a few times in various poses with various family members, Mom and Dad each gave Corey a big hug and kiss and sent the three of us kids on our way down the long driveway. I looked back at Mom. She seemed kind of small—deflated. I don't think she'd been looking forward to this day when all of us were in school all day. Corey's kindergarten really didn't count, since he was home by noon. And I could tell that she was beginning to truly worry about Dana.

The bus didn't come up our lane. It was going to be a long way to walk on snowy winter days, but for now it was pretty. I looked up through the morning light that filtered through the leafy canopy above.

"I'm big today," Corey reminded me. "I'm going to school all day."

"That's right, squirt," Brett answered him. "And pretty soon, you'll understand what a mixed blessing that is." He grinned across at me, and we walked on in silence.

Boarding the school bus was a difficult thing to do. Even at our old school, I never quite got past a little anxiety that there wouldn't be a seat available for Marcy and me to sit together. It never mattered to Marcy, because if there wasn't she'd just ask somebody if they could switch so that we'd have room. I wished with all my heart that Marcy was with me now, especially when I didn't have even Dana with me.

Brett climbed up the steps first and turned, his eyes sizing up the situation on the bus. The smallest kids were seated near the driver and the bigger kids had claimed the back. All eyes were watching to see what we'd do next. Brett worked his way casually down the aisle and chose a seat with the big kids.

As for me, I was much more comfortable sitting forward with Corey, so I pushed him into an empty seat near the front and slid in beside him. No sooner had we taken the seat than the little girl in front of us started a string of questions.

"Who are you guys? Do you live in that new house?"

"Yup," Corey answered confidently. "We were building it this summer, and now we're all moved in."

"What's your name?" the girl prodded.

"I'm Corey. This is Erin. And my brother back there is Brett. See?" Corey pointed back to Brett's seat with a wide wave. "That's him. That's my brother."

Brett pretended not to notice, looking busy adjusting a strap on his backpack.

"What grade are you in?"

"I'm in first grade because this is my first day of school. But it's not really my first day of school because last year I went to kindergarten. It's my first day of all-day school, though."

"I'm in first grade too." The little interviewer in the seat ahead announced the fact as if the two now shared a special position in society. I was beginning to like her. She had a funny, matter-of-fact way of speaking. And I was glad she was conversing with Corey. I had been a little afraid he wouldn't find the new school very friendly, though I couldn't imagine him not being able to chatter away with someone.

I smiled at the girl. She had an upturned nose and a

cute little curly ponytail with a red bow. "What's your name?"

"I'm Rayna. We live in the house next to yours. We built our house too. But Daddy says we paid too much for it. I like it though. I think it's nice."

Corey puffed out his chest and commented, "It costs a bunch to build a house, my daddy says."

These two seemed perfectly suited to each other. I watched out the window and tried not to think about the long day that stretched out in front of me. I wondered what Marcy was doing right now, and whom she'd be sitting with this year on the school bus. I supposed it would be Carli. Then I thought of Dana. I missed her. I hoped with all my heart she would be better soon—maybe by tomorrow.

※　※　※

By Wednesday night it was all I could do to keep myself from rushing into our church in search of Marcy. I forced myself to walk at a dignified pace. Dana followed along behind, apparently much more patient about sharing stories of the new school than I was. Thankfully she had felt well enough to come on Tuesday. I described to Marcy the teachers and the building. I told her about the kids I'd already met and the odd ones I had observed.

Marcy was dramatically empathetic. Then she, in turn, groaned about the classes she'd begun and enthused about seeing some of the familiar faces again. It made me homesick to listen, but I drank it all in anyway.

Dana and Carli were standing near us, speaking in quieter tones. Suddenly out of the corner of my eye I

noticed Carli rush toward the rest room and Dana leaning back against the wall holding her nose. I could only
stare. There was blood dribbling down Dana's hand and
splashing onto her shirt. I hurried over just as Carli ran
back with tissues.

"Dana, sit down," Carli instructed. "Tip your head
back and pinch your nose."

For a fleeting moment I wondered if it was possible
that Carli had actually *hit* Dana. But the ridiculous
thought was immediately dismissed.

"What happened?" Marcy and I asked the question at
the same time.

"I don't know." Dana's voice was muffled behind the
tissue. "Erin, please go get Mom. Please!"

I ran. By the time I reached the preschool room I was
breathless and a little panic-stricken. "Mom." My whisper was breathy and loud. "Dana's nose is bleeding. She
wants you."

Mom hurried out of the room, stopping only to tell
the neighboring teacher to please watch her class. Then
she headed back toward the stairs where Dana was seated.
Already a small crowd of concerned adults had gathered,
and Dana was pressing herself against the wall as if she'd
like it to swallow her up.

"Honey, what happened? Can you get it to stop? Did
you bang it?"

I could see tears forming in Dana's eyes. She looked
frightened and embarrassed. "I want to go home. Mom,
can somebody take me home?"

"Yes, honey, just as soon as we get the bleeding
stopped, we'll take you home."

I saw the blood on Dana's shirt, and I knew she
couldn't go to youth group with Carli now that she had

ruined her clothes. But it hardly seemed fair that the rest of us would have to leave too.

"Erin, please go see if you can find Dad."

I marched up the stairs with Marcy in tow, her questions flying after me. "What happened? Do you know how it started? Did she hit it on something? I've never seen anybody get a nosebleed without hitting it on something."

I assured Marcy that I had absolutely no idea.

We knocked on the door of the boardroom and timidly peeked inside. Dad was seated on the opposite side of the room. When he saw us, he excused himself and moved quickly to the door.

The news of Dana's nosebleed brought an unprecedented response. He flew down the stairs two at a time and sat down beside Dana who, by then, had stopped bleeding. "Honey, are you okay?"

She answered by leaning her head against him and starting to cry. Carli was hovering close, holding Dana's hand.

But the crisis seemed to be over. I breathed freely again. Dana appeared to be okay. I turned toward Marcy, ready now to go to the youth room. But Mom hurried up with a bundle of coats.

"Here's your coat." She handed it to me and crouched beside Dana. "We'll get you home, honey."

People still shuffled about. No one had really left. But Mom was helping Dana into her jacket. We were the ones who'd be leaving.

Dana was the center of attention, and we were all going to pack up and go home without ever going to our activities of the evening. It was unbelievable. There was still so much I hadn't had a chance to tell Marcy.

"Erin, get the boys, please."

I obeyed. But my heart was far from cooperative. It was so unfair. It wasn't my fault Dana had to go home. Why did we all have to go? But even as I was complaining I knew it was unreasonable to expect my parents to make a special trip back.

It was still early when we arrived home, but I headed up for bed anyway. I had finished my homework as quickly as I could after school in anticipation of my first night in youth group. With this milestone stripped away, there was nothing left to do except to watch TV, and I wasn't in the mood for that. I was much more interested in lying in the dark feeling sorry for myself.

Dana walked in and out of the bedroom two or three times in preparation for bed. I ignored her, feigning sleep. She was the last person I wanted to talk to just then. Finally, I could hear her slide her feet down between her sheets and snuggle into her pillow to get comfortable. There was a long, heavy silence, and I thought she must have been drifting off to sleep. Then she whispered across to me in the stillness.

"Erin, I think I'm going to die." The words seared themselves into my mind. Surely I hadn't heard correctly.

I flipped over to face her and whispered back anxiously, "What are you talking about?"

I realized then that she had been crying silently. And I felt horrid for having been feeling and acting so selfishly. On impulse, I slipped out of my bed and crossed to sit down beside her. My voice had softened with sympathy. Suddenly I really wanted to understand what was troubling her.

"There's something wrong with me," Dana said, her voice muffled. "I can feel it. I've been thinking about it for a long time, but now I'm just so scared. I really think I'm going to die."

"Dana, don't say that. You're not going to die. It was just a nosebleed. Lots of kids get nosebleeds."

"But I'm so tired, Erin. I've been tired for months and months. And this summer I kept getting sick. Then the aches started. Sometimes during the night I can hardly sleep I ache so much. I don't know what to do. I get so scared."

"Why didn't you wake someone up? Why didn't you tell Mom and Dad it was that bad? Why didn't you even tell me? I didn't know you were *that* sick."

"I was hoping I could be wrong. I thought I was just being paranoid. But then, the nosebleed. I can't ignore it anymore. Something is very wrong." Her voice broke, and I dropped down closer to her.

"It'll be okay. Mom's going to take you to the doctor. They'll find out what's wrong, and they'll fix it." Tears welled up in my eyes. "You're not going to die, Dana," I repeated with emphasis. "You're not even old."

We sniffled together for a while, neither of us talking. The weight of Dana's words was just too great. I couldn't imagine being thirteen and being scared of dying. It was just too incredible to think about.

"I want you to talk to me, Dana," I whispered hoarsely. "I want you to tell me how you're feeling every day. Even if you don't think you can tell Mom and Dad. I want you to promise that you'll tell me."

"I promise." There was a hint of relief in her voice.

It was some time before we fell asleep, and by then I had crawled under the covers on Dana's bed. It seemed safer if we stuck together.

Dr. Miller eventually chose to refer Mom and Dana to

another doctor—a woman, who was an OB/GYN. It would be a week until they'd be able to see her, and we were all anxious for the day to arrive. In the meantime, Dana walked mechanically through her first days at our new school, colorless and frail. It made me want to throw my arms around her and protect her.

Daddy had asked each of us to pray for Dana whenever we thought of it through the next days, and I noticed that he and Mom spent extra time in the evenings together with their door shut. I imagined that Mom also used a great deal of the school hours praying. I thought back, but I couldn't remember all of us praying so intensely for anything before. Even the new house and the decision about buying the land. It made the knot in my stomach grow tighter, and I worried that my prayers were too vague.

I wasn't sure what you were supposed to pray in a situation like this. Did you *demand*, like the television preacher said, showing God how much faith you had? Or did you let God choose His own answer, trusting in "His good will," like our pastor had suggested? I didn't really know much about either. So I stuck with what I had always prayed. "God, bless Dana. Please make her better soon." It sounded young and a little silly under the circumstances, but I guessed that I wasn't really a "righteous man" anyway, so my prayers probably wouldn't "avail much." I was glad so many other people were praying too, people who were more qualified than I was to ask God for something so important.

On the day the visit with the new doctor occurred, we expected to return home from school to a full report. But Mom still looked distracted and jumpy as she welcomed us to the kitchen for our after-school snack. I

knew without asking that she wasn't content with the results. Though she wasn't offering any information to us.
When Dad finally arrived home, they sequestered themselves in his office, speaking in low voices for some time.
I learned nothing by watching Dana's eyes across the table
as we laid out the plates, and I decided not to press her
for information.

We gathered for supper in near silence. I studied
Dad's face and then watched Mom. It seemed that they
might be ready to make some type of announcement.
Corey cheerfully prayed to bless the meal, and then we
began passing serving dishes around.

Dad cleared his throat. "We need to tell you what Dr.
Britrich suspects is the cause of Dana's problems. I'm
afraid it sounds rather serious."

I watched Brett's eyes dart across to Dana. Corey
seemed somewhat oblivious, but Grandma had begun to
tear already. I swallowed hard and turned back toward
Daddy.

"There are still more tests to be done, but Dr. Britrich
suspects that Dana has something called lupus. It's a dis-
order that affects the immune system—not altogether un-
common in teenage girls. That means her body has trouble fighting disease. Which could explain why Dana has
had so many colds and fevers—and even the rash earlier
this summer. It also explains the fatigue and muscle
aches."

"Is it . . . serious?" My voice trembled.

"It *can* be. The doctor says she thinks this is a fairly
mild case."

Dana refused to look up at any of us as we discussed
her. Her fork stabbed restlessly at her mashed potatoes,
but she wasn't eating.

"What're they gonna do?" Brett's hand was clenched by his plate as he asked the question, the way it had been when Daddy announced Grandpa had died. It made me even more frightened.

"There are a number of medications we can try. They treat the symptoms."

"What do they do to *cure* her?" Grandma's voice squeaked at the end of her question.

For a moment Daddy was quiet. "There isn't a cure yet for lupus. I'm afraid it's something that Dana will contend with throughout her life—if the diagnosis is accurate. As I said, there are still more tests to be done."

Silence fell over us as we attempted to take it all in. I wanted to reach out to Dana. To promise her that it would be all right. But not even Daddy could tell her that anymore. I choked a little and let my eyes drop to my lap. Tears had already begun to roll down my cheeks. There wasn't much more that anyone could say. Our meal proceeded in near silence.

After supper Dana retreated quickly to our bedroom. I followed after a moment or two, anxious to see if there was any way I could comfort her. The door was closed, so I knocked softly and whispered, "It's me."

"Okay. Come in."

Dana was stretched out across her bed, but she wasn't crying. Her fingers plucked carelessly at a loose string on the comforter and her eyes looked hollow.

I approached her cautiously. "Are you okay?"

"No."

I lowered myself onto the bed beside her and waited for her to speak again. Many minutes passed before she was ready.

"It's not fair," she finally whispered. "I thought I was—

I don't know—a *good* person. At least, I thought I was healthy and *normal*. And instead I've got this terrible disease, and my body wants to quit fighting and just die. So I'm going to have to take all this medication to *make* my body go on living. It's not fair, Erin. It's not fair. I had plans!" At last her tears began to flow. The little bed quivered with our sobs.

"It's not fair," I choked out. "It's just not fair."

In the morning, when Dana and I rose, we didn't speak about her illness. We hardly spoke at all. But its presence colored everything, no matter how hard we tried to ignore it. The awful diagnosis traveled with us on the school bus. It was evident in her eyes when we passed each other in the hallway. It was still hanging thick as we traveled home again. I hated this lupus. I hated the darkness it draped across our home. I hated the lifelessness it had inflicted on my sister. And I determined in my heart to hate it forever.

This new loathing stayed with me, even though our family life did proceed with some normalcy. It's not that anyone hated it any less. I saw it in Brett's cold stares whenever it was mentioned. I saw it in the glassy, tearful expression that Mom wore so often and in Dad's tired, pinched face. Even worse, we were each powerless to make it go away. And we were given no choice but to go on as if there had been no diagnosis or dreadful disease. There was still school and church and chores and even play. But each conversation about a doctor's visit or a slight rise in Dana's temperature brought the ugly specter back. And the growing row of pill bottles along the windowsill above our kitchen sink was a constant reminder that we were never to be completely free of it again.

❧ ❧ ❧

I missed Marcy. I still hadn't found anyone in our new school to replace her as a best friend. Not that I really tried. I guess I was waiting for them to invite me into one of the little circles. They didn't. So I just hung back, pretending I didn't care. My grades were the best they had ever been, but that was small consolation. I felt dreadfully alone, and it made it hard at times.

Tryouts for basketball were set to take place before Thanksgiving break. Brett had spent many hours practicing at Travis's house in anticipation. I, however, had no place to practice. We still didn't have the promised concrete pad and hoop at the new house. The possibility that I'd make the team without any practice at all was quite remote, but Brett patted me on the back and tried to be encouraging.

The gymnasium was crowded and noisy when we walked in together. It was easy to see that they'd already divided off the girls from the boys, but kids were still milling around waiting for the tryouts to start. Brett crossed to the far side of the gym and did some warm-up dribbling. His ball-handling ability was what had set him apart on his last team. I think it helped him calm down to show off a little.

I had no such skill to display. So I took a seat along the bleachers until I was called upon. The tryouts were rigorous. First we did several running drills backward, forward, and sideways. Then we split into groups of five and were given basketballs for the dribbling exercises. I could feel my nerves tense as I waited for my turn. Then Brett caught my eye and grinned at me from across the room. It made me feel much better.

The results were not to be posted until the next week-end. I left the gym feeling very little hope, and Brett left certain that he'd have no trouble making his team. He had sized up the competition and remained confident. They were all taller than he, one of them by almost a foot, but he was quick.

For Brett, there were now two sports to pursue. On the one hand, basketball had long been his passion. On the other, he'd discovered a natural ability in skateboarding. As often as he could, he borrowed the car for a trip to the skateboarding park to improve on the various tricks he'd learned. Mom had gone to watch him once and I think had determined that she'd better not do so again. It was breathtaking.

On the Saturday morning when the fall basketball lineups were to be posted, Dad drove Brett and me over to our school. We searched around a little until we found the designated bulletin board in an entryway and discovered the postings that we wanted. Brett's eyes were quicker than mine. He realized first what had happened.

"You made it." His voice was flat.

"No way!" But then my eyes fell on the boys' roster. Brett's name did not appear. He hadn't even been placed on the junior varsity team. "Oh, Brett, I'm sorry."

"It's okay," he muttered and turned for the car.

Dad carried what conversation there was on the way home. Brett had little to say, and I was at a loss for words. We had all expected that he'd make the team.

As we climbed from the car I had finally figured out what I wanted to say. "Brett?"

He faced me reluctantly.

"Thanks. I could never have made my team without

you." There was a sympathetic look in my eye that must have told him how sincerely I meant the words.

"It's okay."

I knew he meant that *he'd* be okay. And I was glad. But I wondered what he would do to fill the place in his life that basketball had always held. I couldn't imagine that he'd be able to stay home with Mom, Dana, and Grandma when he'd always been so involved in sports activity.

I was surprised when Brett announced his solution to the extra amount of free time. Without basketball practice to tie him down, and with mounting expenses for we weren't sure what, he made a declaration that he "needed" a job.

Mom and Dad discussed it one evening in the living room while the rest of us were getting ready for bed. From the pieces of conversation I managed to hear, the only obstacle that could not be overcome in their discussion turned out to be the third vehicle. And for that, even Brett didn't have a ready solution. Mom encouraged him to pray about it, and then we waited, hoping we'd stumble upon an answer.

As it turned out, the answer drove up our driveway in the form of Grandma's old yellow sedan. She had finally made arrangements for someone to deliver the car to her but really had no intention of using it. From things she said I gathered that she supposed it would be best to have Dad sell it. Brett's eyes lit up immediately when he saw it pull in. True, it wasn't exactly what he'd pictured his first car to be, but it had one exceptional quality. It was available.

Without too much persuasion, Grandma said Brett could drive it, so long as he agreed to take her where she needed to go when he could. Brett was beside himself, anticipating the reaction of his school friends when he showed up with a car of his own—sort of. Now all he had to do was find a job, and he'd be living in a style that was the envy of his peers. Basketball had almost been forgotten. And his trips to visit the new skateboarding buddies became regular events.

When basketball season started, things changed for me. It didn't take long to get to know the girls on the team. Once they discovered that I could play fairly well, they welcomed me. Anything to be a winning team, I guess.

Anyway, as time went on and we spent hours in practice, I lost my shyness and they lost their reserve, and I soon felt that I was actually among friends. One girl in particular seemed open to friendship. She lived down the road from us, and her mom or dad, or sometimes an older brother, was quite willing to pop by and pick me up or drop me off before or after practice. It sure made it easier for my folks.

She wasn't a church girl, but she was really nice. And she didn't replace Marcy, but I was really thankful for her friendship. Her name was Belinda Marsden, but on the team we called her Bull. It didn't really fit, because she was the smallest girl on the team. But we all had rather silly nicknames. I think it had something to do with team spirit. Anyway, Coach encouraged it. The tougher the name, the better he seemed to like it. On the court I was known as Squ-walsh. The girls drawled it as if it were about three syllables. It was a little lame—but I'd never really had a nickname before, so I secretly enjoyed the feeling of camaraderie that it gave. I didn't share that with my folks. Only Dana knew, and she sometimes teased me with it when we were alone.

CHAPTER EIGHT

DANA HAD BEEN ON her medications for several weeks, and she still didn't have much energy. She looked pale and seemed to drag herself around. Often I felt she didn't bother to put out much effort at all. She was even losing interest in piano. And on more than one occasion she begged off a church activity. That meant I either had to go alone or stay home. I usually opted to go without her, though I sure didn't like that option. It didn't seem the same without Dana. We'd always done things together.

Her name was mentioned in every prayer time that our youth group had. Carli saw to that. She was constantly calling our house and checking on Dana. Even though their conversations were mostly about everyday things, I got the feeling she was really gathering information to share with the youth group. I mean, Carli was a good friend and loved Dana, but I felt like she was in a mode of caretaking rather than offering friendship. I think Dana felt that way too. She seemed to be drawing away from Carli.

The first question most of our friends asked when I arrived at church was "How's Dana?" My feelings were mixed. Though I appreciated their concern, I had begun to tire of discussing her *all* the time. I prayed for her regularly, did what I could to be helpful at home so that Mom could spend extra time with her, and sometimes chatted with her long into the night. Even rubbed her back when she couldn't sleep. But I wished everything in my life didn't seem to revolve around how Dana was doing.

When I wasn't at home I tried not to think about it. I was beginning to feel more comfortable in our new school. Basketball was going well, and I spent every available minute practicing my shots at the homemade hoop that Dad had set up in the driveway. I was determined to make the starting lineup. The day finally arrived for our coach to make the announcement at practice. At the morning's breakfast table I tried not to let my nervousness show as I spread jam on my toast and listened to Grandma praising Corey for his excellent artwork.

Brett stirred restlessly in his chair and rose to leave without asking permission. "I told Curt I'd give him a ride to school," he stated by way of an explanation.

Dad frowned. "I don't know if it is wise for you to become the new school bus," he commented.

"I'm not—" began Brett, but Dad held up his hand—his signal that he wasn't ready to concede the floor. His voice had taken on the lecture tone.

"Driving is a serious business, Brett. Chauffeuring someone around is a great responsibility. If anything happened—*anything*—you would be responsible. Do you understand that?"

Brett nodded, but he looked glum.

After exchanging glances with Mom, Dad continued. "Since you have already given your word, you may pick

Curt up today. But in the future you will drive straight to school—no detouring to gather up your friends en route. The school bus goes right by Curt's door. I think it best that he continue to use it."

Brett nodded again, but he sure didn't look happy about it. I'd already seen him with his car filled with school friends—both guys and girls—windows down, arms waving, shrieking and laughing their way through the school parking lot. I wondered how Dad would respond if he had seen that. I was sure I knew. But I was just as sure I wasn't going to squeal on Brett.

It did remind me, though, that Dad had a lot more on his mind than just Dana. Other things could not be put on hold until her problem was solved. He had four kids to raise and was expected to meet the needs of all of us.

I guess Dad knew about boys and cars too, for just as Brett was leaving the kitchen, Dad spoke again. "Son."

Brett turned around.

"I think it's great that you want to help out your friends."

I knew there was a "but" coming. I could tell by Brett's eyes that he did too.

"Things can happen in a hurry when you're behind the wheel of a car. Things you hadn't counted on or expected. Sometimes they have long-range consequences. You need the car because you have a job to go to after classes. A car is a tool. Not a toy. I expect it to take you to school, to work, and home again. It isn't to be used for joyriding or running around town. Over the lunch hour it is to stay parked. Understand?"

Brett nodded, his expression grim.

"Tell your friends who ask you to take them places that

your dad has rules. And the first one is, no passengers. Let them put the heat on me. If they really are desperate for a ride, you have my office number. Tell them to call me."

I almost giggled. I knew there would be no calls from Brett's friends to have Dad drive them around over the lunch break. Guess Brett knew it too. I expected him now to really look angry. But he didn't. In fact, I thought he looked just a little bit relieved. Like Dad had shouldered the heavy burden he'd been carrying. Given him some backbone to say no.

Corey came bursting into the room. He'd been sent off to find an elusive library book that was to be returned. "Found it," he almost shouted, even though we were all right there.

Mom took the book from Corey's outstretched hand and tucked it into his backpack. But the found book did not erase the worry lines from her forehead. I knew she was still thinking about Dana, who lay upstairs in our room. She'd contracted another cold. And she was going to miss school—again.

In previous years, Mom had begun plans and preparations for Christmas immediately after Thanksgiving. This year December was already upon us before it was even mentioned. And Mom sighed as she brought up the subject. Not only was much of Mom's time spent with Dana, but most of her energy and enthusiasm had been sapped as well. She tried very hard to make sure that she continued to read with Corey and encourage me with my basketball, but she seemed to have little interest in focusing on holiday preparations.

So Dad and I decided we would take over. Mom declared over and over again that next year would be back to normal. She did, however, also thank us for taking the extra responsibilities out of her hands.

Dad and I gathered a box or two of our favorite things from the attic, deciding to let the rest lie. We did bring down decorations for the tree, but the festive mood in our home would be nothing like Mom usually produced. We set up the Advent calendar for Corey and determined to enjoy a *simpler* holiday.

An e-mail from Grandpa and Grandma Tyler in South America brought some much-needed good news to our house. They were taking a short break from the medical clinic. Grandpa needed to come back home to look into a new drug for treating some disease that was a problem in Bolivia. I heard the name. It was long and sounded funny, so I didn't try to understand what it was all about. I did catch that there were new studies that had been done and some medicine that seemed to be getting promising results. But Grandpa wanted hands-on knowledge about it before trying it on his patients. He was coming to the States and spending three months with doctors who were doing the tests.

Anyway, I dismissed all of that. What was important to me, and to the rest of us, was that they'd be coming for a visit. In fact, they promised to spend Christmas with us. They had never been able to spend Christmas with us before, at least that I remembered, so we were all excited.

Grandma Walsh even seemed to perk up a bit. I wasn't sure if it was because she liked my other grandparents or because she knew Grandpa Tyler was a doctor and someone with whom she could discuss her aches and pains. She had a lot more of them to talk about since Grandpa had died, I thought.

Corey was nearly wild with excitement. He hadn't seen

our Tyler grandparents since he'd been very small, and he could hardly wait. He hauled out photo albums and followed Mom around asking questions about the pictures he found in them. She answered patiently. No—more than that. She answered with enthusiasm—more like she used to be. She hadn't seen her folks for some time either. She was almost as giddy as Corey.

Our days were suddenly measured by how many days *left*—a countdown to arrival. The Advent calendar was not just how many days until Christmas, but also how many days until our grandparents would come, scheduled for December twenty-three.

The doctor had advised that Dana be given extra vitamins to aid in fighting off cold and flu, and with the hope that she'd have more energy as well. I think Mom was anxious to have Dana feeling stronger before our grandparents arrived. The *old* Dana and the *now* Dana were so different, and I think Mom wanted to have Dana back to show off. The Dana who smiled easily. Who tried to take care of other people. Who played the piano well. Who had some spring in her step and sparkle in her eyes. We hadn't seen that Dana for an awfully long time. I couldn't wait for her return either.

The Dana of *now* was quiet and withdrawn—and harder to understand. I wasn't sure how to talk with her anymore, and she didn't seem open to sharing much anyway.

❧ ❧ ❧

We were all to drive into the city to meet the plane that would bring Grandpa and Grandma Tyler home again.

Corey wanted to drag along one of the photo albums. I'm not sure why. I guess he wanted to show Grandpa and Grandma what they looked like or something. Anyway, Mom managed to talk him into leaving it behind on the coffee table.

We were just getting on our coats and were ready to climb into the van when Dana had another nosebleed. This one was hard to get stopped. I could tell that even with his concern for Dana, Dad's eyes were on the clock. It was a long drive to the airport, and if the traffic happened to be bad, we might be late. Dad didn't like being late. Not for anything. It made me feel fidgety just watching him.

Mom had stripped off Dana's coat with the blood spots on it and was working over Dana trying to get the bleeding to stop. She spoke without even looking up. I guess she must have been aware of the clock too. "Maybe you should go."

Mom couldn't hide the disappointment in her voice. I knew she had been counting the days as well. She was so excited about seeing her folks. And she had wanted us all to be there. Together. Her family—to welcome them home. She wanted to hear their "My, how they've grown" words and all those other things that grandparents say when they haven't seen their grandkids for a while.

Dad stirred and looked at his watch. "We've still got a little time," he answered. He knew how much Mom wanted to be there too.

Dana's eyes, above the cold cloth Mom had pressed over her face, looked panicky and apologetic. She couldn't just *will* the bleeding to stop, but I knew she was thinking she was spoiling things for the family. She tried to talk, but it was sort of a mumble. Mom moved the cloth a bit and leaned forward to listen.

I didn't hear what Dana said, but Mom came back with "Of course not. I wouldn't think of leaving you here alone."

Dad reached up to pass a hand through his hair, the car keys jangling with the movement.

Mom looked toward Dad again, and her eyes were shadowed. "I think she'd better stay home, Dave," she said. Her voice sounded a little choked. I hoped she wasn't going to cry. I couldn't stand seeing Mom cry.

"Would *you* like to go?" asked Dad, hesitantly holding the van keys out toward Mom.

"I hate city driving," she responded. I knew it was true.

"Then . . ."

"I'll stay." It was Grandma Walsh who spoke the words. She stepped forward and was already removing her coat. Mom managed a smile and even reached out to sort of pat Grandma's hand. "That's fine, Mother," she said. "Thank you . . . I'll stay. I don't mind."

But her eyes told us all that she did mind. I wondered if her words counted as a lie in God's books. Maybe not. Maybe He understood what she really meant. That though she was terribly disappointed in not being able to go to the airport to meet her folks, she would put Dana's needs first. That was what was most important to her.

I tried not to feel a little angry with Dana—causing Mom to hurt like that. But why did she have to go and have a nosebleed now? I looked over at the coat with its bloodred stains all down the front and felt a little sick. I knew very well that Dana hadn't planned things this way.

"Why don't we all stay?" Grandma Walsh had spoken again. "Let Dave pick them up. Then when they get here, we'll all be able to greet them together. We can have dinner all ready to sit down to."

Personally I had been looking forward to the trip into the city. To seeing and hearing all the commotion of the airport. I loved to watch people, and the airport seemed like an ideal place to do so. I had only been there once before, but I'd found it tremendously exciting. People—all sorts of people—racing around to catch connecting flights or lounging while they waited for their departure time. Talking. Reading. Using cell phones—in all sorts of languages. It was exciting.

Mom seemed to stir and perk up a bit. "It's okay, Mother," she said again. "I'll have the dinner waiting. You go. All of you go. We'll be fine. I think the bleeding's about stopped now."

It was getting late. Dad still dangled the van keys. But Grandma did not put her coat back on. It was clear that she didn't plan on going anywhere.

Wordlessly, Brett shrugged out of his winter mackinaw. Corey took one look at him and nodded, "Me too."

Corey loved excitement, but he hated long car rides. I wasn't quite sure if his decision was a hardship or a blessing.

I sighed. It seemed that I'd be staying too. I could hardly go with everyone else staying home.

"Why don't you go along with Daddy? Keep him company?" Mom asked me. I wanted to. But it didn't seem fair. I shook my head and reached for Dana's coat. "I'll put this in the laundry tub to soak," I said and headed for the utility room without even taking off my own coat.

It wasn't so bad . . . waiting at home. As soon as Mom was sure Dana's nose had stopped bleeding, she settled her on the sofa and tried to get us all perked up again. I was sent to get a bowl of fresh apples and mandarin oranges from the basement cold room, and Corey settled at the kitchen table to draw a picture for hanging on the front door to welcome our grandparents. Brett was sent to the nearby store for mocha pecan ice cream, Grandma Tyler's favorite dessert. Grandma Walsh went to work in the kitchen with Mom, who was soon talking and laughing again. Our world seemed to have been restored. I hoped with all my heart that Dad would not be late. He would be embarrassed if Grandpa and Grandma had to wait at the airport for someone to come to pick them up. It would be awkward enough that he was showing up alone.

But all that was quickly forgotten when we welcomed them later that evening. It turned out to be even more special than we had anticipated, having Grandpa and Grandma Tyler with us. Attending the Christmas Eve service together was really great. I liked the way that Grandpa sang the carols. In a booming voice, as if he meant every word. For the first time in my life I started to really give some thought to what I was singing. Later, over cups of hot chocolate and some of Mom's special Christmas cookies, Grandpa told us what the words would be in the Spanish language. I liked the sound of it all, but I really didn't know where one word stopped and the next one started when they flowed together in the familiar Christmas music. Still, it was fun. Then Grandpa and Grandma sang a new song for us, and Mom joined in. I guess she still hadn't forgotten the Spanish she had learned as a missionary kid, though I had never heard her use it before.

Christmas Day was fun too. We tried to stay in bed a bit later. Mom had asked us to think about the older people in the household, but it was Grandpa who knocked on *our* door and poked his head in.

"Thought it was Christmas," he teased. "We used to get up before the chickens on Christmas morning."

We were out of bed in a hurry after that. Grandma Tyler was already up. She had a cup of coffee in her hand and was sitting in one of the chairs by the fireplace. Dad already had a nice cozy fire going. I could hear Mom in the kitchen stirring about, and then Grandma Walsh's voice let me know that Mom wasn't alone.

Soon Brett came straggling in. He still didn't like to get up in the morning, even on Christmas. Corey and Dad came in with armloads of more wood for the fireplace. Corey, as usual, was talking a mile a minute.

"So how *does* he, then?"

I didn't know who he was talking about, but Dad smiled as he answered Corey.

"Maybe he doesn't."

"But Chad says he does."

"Maybe Chad likes to pretend. That's fine. We'll just let Chad think what he wants to think."

Corey dropped his load of wood in the box Dad had put there for that purpose. Then he shook small wood chips off his shirt right onto Mom's newly vacuumed carpet. She didn't say anything.

"Come over here, sport," said Grandpa, sitting down on the sofa and patting the place beside him. Corey bounded over, a big grin spreading across his face.

"So . . ." Grandpa asked. "Do you think anything under that tree belongs to you?"

Corey nodded. He had already checked out the presents—many times.

"Will you share with me?" Grandpa went on.

"You've got your own. I saw."

"But I bet mine are just grown-up stuff. Socks and soap and stuff. It'd be a lot more fun to play with yours."

Corey looked doubtful for a moment, then nodded his head. I knew he was solemnly agreeing to share his toys—whatever they were—with Grandpa. Grandpa tousled his reddish hair playfully and hugged him closer.

I guessed Mom got her love for life, and for people, from Grandpa. They seemed to always be laughing about something together. Grandma was a bit more reserved. She spent a lot of time reading to Corey or talking quietly with Dana. She asked Brett to drive her—in his car—to the store a couple of times. I could see in his eyes that it made him feel really proud.

Our grandparents even came to one of my basketball games. I had never wanted to play a good game more in all my life. But I fouled out, third quarter. It was embarrassing until Grandpa told me that I'd played a superb, "intense" game. I liked that word, intense. It seemed to justify my being a little too aggressive.

But our time with our grandparents was going to be over soon. I knew that within a few days they would need to travel on to the clinic where Grandpa was going to be working with the others on the new drug. I hated to have them leave. I had no idea when I would see them again. When grandparents live on a mission field, you don't get to see them very much.

❧ ❧ ❧

Though Grandpa loved fun, I knew there was a serious side to him too. It appeared almost every time he looked at Dana. He seemed to be studying her. Once or twice I heard him asking her questions. And I saw his hand go to her forehead several times. He even rubbed her back and asked where it was aching.

Grandma seemed concerned about Dana too. I knew she was a nurse, and I supposed it was quite natural for nurses—and doctors—to want to know things about how people felt. Even so, I wasn't prepared for the little conversation that I overheard the evening before Grandpa and Grandma were to catch the plane for the West Coast clinic.

"I don't want to alarm you," Grandpa was saying to my folks, "but I think you should probe further for the cause of Dana's illness. I know lupus is 'iffy.' Hard to pin down. But some of the symptoms aren't consistent in my view. When I did a little research on the Internet, I noticed that lupus is associated with pain in the joints. Dana is complaining of pain in her bones themselves. That doesn't seem right to me."

I had entered the kitchen to get myself a drink of water. Now I stopped short and listened. It wasn't the words as much as the tone of Grandpa's voice that frightened me.

The four of them were seated around the kitchen table. They had been having a cup of coffee together, but now the cups had been pushed aside. All four faces looked somber and tense. I don't think they even knew I was near.

"What do you think . . . ?"

Mom didn't finish the question. Grandpa answered anyway. "I wouldn't want to guess. There are a number of things it could be. But the important thing is to find out. You can't administer proper treatment until you've diagnosed the proper illness. And it may be extremely important not to lose any more time."

"How do—what should we do?" Dad asked, his voice holding an edge of frustration and worry.

"Well . . . certainly she should have more blood work done. Extensive blood work. That's the place to start."

"Our doctor doesn't think—" began Mom.

But Grandpa cut in, almost sharply. "Then find one who *does*."

Mom's head dropped. I could see there were tears gathering in her eyes. I guess Grandpa saw them too. He reached out and took her hand. "I don't want to worry you, my dear, but I'm concerned or I'd never press you like this. I think you need to pursue this further. I'm not prepared to say—"

But Grandpa stopped. He looked as worried as my folks.

I moved forward and managed to stub a bare toe hard on the leg of the kitchen stool. Four pairs of eyes lifted in surprise. Mom was the one who spoke. "You okay?"

I nodded. But my toe really hurt. Still, I was anxious to get my drink now and limp back up to our bedroom. I felt scared. Really scared . . . and I didn't know why. It was just that the faces around the table all looked so worried.

"Want me to check that toe?" Grandpa Tyler asked, genuine concern edging his voice. But I shook my head even as I grimaced.

Mom sighed. "I thought you were sleeping."

"I tried . . . but I was thirsty." No excuse, I knew, for standing and listening in.

"Come here and give me one more hug," Grandma invited. They had to leave very early the next morning. We had all hugged them good-bye—several times. But one more sounded okay to me. I crossed to Grandma and let her pull me close while I wrapped an arm around her neck.

"You kids will be nearly grown-up when I see you again." Her voice sounded wistful. "That's the hardest part of being away."

Grandpa had reached for my hand. He nodded. "If only we could tie a brick on our grandkids' heads. Keep them from growing up," he teased. I smiled at the thought.

"We have a prayer time together before we go to bed," Grandma explained. "Is there anything special you would like us to pray about?"

I thought about basketball and the big game that was coming up, but it really didn't seem right to ask them to pray about that. I just shook my head. Then I remembered the reason I still felt butterflies in my stomach. "Dana," I said.

I wanted to say more, but right then I couldn't. I felt scared all over again. Grandma's arm tightened around me. "We'll be praying for Dana," she said, her voice almost a whisper. "God knows all about Dana's needs."

I felt a little better as I pulled back from Grandma's arm and kissed her on the cheek one more time. I was awfully glad that Dana's condition was being brought to God's attention by so many people. I'd been told that He was even better at fixing things than my dad.

CHAPTER
NINE

DAD WAS THE ONE who talked to the doctor. I guess
he got some results, because Dana was soon scheduled for
new blood work. They had to go to a distant city hospital
with better laboratory facilities than our hospital had. She
would be staying for a couple of days. Unfortunately, the
date they were given meant they had to be away for one
of my most important basketball games. Previously Dad
had said he'd be at the game. So when he discovered the
scheduling difficulty, he called me into his home office
to talk about it.

"Erin, you know I said I'd be there to watch you play
this game even if I had to take off from work early."

I nodded.

"Well, the appointment for Dana's specialist means
that we'll have to leave home that morning."

I knew I couldn't protest. Not when Dana's health was
at stake. I just swallowed . . . hard. I didn't trust myself
to look up.

"You know what that means?"

I tried to nod.

"This doctor is an exceedingly busy man. If we don't

take this appointment, we won't be able to get another for months."

I still didn't say anything. I wanted to, but the words just wouldn't come.

Dad reached for my hand. "You'll give me a rain check?" He searched my face.

I shuffled a foot. "Sure," I managed. The season was drawing to a close, and there would be few opportunities for "rain checks."

"You understand?" he pressed.

"Sure," I said again.

"It's important that we find out exactly what is the matter with Dana. We can't get her the right help until we know."

I finally looked up. "I know," I agreed. "I want her better too."

Dad squeezed my hand. "There'll be other games," he said. I knew that was his promise that he'd be there. I nodded. Sure there would be other games. But I had really wanted Dad at this one. Coach said I was in line for the Most Improved Player award if I kept on playing the way I had been. I really wanted that award. There was even a chance that I'd be first string for the big game. Kelly Thomas was out with a sprained wrist.

I nodded again, anxious to leave. There really wasn't anything more to say.

❄   ❄   ❄

They didn't have to worry about us kids much as they packed up to take Dana to the hospital. Grandma Walsh was with us, and she promised to take care of things while they were gone. I'm sure it was a relief to my folks, but I still saw a worried look in Mom's eyes. I think Corey was making her concerned. He was already discovering that Grandma was a bit easy to talk into liberties. He'd stretch out his bedtime or eat snacks just before meals or just play in the tub when he was supposed to be scrubbing. And we'd all noticed that he had begun whining when he didn't get his way.

But Mom's concern for Dana overrode any worries about Corey. She would have to take him back in hand once they had seen to the more immediate needs of Dana. Mom hugged us all a few extra times, and finally the car was pulling out of the driveway. I saw Dana wave one last time, and something about it made my stomach curl up in a ball. It was scary to see your sister go off to the city hospital for tests that might bring bad news. How were we to know what the verdict might be?

Then I remembered Mom's last words. *"Keep praying,"* she'd told all of us. *"Remember . . . we have an awesome God."*

That made me feel a little bit better.

Brett was allowed to drive me to the basketball game. I was named in the starting lineup. It was exhilarating. I played a fair game—for as nervous as I felt. Though I wished Dad were there to see me. We managed to win the game, but only by two points. Still—that was enough. In fact, the closeness of the game had made the win feel ten times better.

I had a hard time going to sleep that night. I don't know what was on my mind the most. The basketball game or Dana. My mind seemed to swing back and forth between the two. The good and the bad all mixed up. I tried to pray, but my thoughts kept wandering.

The next morning Grandma's voice called us for breakfast. With Mom gone, I had to make the school lunches, and I struggled with the job. The PTA at our new school was working on getting a lunchroom going that would supply hot meals, but so far it hadn't happened. I sure hoped it would be operating soon. What I could offer to Brett and Corey fell far short of Mom's usual creative cuisine.

The school day seemed to drag. I was tempted to see if Brett would drive me home before he went to his job, but I knew it wouldn't work. So I took the bus as I was supposed to. Corey traveled on the same bus, and I was afraid if I weren't there with him, he'd go and do something foolish for attention. He had taken to showing off among friends.

Things at home weren't much better. It wasn't the same having Grandma looking after us. Corey decided he didn't like the supper of pork chops and green beans, so he talked her into making peanut butter and jelly sandwiches for him. I knew Mom would never let him get away with it, but I wasn't going to argue with Grandma, who said she thought it would be all right. This once.

That night I was brushing my teeth for bed when the phone call came. Dad told Grandma that Mom was feeling pretty tired. It had been a long day—and Dana's tests were just beginning.

I talked to Dad too. He asked questions about the big game, chores, and homework. I answered as best I could, but my heart was still a little sore from disappointment that he hadn't seen it. Then he talked to Corey. I noticed that Corey omitted any report on the peanut butter and jelly business. He did talk about school. Then he asked about Dana. If she was better yet. He sounded disappointed when Dad said she wasn't.

Then it was Brett's turn. He had already been listening to all the other conversations, so he didn't even ask about Dana. In fact, he didn't talk much at all. Just answered Dad's questions. Grandma took the phone again, and I turned and headed off to bed.

But I couldn't go to sleep. It seemed so strange to look across the room and see Dana's empty bed. I could hardly wait till they were all home again and things could get back to normal. I loved my Grandma Walsh and was thankful that she was there to take care of us, but it sure wasn't the same as having the family all together.

In the morning I still felt listless and ill at ease. Without Mom and Dad to make sure we kept up on the daily routine, it was easy to let things slide. Brett had already decided that the trash could wait another day, and I noticed Corey hadn't bothered to make his bed yesterday or this morning. Grandma hardly ever went upstairs, so there was little chance that she'd ever notice.

Strangely, I found that I had wandered to the piano and had taken a seat on the bench. I'd been brooding about Dana, and somehow I seemed closer to her there. Before I realized it, I was practicing. Not necessarily the assigned songs, but at least some of the ones I enjoyed. I even liked the sound of the scales, because it brought a little of the feeling that Dana was home again—the Dana we all used to know.

Before long the half hour had passed, and Grandma called that the school bus would be arriving. I gathered my school books and went to hurry Corey. Brett had already left.

It wasn't until I was seated on the bus that my mind began to plot. If I worked especially hard the next day, I could probably play the recital piece I'd been assigned weeks ago for Dana when she got home. She'd often chided me about not taking my piano seriously, and I was pretty sure it would make her proud to hear that I'd been serious for her sake. It was about the only thing I could think to do as a gift for her. So I determined that I would be ready.

❧ ❧ ❧

When my parents finally returned with Dana, none of us could greet them with the usual excitement. We had already heard the diagnosis, and it had been grim. Mom walked Dana slowly in and got her seated at the kitchen table as Dad retrieved their luggage. We spoke of daily things, and Mom asked questions about how we'd done in their absence, but none of us really paid much attention to the conversation. I was watching Dana's face, wishing there was something I could say to her. It didn't seem the least bit appropriate to bring up the recital piece now.

There was little that I understood about the medical jargon Dad had reported over the phone. Many of the words I hadn't understood at all. The only one I had even heard before had been "leukemia," and it had an eerie sound. I had never known anyone with that disease. Somehow, it seemed even more frightening than lupus had. At least the expressions on the faces of people who were old enough to understand had given that impression.

I'm sure Dana was scared too, but she had become difficult to read. She didn't say much, and she looked even paler than when she had left. I decided to save my questions until we were alone in our room.

When we retired that night, I mentally fumbled through the questions I wished to ask. Dana hadn't seemed anxious to discuss her experiences earlier, but I hoped to be able to coax her to open up a little to me.

I dropped down beside her bed, where she was already resting, and leaned against it. "Want to talk about it?"

"Okay." Her eyes looked a little pathetic as she said, "I guess I don't mind." It took her some time to gather herself and continue. "It was really scary. There were so many doctors and so much that I didn't understand. Once my blood tests came back, I guess everybody realized it wasn't lupus. That I had leukemia. I really didn't want to ask what that meant. I don't know much. But it's bad, Erin. It's really bad." She lay on the bed, staring at the ceiling for a while.

"The worst thing was how much blood they took," she finally continued. "I thought I wouldn't have any left by the time I got home. Just look at my arms." She drew them from under the covers and showed me the marks where the needles had gone in.

"Did it hurt?" My eyes were welling up with tears.

Dana nodded. "Every time. I tried not to think about it, but it was hard. I had to stay in the hospital too. Mom and Daddy had thought we could all stay in the hotel together and just go back and forth from the hospital, but the doctors said they wanted to monitor what I was eating and begin records of my other statistics, so they had to admit me." It was strange to hear her use medical terms. It didn't sound at all like the words that should have been coming from Dana.

"I felt like a lab rat, the way they poked at me and did

things without even asking if they could, or even telling me what they were doing. And it was even worse when they tried to make me laugh. I never felt like laughing—not once—the whole time I was there. And it was awkward to have someone trying to make me.

"It was so much worse when Mom and Daddy weren't there. At least they didn't leave very often. I think they had to go talk to the doctors sometimes. But they even took turns staying with me at night just so I wouldn't have to be alone. Erin, I don't think I could have slept at all if I'd had to spend a night there alone."

I tried to swallow, but my mouth had gone dry.

"There was one needle—you just wouldn't believe how long it was. They put me out before they stuck it in me, but I saw it before I fell asleep. They stuck it all the way into my hipbone. It still hurt when I woke up. And I just hung on to Mom and cried. I know that sounds like I was a baby, but that was one time I just lost it."

We were both crying now. I wished with all my heart that I could do something—anything—to make it easier for Dana.

"But I don't understand. How come they were wrong? They thought you had that other thing—lupus," I finally managed to ask.

"I don't know. I don't think anybody knows for sure. My lab tests might have been wrong. It's even possible that the lupus turned into leukemia, or something like that. I didn't ask many questions about that because it doesn't really matter. I've got *this* for sure.

"They've started me on some different medicine. One makes me very nauseated. And my nosebleeds are even worse at night now. I wake up and can hardly breathe. And the aching is even worse. Sometimes I hurt so bad I can't sleep. Pretty soon I'll have to go back to a specialist and start chemotherapy. I hate that. From what Dr. Rutherford described, it's just awful. They inject stuff into me that kills all the cells in my body that make new cells quickly. But it doesn't just kill the bad cells. It also kills cells in my stomach, and my mouth. Dr. Rutherford said it would make me nauseous and I'd probably get mouth sores and stuff. I'll have to go to a different hospital a long way from here, and I'll have to go back three times a week for five or six weeks." Her voice took on a strange pitch. "Erin, they told me my hair might fall out."

All I could do was stare at her in horror. Dana's beautiful hair! I couldn't even imagine her without it.

Word must have gotten around quickly, for we soon started to get plenty of phone calls. Then Pastor Dawson came to visit, and he looked very somber, not even attempting to tease Corey like he normally did. The next thing I knew I was opening the door to casseroles and loaf cakes. That scared me even more. That was usually what Mom did when someone in a family had died. I kept thinking about what Dana had whispered across the room that night in the dark . . . about dying. It had sounded preposterous then. Now it took mental effort to keep it out of mind.

Next our youth pastor came and talked to my folks. He said that the youth of the church were remembering Dana in prayer. I heard them discussing the details of Dana's situation and then, for the first time, heard them use the word "cancer." Surely leukemia wasn't the same thing as cancer. I knew about cancer. Trisha Morgan's grandma had died from it. So had Mr. Perkins, my sixth-grade science teacher, and Jessie Landry, who had been only in her thirties at the time. If everyone had exclaimed over and over that Mrs. Landry had been so young to have fallen prey to this disease, how could cancer possibly have touched Dana? Cancer was a frightening word—far worse to me than leukemia.

"But God can do wondrous things," I heard over and over, "and these days treatments are curing many children with leukemia." I clung to that . . . with my whole heart. We just had to pray. I started praying even more and more fervently. I begged God to make Dana better—and by the end of basketball season in February too. It looked as though we might make the finals. I was sure she'd want to see the playoffs. Why not pray for that? God could do it. This time, I was determined to believe hard enough. No more vague prayers. I was ready to be specific. If God commended the friends who had carried the paralytic man to Jesus and then ripped off a roof just to get them together, then I would do the same for Dana—figuratively speaking. If prayer was what was lacking, I would pray like I'd never prayed before.

I secretly hoped that we'd waken one morning to see her bouncing through the house as she used to do—completely restored. But, in the meantime, the treatments proceeded. Mom and Dad were talking to doctors again, and Dad was searching the Internet to discover as much information as he could about Dana's condition and the medical procedures that would follow.

"Well, you know they've made considerable advances in chemotherapy. And the new drugs can counteract many of the side effects," I heard Mom say to Mrs. Ramsay, the prayer coordinator, who was calling again for an update. "I'm told that it's not as bad as it used to be."

I listened while I unloaded the dishwasher. Mrs. Ramsay must have been talking, because Mom was listening and saying, "Uh huh," and periodically nodding. Mrs. Ramsay was a nurse. I figured she probably knew much more about this than Mom. "Well, yes. They do. Yes. They can. . . . We realize that they can go further if they need to, but we're praying that the chemo will be all that's necessary. Sometimes it is . . . yes. She's to start the first series next week. The sooner the better, of course." Mom looked spent, but she labored through the conversation dutifully. "No, we're not looking forward to it, but it's certainly better to be able to begin some type of treatment. . . . I don't know if Dana really knows what to expect. The doctor said they'd talk to her on the first visit. . . . Yes . . . I'm dreading it. . . . Well, thank you." Mom wiped a tear and drew the conversation to a close. "We're really learning again how important it is to be part of the church family. It's so good to know that folks are praying. We need your prayers. Yes . . . thank you. We appreciate it so much. Yes . . . we'll keep you informed. Bye now."

When Mom finally hung up and turned from the phone, I saw that she was still blinking back tears. The feeling I'd had the night Dana and I talked together in our room had returned. Now Mom's broken conversation gave me the added fear that the treatment might not even work—that it might be necessary to do more than that. How could that be? Medical therapies were supposed to fix things. Mom and Dad had been so anxious to discover what was wrong with Dana so it could be fixed. Well . . . it had a name now, and there were treatments for it. If the doctors couldn't fix it, then I was dubious that all this medicine and chemotherapy were God's answer after all.

Dad spent a lot of time checking e-mail. He and

Grandpa Tyler, who had already left for Bolivia again, seemed to be sending daily messages back and forth. The worry lines on Dad's brow were never completely absent anymore, but they were even more pronounced when he thought no one was looking.

I'd seen it happen. Once I went to his office just after he had an e-mail conversation with Grandpa. He didn't know I was there. He was sitting, his head down, his eyes shut and his hand rubbing back and forth over the nape of his neck. He looked so tired. And so old. I just stood and stared at him, and wondered if this was how Grandpa Walsh looked before his heart quit and he died. The thought sent cold chills through me.

Dad must have sensed there was someone in the room, and he opened his eyes. As soon as he saw me, he straightened in his chair and managed a smile. But the *old* look didn't really leave his eyes, even though he tried to be normal.

"So . . . how's basketball?" he asked. I knew he was trying to make me forget what I had just seen.

I went along, pretending that I might have just entered the room. "Fine," I said, attempting to make my voice sound light. But it really didn't work well. I was glad when the pretend conversation didn't last long, so I could leave the room. I had forgotten what had brought me there in the first place.

CHAPTER
TEN

COREY GOT THE SNIFFLES. It wasn't really surprising, since many of his schoolmates—including Rayna, whom he always sat with on the bus—had been home with colds. The cold symptoms were hardly noticeable at first, but soon he was sneezing and dripping. Normally sniffles didn't throw our household into panic. They came—and eventually went. But that was before Dana's problems. Now we were all concerned. Dr. Rutherford had warned that if Dana picked up any type of sickness before her treatment began, they might be forced to delay the entire procedure. There had been a discussion between Grandma and my parents as to whether or not we kids should be around Dana. Grandma maintained that it was better to keep us apart, but I don't think Mom had the heart to impose quarantine. I'm sure she thought it really wouldn't be good for Dana or the rest of us.

The time leading up to the treatment had been spent focusing on cleanliness and sanitation. Our house took on the strange smell that I associated with a hospital ward from my trip in to see Mom when Corey was born. It was rather a strong medicinal odor that I didn't like. We washed our hands so often that mine began to chap and bleed. Every time I caught the basketball the chapped places on the backs of my hands smarted. I tried not to resent it, but, I had to admit, it was very difficult. Especially since Dana seemed closed off again. She kept herself distant and guarded, even when we were alone. I wondered if it was because she was afraid. But I didn't ask. I just hoped she'd let me know when she was ready to talk.

Instead, I stumbled through halfhearted conversations about unimportant things in an effort to cover up my feelings of discomfort. It seemed to help her relax a little when I talked about homework deadlines and team stats. I knew she couldn't really be interested, but she responded best to those everyday events. It made me feel cold and unsympathetic, though. Here she was, battling serious medical problems, and I could only offer my complaints about a difficult term paper that was coming due.

Now, after all the efforts we'd made to keep her from catching anything, Corey had brought home that cold virus. And of course it wasn't long until Dana picked it up. Dad called Dr. Harrigan at the cancer treatment center to let him know, and he advised that the treatment be postponed. It was a momentous setback. Dr. Harrigan also cautioned that Mom keep a close eye on Dana's temperature. We would know soon enough if the bug had overcome Dana's collapsing immune system.

By Wednesday, her temperature had begun to spike. Mom insisted that Dad take the rest of us to the usual family activity night at the church, but we weren't really interested. We only went because it seemed to ease Mom's mind somehow. Maybe the normalcy of it.

It was a very quiet ride, until Corey broke the silence. The rest of us had been so lost in our own thoughts that we hadn't realized how pensive he'd become in the last few days.

"Daddy, I'm sorry."

Dad turned to him, puzzled. "What do you mean, son?"

"That I made Dana sick. I'm sorry." His lip quivered a little.

"Corey, did you think it was your *fault*?" Daddy sounded shocked. "It wasn't anybody's fault. There was nothing you could do."

"Maybe I shoulda washed my hands again. But, Daddy, I didn't even *see* the bug." He was crying now, and I think Dad was too, because he coasted to the side of the road and stopped the car. Through my own tears, I could see him pull Corey to him and hold him for the longest time. Even Brett began to sniffle.

It was then that I made my decision. There were so many people watching out for Dana. There were doctors, nurses, parents, and grandparents. But Corey had been overlooked for a long time—though no one had meant to do so. I decided that I would be the one to look after him. Never again would I allow my little brother to be alone and scared and feeling guilty about things he didn't even understand or couldn't help. Dana wasn't talking much anyway, so I'd concentrate my energy on Corey, who had in his own way become a victim of this sickness too.

After that Dad allowed me to take Corey along wherever I went, and he became somewhat of an amusement to my friends. His vivacious personality made everyone fuss over him. He found himself once more in the familiar role as the center of attention.

Brett had picked up on my technique too. He often asked Corey if he'd like to go for a ride, and together they would be gone for long hours at a time. We weren't sure what it was they found to do with themselves, but we were certain that anything was better for Corey than to stay in our house with Dana's illness pressing down on it.

❧   ❧   ❧

The first week of Dana's bout with the cold virus turned into two. She was now sleeping in the empty guest room, and she hardly left the room. I was able to sleep through most of the nighttime activity, but Mom must have slept very little. Just as it looked as if Dana was recovering from her cold symptoms, Mom made a gruesome discovery. One day, after Dana had complained of pain, Mom found that Dana had developed an infection deep under the skin of her upper right arm. It had set in quickly and was now swollen and painful. Mom tried to treat it and then wrap it protectively so that it would cause as little pain as possible, but it pressed against the bed as Dana lay on her back and throbbed when she tried to raise her arm.

Dana did not describe to me what she was going through. She may have confided in Mom, but she certainly shared her struggle with no one else. I was sure if I were in Dana's place, I would have verbalized more—probably complained more—but then there had always been a marked difference between the two of us.

Sometimes it actually made me angry that she was being a martyr and suffering in silence. Then I was disgusted that I'd allowed myself such selfish thoughts when I considered all that she was going through. I felt like an emotional Ping-Pong ball, my feelings shooting off in one direction and then ricocheting to the exact opposite, seeming to become even more chaotic with every turn.

I had almost convinced myself it would be easier to bear if Dana could just seem *real* again—if she could allow herself to cry or scream and fight. At least I'd feel like she was still a person. Then I heard her groan while Mom was redoing the bandages on her arm, and I had to flee from the room, even stepping outdoors to escape the thought of her pain. It was almost too much to bear.

Finally, the cold and the infection seemed to have receded, and Dad called Dr. Harrigan back to set a new date for the treatment. Dana had weakened, but she claimed to be anxious to proceed. Mom, on the other hand, looked haggard and tired as she struggled to keep up with everything.

She seemed only too willing to let Dad make the arrangements with the doctor. She no longer hovered at his elbow, straining to hear every word that was said. Maybe she was just afraid that something would happen to upset the plans again. Every day of delayed treatment made Dana's situation more precarious.

❀　❀　❀

Dad finished his calls and entered the kitchen. He stood stiffly by the door as if he were gathering courage to speak. "She can begin treatments next Tuesday," he said, looking over at Mom. "We'll need to check her into the cancer treatment center on Monday night—so long as she doesn't have another setback. But it's a long drive, so we'll have to leave pretty early."

Mom silently dropped into a kitchen chair. To the rest of us, it meant that the treatments would finally proceed. To Mom, it no doubt also meant that she would need to begin again the extensive and tedious process of trying to make sure nothing happened to change the new schedule.

"Angela." Dad's voice was tight, and he didn't look up as he spoke. The expression on his face was one I hadn't seen before. "I've made arrangements for you to spend some time at a hotel."

"That's fine. Will it be the same one as last time?" Mom was clearly not comprehending Dad's meaning.

He took another deep breath, then continued, emphasizing each word. "For you. Alone. Now."

"Mother can't manage—"

"Mrs. Ramsay will be here tomorrow morning. She's a nurse, so there's no reason she isn't qualified to care for Dana while you're gone. And this time I'm insisting that you go. I'm not taking no for an answer."

Her head came up and her eyes darkened. "What do you mean?"

"I've told you repeatedly that you need to take a few days off and get some rest if you expect to be able to continue to help Dana. She'll need you next week even more than she needs you now. You just can't keep up this pace. You absolutely cannot."

A flush crept over Mom's countenance that I recognized as anger, and I was suddenly afraid. "You know I don't have a choice." She said the words one at a time, as if she were trying to strike Dad with them.

"No. *I'm* not giving you a choice. I'm insisting—and I've already called Deb Ward to pick you up at nine-thirty in the morning. Your bag is packed and you're ready to go. If you back out this time, you'll have to explain it to Deb in the morning."

Dad held his ground, deliberately using Mom's friend as leverage. That was a tactic I had never seen used in my household before. We'd always considered family privacy to be a virtue. Nor had I heard Dad openly confront Mom in such a manner—and seen her flash of anger in return. I'd never witnessed a fight before—not like I was seeing now.

I grabbed Corey's hand and hurried him out. There was anger—cold and hard—in the room. I didn't care how it would end, but I didn't want to be there. In my fear and frustration, I even hoped that she *would* go away. That she'd take the ugly expression she had allowed to mar her face and go far away from me—and Corey. And she could take Dana too, for all I cared. We would be better off without them. Maybe then things could return to normal.

I headed outdoors, pulling Corey along with me. He trembled a little, so I had him climb on my back piggyback style and walked toward the field. There was a ramshackle tree fort that he'd begun to build. I decided it was as good a diversion as any. Thankfully, his mind was easily distracted from the scene he'd just witnessed. If only I could erase it completely for us both.

We stayed in the fort until Corey complained of being cold and hungry. I admitted silently that I was too. I knew we had to go back in, and I reluctantly climbed down the makeshift ladder, then stood beneath while Corey shivered his way down.

There was no one in the kitchen, for which I was thankful. I warmed some leftovers for both of us, and we ate rather quietly. As soon as we were done, I stuck the dishes in the dishwasher and guided Corey up to bed.

The next morning there was little conversation as a breakfast of sorts was assembled and eaten. I noted there was no embrace between my parents before Dad left for work. He hesitated for a few moments before letting himself out the door, but Mom turned her back and refused to even look his way. At last he kind of shrugged his shoulders and left. I knew he was hurt. It made me angry with Mom.

Mrs. Ramsay arrived and was given complete instructions on Dana's care, even though she was a nurse.

Then Mom waited in the living room for Mrs. Ward. She seemed to have even shut us out. I tried to speak cheerfully with Corey while I scrounged a brown bag lunch for the two of us. Brett had wisely decided to spend the night elsewhere. I wished I had been able to go along.

I had been struggling with recent school assignments. The work wasn't any more difficult than it had been before, but my mind just wouldn't focus on it. I tried to concentrate on the pages of my textbooks, but my thoughts were cloudy and grim. Dana's face was never really out of mind. Only the rush of a basketball game was able to erase her image for a while.

Mom was gone when we returned from school. Both Corey and I were feeling awkward now that Mrs. Ramsay had taken charge of Dana. Even Grandma felt out of place and inept with a new caregiver around. She spent most of her time in the kitchen baking more goodies than we would eat in a week.

With Mrs. Ramsay supervising Dana's care, we were rarely allowed in her room. We were told that Dana moved around upstairs during the time we were in school. Mrs. Ramsay was careful to spray a generous amount of disinfectant throughout the rooms Dana used, but she seemed to think it was important for Dana to get as much exercise as she could manage. I guess that, being a nurse, she wasn't as easily swayed from what would be good for her patient just on the basis that Dana didn't feel up to following the prescribed regimen. I knew Dana had sometimes bucked Mom when she'd been asked to walk around a bit. She said it hurt too much.

Mrs. Ward told Dad on the phone that Mom slept the entire first day and on through the following night. Mom finally allowed Dad to speak to her on Friday morning, and I think the two of them began to patch things up. When Mom returned on Saturday afternoon, she looked much better. On Saturday evening Dad asked Mrs. Ramsay to stay for just a little longer while our parents had dinner out together. It must have been just what they needed, because they were laughing when they came home. It sounded odd. We hadn't had anyone laugh in our house for several weeks—ever since Dana had caught her cold from Corey.

Mom readily admitted that the rest was just what she had needed. I supposed that Dad had forgiven her for her angry response to his "taking charge" and for the ugliness of her reactions toward him. I hoped that I'd be able to do so too—someday.

Then the day arrived when Dana was to be taken for her chemo treatments. Her temperature was a little high, but no one seemed worried. She rarely had a normal temperature. We hugged her good-bye, turning our faces away so we wouldn't breathe in her direction, even though she wore a mask over her nose and mouth for protection. It was difficult to see her go—a strange mixture of joy that she'd finally be able to begin the road to healing, and yet fear of the unknown agonies that treatment would bring. I watched the car leave the driveway and turned to go attack the recital piece I'd forsaken all the time she'd been home. It brought a small measure of comfort.

CHAPTER
ELEVEN

I'D HAD NO IDEA what the chemotherapy treatments would do to Dana, but I have never in my life seen anyone as sick as she was. She was so sick, in fact, that I was moved out to the living room couch, and Mom used my bed so she could be near Dana day and night. After a few days of this, I wasn't sure who looked worse, Dana or Mom. They both were pale and worn out. I wondered if what Dana had was contagious—Mom sure looked like she had caught it. How would Mom ever have managed if Dad hadn't made her rest up first?

And then that awful thing began to happen. Dana started to lose her hair. She had said she might, but it was not what I'd imagined. It just seemed to come out by the handfuls. There on her brush—on her pillow. All that beautiful russet hair that folks had always noticed and complimented—it lay all over the place. It didn't look nearly as pretty in clumps as it had on Dana's head. I'm not sure what I'd pictured, but I had no idea she meant she was destined to lose it *all*.

Dana cried. She wasn't one to spend much time in crying, but I think the sight of all the hair around her, and the bald spots getting bigger and bigger, made her feel rather sick in a different sort of way. I noticed her deliberately avoid mirrors. She wouldn't even lift up her eyes when she went to wash or brush her teeth.

Though I tried my best to pretend it didn't bother me, I found it disgusting—and I was embarrassed for Dana's sake. Her bald head was so . . . gross. Shiny and bare and sort of bony. It made me feel sick inside just to look at her. Now I knew she wouldn't be going to school for some time. Not even if she did feel better. Dana would never leave the house looking as she did now, and I didn't want kids laughing at her and calling her names— or even staring. I knew there were those at school who would be cruel with their teasing. I wasn't even sure that all the members of our youth group would understand.

Dana's stomach finally began to settle and grow accustomed to the treatments. She started drinking specially prescribed vitamin drinks that supplemented the IVs Mom said she was getting at the cancer treatment center. Mom just shook her head as she described the number of medicines that the IV pumped into Dana's shrinking body along with the much-needed nutrition.

At home she tried eating bland things, but there was little she could keep down. The mouth sores that plagued her made this even more difficult. So she worked at sipping her special drinks almost constantly, and I hoped that altogether this would keep her from starving. But I couldn't bear to ask questions. I don't know how Mom had the nerve for her nursing role when it came to giving needles.

After five long weeks of this, the treatments were finally completed, and Dana's appetite began to pick up— very slowly at first. She started with things that had been her favorites—ice cream and puddings and such. Gradually she added more. I was so relieved to know she was beginning to eat again. Even though she was home in her own bedroom, the rest of the family saw her infrequently. The Dana I was allowed to visit occasionally was thin and colorless. But each time I went in, I noticed slight improvements. Her eyes began to look just a little brighter. Then her cheeks had a little more flush. Finally I could tell that a smile came easier, and I heard her laugh again. It was like watching a flower blossom—ever so slowly. I began to wonder if her seclusion had more to do with how she looked than how she felt. I could understand either. I could see that she was still weak, and I tried not to resent that we had to continue the strenuous cleanliness program. Dana had to be careful.

With Dana's gaining strength, the day finally came when she walked downstairs to sit with us at the breakfast table.

Our breakfasts had become a hurried affair, each family member finding a bowl of cold cereal or, on occasion, popping some toast in the toaster. Corey often went for a handful of cookies or grabbed a couple of Pop Tarts if I wasn't there to head him off. Mom was busy with Dana in the mornings and couldn't be two places at the same time. But now that Dana was back at the table again, I wondered if we would change back to our more usual routine.

On her first trip to the kitchen, Dana wore a rather cute hat Mom had bought. It improved her appearance greatly, and we complimented her over and over. That pleased Dana. It had been so long since she had felt attractive at all. In the days that followed, Mom and Grandma made up some more hats. Crocheted ones.

Knitted ones. Cloth ones. They made her one for almost every outfit she owned. Some of them were very attractive. Dana started wearing them almost all the time—and soon had made several appearances outside our house. Just a car ride with Dad at first. Then they stopped at the post office to purchase stamps. Next came a restaurant with Mom and me.

Finally, Dana felt well enough to pay a visit to church. A round of applause from the congregation greeted us when we all arrived and filed into a row as a complete family again. Dana blushed deeply, and I couldn't help but stare at the color glowing on her cheeks. The people who had not watched Dana fade could never have understood how lovely she looked on that particular morning.

❧ ❧ ❧

Brett made his announcement while the two of us were riding together on a Saturday morning. His words made no sense to me at all.

"I'm not going to church anymore."

I was shocked. And the tone with which he had spoken seemed so oddly matter-of-fact. I wondered what he imagined my response would be.

"Are you crazy?" There didn't seem to be adequate words.

"I'm just not going. That's all."

There was something he wanted to say to me. Why else would he even bother to clue me in before he made his declaration to Mom and Dad? And, if I was certain of nothing else, I was sure that this had not yet been announced at home. I could not possibly have missed the fireworks that the event would have lit. I decided to call his bluff. "So why are you telling me? What do you want *me* to say?"

He responded rather casually, "I guess I just wondered how you thought Dad would react."

"You and I both know how Dad'll react. He'll blow. He'll hit the roof. What do you think?"

"Well, I hoped he'd think it was important for me to decide for myself if church is the place I want to spend my life. I *hoped* that he wouldn't want to watch me sitting there hypocritically every Sunday."

"Oh, please! You think you can lay this at Dad's feet and he's going to say something like 'fly—be free'? Are you crazy?" I said again. I knew this wasn't very diplomatic, but it was all I could think of to say.

Brett scowled. I guess he'd really pictured the scene as something matter-of-fact like that. "Well, I thought I'd at least get some support from you."

"Why?"

"Because you're going through all of this just like me. You see how they've treated the rest of us. None of us matter anymore. Just Dana. They don't even bother with Corey."

"What do you want them to do? Should they send her away? Should they leave her at the hospital so they can get home and pay attention to you? You're almost seventeen! Do you really still need a babysitter?"

This time I'd struck a nerve, and I wished immediately that I could take it all back. The truth was I knew exactly what Brett meant—because I'd had all of those feelings too. The anger. The resentment. I fought it all the time. Why wasn't there more equity in the way we'd been treated? At the very least, I reasoned, we had *two* parents.

Couldn't one of them have spent more time with the rest of us? Why did Dana get them both?

But why this? Why had Brett felt he could improve the situation by leaving the one place where people were willing to put him at the center and listen to anything he wanted to say? There were pastors and youth workers who would have crossed almost anything off their busy schedules just to listen to Brett or me express our feelings. We'd been told that any number of times—all we had to do was call. Day or night.

I watched him grip the steering wheel and realized that I hadn't even seen him for weeks. We had shared family meals together—such as they were—driven places in the same car, and passed one another in the hall at school. But I hadn't truly *seen* Brett for a very long time.

It made me remember the morning he'd left the table after he'd been hurt because we hadn't invited him to the costume party. Dana had been the one who had made things right then. I had been completely inept about how to proceed.

"She's lots better. It might be over," I finally whispered.

"It'll never be over." His words resounded with defiance. "Dana will always need them. She'll always win."

We spent the remainder of the drive home in silence. In the days that followed, I wasn't surprised to see that Brett was spending less and less time at home. But it hurt me deeply that no one else seemed to notice. He hadn't found the courage to defy Mom and Dad on the church issue yet. But I had a feeling the crisis might be looming in the not-too-distant future.

❧ ❧ ❧

Just when I thought things might be returning to normal, Mom announced in May that Dana would undergo a second series of chemo. I couldn't believe it. They were going to put her through all that again. Perhaps we'd be able to take some pictures of her fourteenth birthday before the treatments, Mom went on, and I knew she was thinking that with the chemo, her fuzz of new hair growth would fall out again. Well—at least we wouldn't be shocked when she lost her hair this time. What little she had was short and not particularly noticeable.

Dana seemed to accept the hair loss with a shrug of her skinny shoulders. "Sondra said it's always the worst the first time," she noted simply. "Then you get sorta used to it." I nodded my reply, trying not to shudder. I wondered why a teenage girl should have to get used to such a thing, but I said nothing. I knew my comment wouldn't help anyone feel better about it.

But she was just as sick again. I was glad I didn't have to share our room. I couldn't stand to see her so ill. I had thought the treatments were to make one better—not worse. The whole thing seemed so backward to me.

Dana tried to explain it to me one day when I was rooting through my drawer, trying to find a clean pair of gym socks. Mom hadn't been able to keep up with the laundry, and my attempts at filling in were rather sporadic, what with school and all.

"Wear a pair of mine," Dana managed to utter loudly enough for me to hear.

"No, you might need—" In her condition, Dana would not be needing her gym socks.

She shook her head. Her red-checked hat went a bit askew. "No," she insisted, her voice so low I could hardly hear her. "Not for a long time yet." She carefully rolled onto her back, a grimace crossing her face.

"They might try a different kind of drug once my chemo is over this time—it's supposed to reduce the recovery time and the side effects. Dr. Harrigan says that someday maybe they'll be able to cure all cancers without making people so sick. I wish you could meet him, Erin. He's really nice. And you'd like Sondra too."

If she expected me to be excited about some obscure future hope, I wasn't. I wanted a cure right now. For Dana. A cure that wouldn't make her feel so terribly sick. A cure that would get our family back. And Dana back. I could hardly stand to look at her. She was so . . . different.

I pushed my drawer shut rather noisily and pulled out Dana's sock drawer, helping myself to an old pair of her gym socks.

"So is this the last time you'll have to take all these drugs?" I asked her.

"I don't know." Her voice sounded very tired.

"Didn't they tell you?" I was impatient with those who were treating her. First they weren't sure exactly which disease she had, and now they weren't sure how to make it go away.

"No," said Dana quietly. "They don't know."

That made me angrier. They *should* know. What good were doctors who didn't know anything? I whirled around, trying to release a little of the pent-up emotions I was feeling, but she had closed her eyes and her face looked pinched and pained. I knew another bout of nausea was sweeping through her. I made a dash for the basin she used so frequently and yelled at the top of my lungs, "Mom! Come quick."

I could hear Mom running, but before she could even get there, Dana was making use of the basin again. I slipped out the door, clutching the socks and feeling guilty and angry and sorry all at the same time.

CHAPTER
TWELVE

DANA'S HEALTH DID NOT PICK UP again as quickly after the second series of treatments, so Dad suggested hiring a part-time nurse to be with her in the mornings so Mom could get some sleep while we were at school.

Since summer vacation would arrive in two short weeks, Mom didn't fight the idea. I think this time she realized immediately that he was right. But even though Dad had good medical insurance through his company, we all knew it would be difficult to pay for such an expense, especially on top of the mounting medical costs.

The fact of the insurance was gratefully mentioned often during times of thanks in our family prayers. I wondered what people did who had none. It never occurred to me before to even think about such things, but it was only one in the unlimited number of ways that my life and thinking had been reworked by Dana's illness.

It had helped all of us to focus on the completion of this new round of treatments and the hope of seeing Dana improve again. But it was disappointing now to see it taking place so slowly. We were anxious to see the color come back to her cheeks and hear the bright laughter again.

The e-mail with our grandparents, the Tylers in Bolivia, became more frequent. They talked often about coming home again but did not know the best time to do so. Mom would express her desire for them to hop a plane and come right away; then, when Dana seemed to brighten just a bit, she'd wonder if she was being selfish and tell them they should stay and take care of the sick at the mission clinic. Up and down she went. Back and forth. I figured it must have been tough for Grandpa and Grandma.

We all knew they were badly needed in Bolivia. The other doctor in the clinic had returned to Canada with his own medical problem, a herniated disk. Grandma was now more than a nurse and served as Grandpa's assistant. The mission was scrambling to try to find another doctor but, so far, had gotten little response. Mom said it was really tough to get trained people for a place like the Bolivian mountains to work in a poorly equipped village clinic. Grandpa and Grandma's jobs were even more important than we had understood.

Slowly, ever so slowly, the medication seemed to be having its desired effect and Dana began to show improvement. The daily e-mail updates were more optimistic now. And the heaviness began to lift from the house until you could feel the difference in the air. I felt released somehow.

And then one morning Mom appeared in the door to the kitchen.

"Look who's here." Mom was holding Dana's elbow as they carefully made their way to the breakfast table. We laughed. The newest hat she sported had a series of animals stitched on it as if they were following each other around the rim. Monkeys and tigers, galloping horses and slithery snakes—a Noah's Ark on her head. I remembered the Ark represented safety. And there was the rainbow of promise. . . . Well, anyway, I liked the hat. The colors were bright and cheerful.

"Where'd you get that one?" Corey pulled Dana's chair out and got a closeup look at the animal parade. "I like it." He echoed my thoughts exactly.

Once Dana was settled at the table, she answered, "Grandpa and Grandma Tyler sent it. They sent something for each of you too."

Mom produced a bag.

"Oh boy, presents!" Corey had already bounced back into his seat and was eyeing the bag. "Is there one for me?"

"There is"—Mom smiled at Corey—"but why don't you be the one to hand out the gifts to the others first?"

"Okay," he agreed, a bit subdued. But he was soon thoroughly enjoying his job, reaching deep into the bag and pulling out the wrapped gifts one at a time. The responsibility required him to read out the name on each tag. "This one says Dave. That's you, Daddy." He delivered the lumpy package to Dad and studied the next tag for a moment. "And this one says A-an-ge-la, I think. Is that you, Mommy? Here you go." We all chuckled at his in-charge manner.

"We'll open them at the same time," Mom instructed, her eyes twinkling. Dana seemed to have an idea what the surprises were because her eyes were twinkling too.

"This one's for Brett. I guess we have to save it for later." He put the package on the counter. Brett was gone most school mornings before the rest of the family sat down for breakfast. And he wasn't home much of the time after school either. "And this one is for me." He plopped it onto his chair. "So the last one is yours, Erin." Mine was particularly cumbersome.

"Okay, now we can open them."

Mom left hers in her lap and looked around the circle at each of us in turn. Paper shredded and exclamations rippled around the table. I had been given a hat. And when I looked up, I saw that we each had a hat. But what an odd assortment they were. Daddy had a bright orange hard hat. In big letters on the front it read, "Danger, Man at Work." He laughed and set it snuggly on his head. Dana giggled back at him.

Then Corey discovered a safari pith helmet with a little water bottle snapped onto one side and a plastic knife on the other. He grinned and held it out for Dana to see.

My hat was a wide-brimmed straw one, with a band of printed ribbon and a whole bouquet of silk flowers tumbling over the rim. There were even little plastic fruits mixed in for good measure. I set it on my head, but it teetered and slid off. We all laughed together.

Mom opened hers last. She must have forgotten it in her enjoyment of watching the rest of us. Inside the wrappings was a gold plastic tiara with colored plastic jewels glued to the front in all different colors. Her eyes teared up a little, but she placed it on her head and we all laughed again.

Corey had made a trip around the table to view each hat up close. "How did they do it, Mommy? How did Grandpa and Grandma Tyler send the presents?"

Mom directed her answer toward Dad, a sparkle in her voice. "They sent some money to some friends of theirs with instructions about what to look for, and those friends went shopping. The hats were wrapped when they arrived, but Dana and I figured out pretty quickly what they were. There was a note attached that told us to wait until Dana's first breakfast with the family after this series of treatments. Wasn't that nice?"

Dana and Mom had apparently shared the anticipation of this morning. It must have been good for them to have a surprise tucked away as they struggled together through the last of the chemo series. I thought it was awfully nice for Grandma and Grandpa Tyler to go to so much trouble.

I smiled at Mom. "It's almost like they paid us another visit."

"I know." Mom must have been thinking the same thing as she lightly fingered her golden crown. Even at my young age I could see that it carried a powerful message from her dad about joy and hope in the midst of this "trying of our faith."

Breakfast that morning was a rollicking affair. Periodically someone's hat would slip and almost land in the breakfast casserole that Mom had made the night before. I had assumed she was planning a good hot meal again and was more than willing to help out by popping it in the oven in the morning according to her instructions. She had given no indication that it would turn out to be party fare.

We laughed and made jokes until we realized with a jolt that we had already missed the bus. Dad said it wasn't a problem, that he would drive us to school on his way to work. He reached for the Bible and took time to read a short Scripture passage and pray with us, especially thanking God for the welcome improvements in Dana.

She smiled over and over, her eyes sparkling with joy,

though she looked as if she'd already spent most of her energy for the morning. It was so good to have her back again. And I wished with all my heart that I'd never have to see her suffer through a treatment again. I kissed her lightly on the cheek before dashing out the door.

❧   ❧   ❧

My English final exam was passed to me, and I unfolded it to survey my grade. My heart sank when I saw my score. My schoolwork had suffered over the last semester. I had never done this poorly before. I stuffed it under the cover of my algebra text and tried not to think about it anymore. I had warned Daddy that I was anticipating a pretty significant drop in my grades, but even I hadn't realized it would be as bad as this.

I wondered how Marcy had done on her finals, and the old ache of loneliness came over me again. I decided to call her the minute I got home.

I noticed Brett's car in the driveway—odd, because he was normally at work during this part of the day. Corey rushed into the kitchen in front of me, and we discovered Mom and Dad sitting at the table with Brett, a hot look of anger on his face.

The discussion stopped as we entered.

"Erin, please take Corey upstairs for a little while. Maybe you could read to him." Mom's voice was strained, and she sounded tired again.

We left, and their voices resumed when we reached the top of the stairs. It sounded like they were arguing. I hoped Brett hadn't told them he was quitting church. Or maybe he'd received a poor grade too. That might explain a lot, but it was odd that it would have brought Dad home early from work. We all knew he was struggling to catch up. He'd been gone a lot when Dana was going in for treatments.

Dana was in our room, typing at the computer Uncle Patrick had delivered for her. Now she had her own e-mail address and, apparently, a number of pen pals. She looked up at us as Corey and I entered.

"Hi. I thought you must have come in. It got quiet all of a sudden downstairs."

"What's going on?"

Dana looked back at the computer screen, then clicked the standby mode on the monitor. Apparently she felt it would take some time to explain. "Corey, why don't you put your school books on your desk? Then get your reader and bring it back, okay?"

"Okay."

I wanted to tell him not to hurry.

Dana turned her chair to face me. "Brett came home partway through the afternoon and surprised Mom—or maybe *she* surprised him. We hadn't heard him drive up, and it turned out he'd sneaked into the kitchen and was looking through the cupboards. Mom showed up just as he took some money and put it into his pocket. They argued a little, and then Mom called Daddy at work.

"When Daddy came home, they started arguing all over again. He wanted to know why Brett was home in the middle of the day. Brett said he didn't need school. I think he's been skipping some of the time. And Daddy wanted to know why he was stealing. Brett said he wasn't. That he was going to pay it back. It got pretty ugly for a while."

"What did *you* do?"

Dana shrugged and gave a heavy sigh. "I stayed up here. I know he doesn't like me. I know he thinks this is all my fault. So I just stayed out of the way."

It was awful to hear her say the words. "What makes you think that?"

A tear welled up and rolled down her cheek. "He said so."

All at once I was angry too. I wanted to march right downstairs and tell Brett what I thought of him. I wanted to yell at him and fight with him and make him pay for what he'd said to hurt Dana. I stood up, my jaw clenched.

"It's okay." Dana rose to face me. "He doesn't like me *right now*. And I don't really blame him. I've had so much of Mom and Daddy's attention for so long. He just wants to be noticed too."

"But not like this. He has no right—"

Dana didn't let me finish. "It's not about rights. It's about feelings." Her eyes were earnest and pleading. "And he *has* those feelings whether we want to let him or not. We won't be helping Brett if we get angry too. It'll just make everything worse. We've got to pray for him, Erin. And, too, we've got to love him. Otherwise we might lose him. And I don't want to lose my big brother."

If you only knew, I found myself thinking. Stories had been filtering back to me through school friends—reports of some things Brett might be involved in. I'd even heard talk about some of his friends using drugs and stuff. I couldn't say that to Dana. All I could do was stand and look at her.

I had been wrong when I'd thought earlier that the old Dana was back. Now I realized just how much she'd changed—not only the physical changes from her illness, but the fact that she had matured far beyond the simple passage of time. I needed to stop thinking of her as frail and weak, because I suddenly recognized the enormous amount of strength she'd gained—inner strength.

She had just had her fourteenth birthday in the midst of her last chemo, but in a way she seemed almost an adult. She used words I could not fully grasp and had a look in her eyes as if she were fourteen going on forty. She didn't fit the mold of what it was to be a teenager.

Corey came back into the bedroom and crawled up onto my bed, the one Mom had been using for so long. "Okay. Which one of you guys is going to read with me?" His anxious look begged for more than a story. The voices downstairs had not ceased.

"I will. Dana, go ahead and work on your letters." I curled up with Corey and began the torturously slow process of phonetic reading. Corey's tongue wrapped every direction around the sounds before stumbling upon the correct pronunciation. Even so, I couldn't help but notice how much he'd improved. I forced myself to smile and encourage him. His effort to concentrate probably kept him from hearing the argument downstairs. But I could hear it—rising and falling for a long time. Mixed in were Corey's tortured attempts at reading and the sound of Dana clicking away at the computer. The combination was almost more than I could stand.

❈　❈　❈

The next evening our youth pastor paid us a visit. There were no casseroles preceding it as had happened before his last call, and the mood was a little tense and secretive this time. Brett had agreed to the meeting, but he was slumped in a corner chair in defiance. Apparently he'd decided on his course of action and had determined that he would not be moved from it.

Their discussion began in the early evening and went rather late. Upstairs I tucked Corey into bed, singing to him for a while. He loved this little ritual. Then I went to Dana's room and threw myself down on her bed. She was back at her computer again. I flipped open my geography book, knowing that I wouldn't be able to study for my last final exam. But at least I wouldn't be alone.

The rest of us were told very little about the meeting with the pastor, and Brett still wasn't around much. I did manage to gather that his behavior could largely be traced to the new set of friends he'd found since he began skateboarding. In fact, Travis was the only past friend who seemed to be sticking with Brett. I think Brett might have dropped him too, had Travis been willing to let him. But Travis called at least once every week with some excuse to get together.

I also found out that Brett had lost his grocery-store job a month before, and he had been in some trouble at school. He tried to defend himself by saying he hadn't *intended* to let it all happen—that he had tried to get out of some of the marginal situations himself. But I could tell that Dad was very disappointed. I was also well aware that my parents had enough to deal with right now—with Dana's illness and all—without this kind of difficulty with Brett.

We were informed that counseling appointments had

been set up for every Tuesday night. Brett would be going alone for a few weeks and then Mom and Dad would be joining him. I was afraid Dana would take the blame and feel it was her fault, but she seemed relieved. She figured things the way I did—that it was Brett's way of getting his share of the parenting. At any rate, he had them noticing him now.

❄   ❄   ❄

There were still frequent trips to the cancer treatment center for Dana and Mom. I was never invited to go with them. And to be honest, it would have been a struggle to make myself go—but I would have felt guilty if I had declined. To my relief, Dana seemed to have no interest in sharing her private world with the rest of us. I wondered what the reason might be. But mostly I was just glad to be excused. Besides, I was often needed to take care of Corey. Mom preferred that I supervise Corey since Grandma's soft heart made it difficult for her to enforce the rules.

I also assumed that Mom knew she couldn't drag us all along and still give full attention to Dana and to her doctors. So I usually asked for permission to spend my summer days with Marcy, and Corey came along. Brett chose to fend for himself at home—especially now that his use of the car had been severely restricted.

One day as Corey and I passed a yard where a small boy played with a puppy, Corey got it into his head that he wanted a dog. When Dad got home, Corey explained that if he just had a puppy of his own, he could be so much happier because he'd have a friend. Dad was unconvinced and quickly brushed him off by saying it wasn't the right time to train a puppy—we all were much too busy for such a responsibility.

So Corey went to Mom. Mom's reaction was much softer and gentler—but it amounted to the same thing. It was just not the appropriate time to be taking on a puppy.

I'd never seen Corey throw a temper tantrum. I suppose in the past we had showered him with so much attention that he didn't feel such a display was necessary. And then, when Grandma had taken over much of his care, she had given him pretty much whatever he wanted. When summer arrived and I was watching him most of the time, I had fallen back on diversion tactics instead of saying no to him outright.

Now Corey was face-to-face with a denied request. One upon which he had set his heart. And, I assume as I look back on it, in a dreadful expression of all the stressed relationships that he'd recently seen displayed in our home, he pitched a fit. It was painful to see. Mom was shocked. Dad came immediately.

They managed to remove him to his own room and to get him quieted down. Then Dad explained to him that his behavior was absolutely unacceptable and that it was not to happen again. Corey was sniffling and hiccupping by then, though his heavy crying had subsided. He was put to bed, but I heard Mom and Dad both expressing how much they loved him as they turned off his light and closed his door.

Then I heard the two of them walking to their own room and the door closing softly. This was followed by the muffled sounds of my mother crying quietly. I knew she was trying to hide it, but I couldn't help myself. I tiptoed up the hallway and rapped gently to see if they would answer. When Dad's voice did, I pushed the door open.

Mom was lying on their bed, and Dad was sitting next to her. I moved over to them sheepishly and gently touched her arm. "It's okay, Mom. It's going to be okay."

She gave a wobbly smile through her tears and whispered that she knew it would. That it was just so much to happen all at once. I agreed with her and added, "Don't worry about Corey. He'll be himself again tomorrow."

She nodded, and I left them alone. I was pretty sure she just needed a good cry. But I couldn't have stopped myself from going to her. I wanted one of her children to remind her that she was loved. And I believed with my whole heart that we each loved her deeply—even Brett.

CHAPTER
THIRTEEN

I WILL NEVER FORGET the summer of my thirteenth year. So many things seemed to happen at once that it made my head spin.

As my birthday was drawing nearer I could sense that something was going on. Dana and Mom seemed to always be sending each other little signals and whispering together until they knew I was approaching. I was sure something was up.

Marcy and her mom came to pick me up the morning of my birthday and managed to keep me busy for the entire afternoon. When I arrived home in the evening, our whole yard was like an outside carnival with streamers and balloons and party decorations. Then cars started arriving, mostly occupied by friends from church. Not just the kids my age, but entire families. We had a huge BBQ in our backyard. Mothers brought salads and other side dishes, and the gifts began to heap up on the table Mom had placed there for that purpose.

It was the grandest celebration I had ever seen. Even bigger than Dana's thirteenth party had been. And Dana seemed to enjoy it even more than I did. Wearing a cute summery hat decorated with flowers, she pretty much took over as hostess, then cheered and exclaimed over every gift I opened. She was right beside me when I made the first slice into the huge birthday cake.

And Brett came. I guess that was my very best present. He stood back and didn't mix much, but he did give me a smile and a little wave. He even handed me a gift—personally. In typical Brett style, it was tucked in an obviously used brown paper bag. But inside I found a brand-new basketball. I hugged Brett and almost cried, I felt so good. There was something in his eyes that seemed to say he hadn't decided to completely abandon us.

After the party finally ended and all the cars had left, I just sat and stared, thinking back. Mom was busy trying to clean up leftover food, and Dad was gathering limp streamers and stuffing them into a black trash bag. Dana had been sent to put Corey to bed, and I just sat—and looked and thought. I guess I still couldn't believe it had all really happened. It was in such contrast to our entire last year. I was reminded of what a difference it made when everyone in the family was well and family plans could be made—and carried out. When life wasn't all pills and shots, and basins that needed emptying and sheets that needed washing.

I looked over at the heap of presents I would have to make room for in my room—*our* room, actually, since Dana and I were together again. Deep inside I recognized a truth. Not one of the items, no matter how special they were, compared to the best gift of all—the inexpressible feeling of things finally being right with my world, of our family laughing together and loving each other.

Dana was much better. The terrible bouts of intense illness after chemotherapy were now behind us. Gradually—oh, so gradually—she had begun to feel more herself. And then the good news from the doctors. Her white blood cell count was to an acceptable level and a list of other factors was checking out okay. She was medically "in remission." That in itself was enough to make our home seem like a brand-new place. Not a return to how things had been. I realized that things would never go back to the way they were before Dana got sick. I knew by now it was unrealistic to ever think things could. We had all changed so much over the year of her illness. It was different. *We* were different. But it was good. After all the family had gone through together, it felt like we had been released to live again.

And nothing was said about money and bills. I knew Dad must still be struggling to get us back on track financially and in every other way, but at least now he could see there was hope. He was able to return to a regular work-week schedule and gradually was catching up on the things that had been pressing. It was a relief to see some worry lines begin to leave his forehead. He even took some time on Saturdays to do things with the family. Like Corey's soccer games and little trips to movies or on picnics. It was wonderful.

For a time Brett continued his sessions with our youth pastor. But as the summer passed, it became tougher and tougher to get Brett to keep the counseling appointments, and finally they were dropped altogether. We all hoped he would find good things with which to fill his time.

There had been improvement in his attitude, but we all knew he hadn't returned to his old self. He was still too sullen at those rare times when he was actually home with the rest of us. In August he moved his belongings into the basement, where his promised room had never materialized, and he began to leave early in the morning and come home late at night—sometimes after everyone else had gone to bed. We prayed for him often, and Corey was relentless in asking for his involvement with family plans.

Corey seemed to be about the only one he'd talk to. Brett still called him Squirt and gave him occasional rides in his car. Corey loved it. He'd sit up there in the passenger seat, his hand thrust out the open window to catch the breeze, and grin from ear to ear.

I think it made Mom nervous when Brett took Corey off like that, but she held her tongue. She was convinced Corey was the family link that kept Brett still with us. In all fairness to Brett, I'm sure he would not have tried to influence Corey to rebel as he had. In fact, I think their relationship had just the opposite effect. I heard Brett telling Corey that it was important for him to go to church with the family. I didn't know how Brett could say that when I knew what he was planning at some point down the road. Corey didn't seem to question it, though.

Brett had found another job and was working in the city as a sorter and loader for UPS. I think he liked his job. He said it made muscles. He had grown so much over the last year—not taller as much as bigger. Sometimes I felt a little afraid of him—he almost looked like an adult. He was shaving too. Not just because he wanted to—it was actually necessary. And now he was into body building. I understood from Marcy, who heard it from some of her friends, that Brett spent a lot of time in the local gym working out. I knew he liked short-sleeved tight T-shirts, and he often rolled up the little bit of sleeve they had to show off his biceps.

So Brett was still in our lives—yet in a way he wasn't. He never had breakfast with the family, was rarely home, and drove himself to church. But he really didn't make many waves either. He just closed us out. I hated that feeling. I was awfully glad he was still in touch with Travis.

I knew Dad and Mom hoped Brett would settle down and show some interest in school again. Brett would be a senior in the upcoming school year and had some serious work to do if he wanted to graduate with reasonably good grades. Dad had established a college fund for each one of us, and though it wouldn't pay for all of Brett's schooling, it would go a long way toward helping him through. I think Brett would have liked to blow the money on a cooler car—or maybe on finishing his room downstairs. But Dad was firm about that. It was a college fund. That was the only way the money would be released.

❦ ❦ ❦

On one of those famous *lazy* days of summer, Dana and I were sitting on our back porch sipping lemonade after a bike ride. Grandma came out with her own glass to join us. She had made a few trips recently to spend time with some of her former friends. That had been a blessing. Though Corey always missed her, we could live and breathe without worrying how our noise and bustle would affect an older person. I think Mom breathed a deep sigh and enjoyed the quiet. Mom still had a ways to go to be back to her old self. I think she was even slower to recover than Dana.

Anyway, Grandma was back with us again, and she came out to the porch, pushed back one of the wicker chairs, and sat down. I thought she looked just a little bit brighter and more cheerful than normal. I guess Dana noticed it too because we both just sort of fell silent and looked at Grandma.

"I've been thinking," she began, "how would you girls like to be junior bridesmaids?"

It seemed like a very strange question—especially since we didn't know anyone who was getting married. But Dana was nodding her head, with its hair returning nicely, as though the question made sense. "It would be fun," I heard her say and wondered what she was talking about. She and Grandma exchanged smiles. I just frowned, trying to sort out the strange conversation.

Grandma beamed. She reached down and smoothed out her new linen skirt. Her rosy cheeks and sparkling eyes made her seem a lot younger.

"Ben and I have decided to be married."

I don't suppose there was anything she could have said that would have shocked me more. In the first place, I didn't even know who Ben was. There had been no hints, as far as I could remember, about a suitor or a possible marriage for Grandma.

What about Grandpa? was my first thought, and I quickly reminded myself that Grandpa had been gone for two years. He wouldn't be caring about whether Grandma married Ben or not.

I noticed Dana had straightened up from her relaxed position in the matching wicker chair. Her eyes reflected my own surprise, but she asked softly, "Who is Ben?"

Grandma flushed an even deeper pink. "You'll soon see," she said. "I've invited him over to meet the family on Sunday."

"Does . . . does Mom know?" asked Dana.

Grandma brushed at her skirt again. Then she looked up and her eyes were bright. "Your mother knows. I just had a nice long chat with her and David." Grandma was one of the few people who still called our dad David.

"And it's okay?" I blurted out before I could check myself. "They said you can marry Ben?"

Grandma chuckled like a schoolgirl. "Well . . . I don't suppose I needed to ask their permission," she said. Then she sobered somewhat. "But I did want their blessing. And yes . . . they gave it."

I suppose we should have been congratulating Grandma and telling her how happy we were for her and all that. But I'm sure Dana was as dumbstruck as I was. Neither of us could think of a thing to say.

"So . . ." she prompted. "Junior bridesmaids?"

I tried to regain my wits, but it was Dana who spoke. "That would be fun," she said. "We'd be honored— wouldn't we, Erin?"

I managed a nod . . . and finally a smile. Maybe it would be fun. But it would seem strange. To be bridesmaids at your own grandmother's wedding. I wasn't sure what our friends would say. You picture yourself as the bridesmaid for your sister or your best friend. But your *grandmother*?

Grandma Walsh didn't waste time in preparing for her wedding. It seemed that she and her Ben had already been making plans.

We met him, just as Grandma had promised. He wasn't at all like Grandpa Walsh. That disappointed me a bit. He was shorter and stockier and had gray hair, what there was of it, and sort of washed-out blue eyes. He wore heavy glasses over them so you couldn't really see the color. But he was pleasant enough, and he sure made

Grandma perk up. She had always been talkative, but now she was almost giddy.

The wedding, two weeks later, was a small affair. Grandma had one of her lifelong friends as her matron of honor, and Dana and I were junior bridesmaids. Corey was the ring bearer, even though Mom thought he was getting a little big for that role—he was seven now and had shot up to be quite tall for his age. Corey didn't seem to mind.

Ben, or Mr. Paulsen as I had decided to call him, since I didn't suppose I would ever be comfortable calling him Grandpa, had one of his friends as his best man and a couple of his grandsons as his attendants. One of them was rather cute, but the other had an acne problem and seemed dreadfully self-conscious. Dana and I made no real attempt to get to know them, and they were both so shy I think they were relieved that we didn't talk much.

Brett went with us to the wedding. He even wore a suit. I think Brett rather liked Grandma. He didn't say much, but I saw him give her a big smile. And he did arrive with a gift, all fancily store wrapped. I knew Brett, who was all thumbs when it came to artsy things, wouldn't have been able to wrap it like that.

A small moving truck had already come to our house for the things Grandma wanted to take with her into her new life. She had given a number of personal items to Dana and me as she had sorted through. I half hoped she'd pass me the special picture of Uncle Eric—but she didn't. She gazed at it long and hard, and I could see a tear form. Then she carefully wrapped it and tucked it in her suitcase.

It was strange to go back home after the wedding and not have Grandma in the house and to know she wouldn't be coming back to stay again. I didn't even want to look toward the door that led to her rooms. I knew what it looked like in there. All her little knickknacks and personal items were gone. Only a few pieces of furniture that she no longer wanted remained behind. I wondered what we would do with those rooms now. Maybe Mom and Dad would take them over and Brett could move up from the basement to their old room. But nobody brought up the subject, and I sure wasn't going to do so. We all made our own adjustments to Grandma's rather sudden departure and those empty rooms.

CHAPTER
FOURTEEN

WHEN SCHOOL OPENED again that fall, Dana was feeling even stronger and was back to attending classes regularly. But she had lost so much school time we all wondered what the year would bring. Mom spoke with her school counselor, and they decided to have her proceed into ninth grade. She would begin high school and I would stay in junior high. Though I knew it would be a year during which she'd be diligently laboring to catch up, I still felt a little blue about being left behind.

I guess I still missed Marcy—even more than I realized. She had taken up with Sarah Brown, a new girl from church who went to the same school. She said that we were still best friends, but I could tell things had changed. There really was no one in my school, not even Bull, to whom I felt close enough to talk to about girl things and growing up and all that. In the past, I would have shared my questions and doubts and fears with Dana. But she already had her hands full trying to get back on track with her own life again. I felt sometimes that I was floundering. Trying to sort out my feelings and frustrations on my own. Whether I was still a kid or had to be an adult. It was all confusing—and rather lonely.

The kickoff event for the youth was an all-night party at our church. Dana and I arrived on Friday evening and threw our sleeping bags and pillows down in the classroom designated for the girls before going to join the rest of the group in the gym. We played some basketball, then ate pizza. Most of the kids, including Dana, left to watch videos, while a few of us stayed to shoot hoops. It quickly turned into a contest.

Since Marcy had little desire to play, she sat chatting with Sarah on the sidelines, and they cheered periodically. After some time I quit and dropped down onto the bench beside them.

Marcy leaned closer so she could be heard above the din and shouted words that echoed through the large room. "Sarah and I are going to watch videos. Are you ready to come?"

"In a minute. You guys go ahead. I'm going to get a drink first."

I wandered out to the drinking fountain and tried to cool down a little. In a moment I was aware that someone had approached from behind. It was Graham Dawson, the pastor's son, younger brother of Travis. I couldn't believe how tall he'd grown. I guess I hadn't really noticed him for a while.

Now I turned toward him a little. "Hi." I supposed he had just come to get a drink himself.

"Hi, Erin," he answered. "How'd the game go?"

"Okay." He hadn't moved toward the fountain yet, so I decided it was awkward not to continue the conversation. "Were you watching the video?"

"For a little while. But I've already seen it."

I nodded, mute.

He still hadn't gone for his drink. "How about you? Are you going in to watch it?"

"I think so. But I've seen it too. I was just going to be with Marcy and Sarah."

"Ah." He seemed to be undecided about how to continue. Then he stepped a little closer and asked, "Have you seen the church web page? Dad's been working on it for a while, and I've helped—some."

I shook my head.

"I can show it to you."

I couldn't figure out what was wrong with Graham. But I decided I'd go see his web page and then catch up with Marcy. It wasn't as if I'd be missing anything.

Graham led the way into his dad's office and flipped on the computer. He maneuvered the mouse and clicked repeatedly until the web page flashed up on the screen. And I had to admit it was neat. Parts of it moved or flashed, and there was a cute church-mouse character at the top of each screen like a little tour guide. It surprised me that I was interested.

"How'd you do that?"

He began to explain, and then showed me how easy it was to reset the colors, even letting me try. Before long our little tour-guide mouse was green and then red. We began talking and laughing about other things too. I discovered that Graham had a great sense of humor. And I lost track of the time.

"I wondered where you were." Marcy was in the doorway. "You never showed up," she scolded. Sarah peeked over her shoulder and smiled.

They made me feel a little embarrassed, so I hopped up. Graham shut down the computer and then followed me out the door, pulling it closed behind him.

"See ya," he smiled down at me.

"See ya. Thanks," I answered and walked off down the hallway with the two girls.

Marcy nudged me. "Hmm. You and Graham in a room by yourselves. That wasn't what I was expecting."

I frowned at her and whispered hoarsely, "Be quiet. He'll hear you."

"Hmm," Marcy repeated, and fortunately let the matter drop.

❀ ❀ ❀

Brett continued to take Corey with him on private excursions. Mom was still concerned, but she seemed to think it was better not to interfere. Corey was seven now, and Mom was counting on him to tell her anything she needed to know. And she was also relying on Brett's judgment where Corey was concerned. I had serious doubts about the arrangement, but I didn't vocalize them. Corey did often speak of seeing Travis. I think that made us feel a little better. We were all aware that besides his part-time job and school, Brett had few responsibilities. This left him many hours that we couldn't account for.

We went to Uncle Patrick's house for Christmas, and Grandma and Mr. Paulsen joined us. It was good to see her so happy. She talked openly about their home together and how much she liked her new community. Even Auntie Lynn seemed to appreciate the fact that Grandma had found happiness again.

Among her other comments, Grandma mentioned that they had begun attending church, and I noticed Dad suddenly grow interested in the conversation. But then

Mr. Paulsen laughed and said it couldn't hurt to cover all the bases, and Dad's expression fell. I knew we'd all continue to pray for both of them.

My grades had improved a great deal. I was back to the level I had been accustomed to before Dana's illness began. And I was enjoying my classes too. In addition, the basketball season had started again. My family sat in the center of the stands for some of my games, shouting and cheering us on. Now and then Brett was there beside Corey. It was so good to have everyone together and happy.

One February morning I came down for breakfast and sniffed deeply. Mom had made bacon and eggs—on a Saturday, no less. We usually had to fend for ourselves on what she referred to as her "morning off." I joined her in the kitchen, said good-morning, and took the stack of plates that needed to be set around the table. I could hear her humming to herself. Then I caught an odd whimpering sound. Mom hummed a little louder.

"What was that?"

"What was what, honey?"

"That sound. It sounded like . . . crying."

Her reaction seemed far too subdued. "I don't know what you mean."

It came again. From the garage. All at once an explanation began to bubble out of Mom. "Oh, Erin. Don't tell. Please don't tell. Dad and I want it to be a surprise. We got her for Corey. I just thought it was time."

I moved past her and opened the door to peek into the garage. My eyes fell on a whirling, squirming mass of black fur that scurried across the floor. Before I could stop myself I had jumped back in surprise.

Mom laughed at me, and then laughed again with

pleasure. "What do you think?"

I couldn't believe my eyes. They had gotten him his dog. "Does Dana know?"

"Sure. She helped me pick it out this week. We could hardly keep from telling you, but we wanted you to be surprised too. It seemed more fun that way."

They had surprised me, all right. I was shocked. "Is it going to live in here? With us, in the house?"

"Oh, she'll be in and out for a little, while she's young. Once she's bigger we'll keep her outdoors."

"It's a *she*?" I stooped down to run a hand over the wriggling puppy. "She is sweet."

Then we heard Corey approaching. I closed the door quickly and resumed setting the table. As usual Corey chattered away as he entered the kitchen. There was little chance he'd hear a whimper from the garage—just so long as the little thing didn't decide to bark.

We didn't have to wait long. Dad arrived at the table, and then Dana. Mom placed the plate of bacon in front of us and then announced, "We have a little surprise."

Corey speared a slice of meat and dropped it onto his plate. When no one else moved, he looked up from under his mass of red-blond hair and dropped his fork back down beside his plate. "Oops. Sorry. I should wait."

Dad spoke. "I think you need to take a look in the garage."

"I thought I did put my bike away, Daddy. I really thought I did. I don't know *how* it got out." He was walking obediently to the door, still trying to defend himself. Then he heard a noise. "What's that?" He shot a look back at us and reached for the doorknob. We had already begun to follow him.

"What—?" The puppy made a dash for him before

he'd even had a chance for a good look. "A puppy! You got me a dog!" Two little bodies wriggled in a mass of movement. The rest of us stood and watched in awe.

From then on, the little black furry body was at Corey's side every opportunity. Corey named her Max after a dog in a story he'd read. We tried to tell him that it wasn't quite appropriate, that it made her sound like a boy. But Corey just responded by saying, "Some girls are called Max when their name is really Maxine. Katie Brewer has an Auntie Max." Who could argue with those facts?

The only trouble with Max was the yipping she did when she wanted to be let in. And she *always* wanted in. I could never prove it, but I had a theory that Mom kept the pup inside while she worked at the kitchen table. She now had a part-time job transcribing some kind of medical files. Max seemed so surprised when she was relegated to the garage after supper. And she seemed especially fond of Mom—next to Corey, of course.

Max grew more quickly than we could believe. In a week or two, she'd almost doubled in size. Even Mom was surprised. Then she seemed to double again during the following month. When Corey walked her on the leash, she already pulled him along behind.

He worked with her every day in the driveway, the big melting mounds of snow on each side making it messy to work anywhere else. He taught her to sit and stay and come. We were impressed. She picked up on his commands quickly and seemed eager to please him. But once they struck out together on a walk, she had little patience for being made to move quietly beside him. She sniffed and loped and darted back and forth. Corey tugged back on the leash, but it did little to slow her down. I supposed he'd have to do some more growing of his own before he could adequately control her.

That was when Brett stepped in. How it was he felt qualified to train a dog, I wasn't entirely certain. But at least he had the necessary strength. He took the leash from Corey and looped it several times around his hand so that it was much shorter. Then, in a deep voice, he commanded Max to "heel."

She wiggled a bit, trying to scoot away from him, but was given no choice. Brett began walking forward. Max fell in beside submissively, until she lunged away at a squirrel darting along the branches of a tree. Brett jerked the leash up, hard enough to bring her to a stop, and then commanded her again. "Heel." Max cast a curious look upward at him but fell back in step alongside.

"You did it, Brett. You made her walk with you." Corey trotted along beside them and cheered.

"Oh, she hasn't learned yet. She needs a lot more practice. But I think she's smart. She'll catch on. You're just not quite big enough to make her obey. It's all right, though. She'll catch on."

Corey's face was beaming with admiration. "You did it, though. You made her."

❧   ❧   ❧

It was spring break, and Travis had been over often. In fact, he'd called Brett immediately when break started, asking when they could get together. Now Travis had stopped by on a Saturday afternoon to help Brett with his car. From the kitchen, where I was completing homework I'd been procrastinating on, I could hear a third male voice. It couldn't be Dad—he was out shopping with Mom and Dana—so I went to check it out and found Graham with the other two. It made me blush a little.

"Hi, Erin." He had already noticed me in the doorway.

"Hi."

Brett and Travis moved off toward Brett's car, some of Dad's tools in their hands, but Graham made no move to follow. Instead, he stood in the entryway and attempted to explain his presence. "I came with Travis. They're going to work on Brett's car."

"I know."

He waited a little awkwardly for a moment. I couldn't think of anything to say either.

"How's your dog?" He suddenly asked, no doubt glad to have thought of a coherent question.

"She's good. Want to see her?"

He seemed relieved. "Sure." So we headed out into the garage, where Max was penned, and let her out to run behind the house.

Graham didn't look as if he was planning to join Brett and Travis. We played with the dog for a while, chatting about church and our youth group calendar. Then he followed me back into the house. I wasn't sure what to do. I had homework spread out all across the kitchen table, and I needed to get back to work.

With a motion toward the opened books, I informed him, "I'm finishing an algebra assignment." I tried to say it casually, but I hoped he'd catch on.

"Oh yeah? I like math. What're you doing?"

I showed him my textbook and the page I was working to complete. Instead of heading out, he pulled up a chair and offered to help with the assignment. The truth was, I could really use the help. Graham had a quick mind for math—and computers and science. I enjoyed English and history classes much more. Math required extra effort—especially when it came to story problems. The kind that started, "If a train is heading west at eighty miles an hour, and another train is heading east . . ." made my head spin.

"All right. I'm stuck on question six," I told him.

Graham leaned forward over my book and read it aloud. Then he began an explanation, asking me questions until I understood the direction he was headed to find the answer.

It wouldn't have taken nearly as long to finish my assignment if we hadn't stopped for something to drink, then chatted about what was going on back at his school—which was my old one. He had a couple of "Marcy stories" she had somehow neglected to share with me. I laughed at her school antics, secretly wishing I could have participated. He even updated me about the church web page and his plans for it. With all of the extra talk, I still had moved more quickly than usual through my assignment because of the help Graham had given me. We were on the last question when the door from the garage opened and Brett and Travis entered.

They looked over at us, and then glanced at each other, apparently struck by the same thought, though neither expressed it.

Brett opened the refrigerator. "Want something to drink, Travis? You can wash your hands in the sink. Mom's got soap on a shelf behind the cupboard door on the left."

I laid down my pencil. "I think I can finish the last one myself, Graham. I guess you're ready to go." My voice was low in an effort to keep Brett from hearing, but I knew he and Travis were listening.

"It's all right. I don't think we're in a hurry."

"No, I can do it. You've already helped a bunch."

"Go ahead and help her," Travis called over to us. "Brett and I can go shoot some hoops."

"Yeah," Brett agreed. "Take all the time you want *helping* my sister."

They grinned at each other and left again through the garage door.

"Sorry, Erin. I didn't mean to embarrass you."

"Oh, I'm not embarrassed," I hastened to answer, trying to hide the fact that I was. "Brett just acts that way sometimes."

We finished the last of the assignment, and I began closing the books. Graham took our glasses to the sink and then walked back toward me.

He cleared his throat. "I wanted to ask you. Would you like to catch a movie with me sometime? Even tonight—if you're free. I mean, I'm going with my parents, but I already checked to see if you could come along. We wouldn't have to *sit* with them."

I smiled. "Now that I'm done with my homework, maybe I could."

"Can you call and let me know? We could pick you up around six. That way we could get something to eat first."

"I'll ask my parents. And I'll call you."

"Okay."

We walked outside together, and I waited on the porch with him while Brett and Travis finished their game. They were puffing and sweating by the time Brett finally conceded defeat. But they grinned at each other again.

I waved good-bye as Graham got into the car with

Travis, and turned to go back into the house. The clock said three-twenty. Mom and Dad had planned to be home by four. I could hardly wait to tell Dana that I'd just been asked on my first date. And with Graham—well, Graham *and* his parents. But I still could scarcely believe it.

CHAPTER
FIFTEEN

I WAS TOTALLY UNPREPARED for the report Dad and Mom brought back from a routine trip to the cancer treatment center in May. We all knew Dana had not been feeling quite as well, but we supposed that it was another flu bug—or at the most, that her medication required adjustment.

Dana went immediately to her room, and Mom followed a few minutes later. When Mom returned, she and Dad gathered the rest of us in the kitchen to bring us up-to-date. I could see that Mom probably had spent a good deal of the trip home crying. I noted that Dad's hand trembled as he reached up to run fingers through his hair. I knew, even before he spoke, that something wasn't right. And then he said it. Right out front. "We have bad news. Dana's cancer has returned."

After extensive tests and consultations, the doctors had called in our parents and informed them that Dana's leukemia was no longer in remission. *It was back*. Back, and they feared, more invasive. She had been free of the disease for almost exactly one year.

I wanted to deny it. To argue. It couldn't be. *She was*

in remission. The doctors had said so. Her blood count had been fine. Didn't that mean she had been cured?

But I just stood there and stared.

Corey started to cry. I wasn't sure if it was because he understood better than I what it all meant—or that he didn't understand at all.

Brett, who had been summoned up from the basement, pushed back from the table and started for the door. Dad called him, but he didn't turn around, just kept walking, his jaw clenched as though he was deeply angry. I stood. I wanted to run after him, to go with him—but my legs wouldn't work.

"Erin?"

I heard someone speak my name, but it didn't really register. Then it came again, along with a touch on my hand. It was Dad. "Erin . . . are you okay?"

I shook my head to clear the cobwebs. I wasn't sure. We'd likely have to go through all the months of agony again. The disruption and pain and weariness and uncertainties . . . and the struggle to pay bills. I shook my head again.

Dad gently guided me down on the chair that Corey had vacated for Mom's lap. For a moment I wished I were small enough to be held and cuddled like that. But Dad was speaking to me again. "They are still undecided about just what approach to take. We need to take Dana back to the cancer treatment center, and they'll do more tests to assess just what has been affected. After they get that all figured out, they'll know better how to progress with the treatments."

My eyes traveled beyond the kitchen to the door into the little suite where Grandma Walsh had stayed. Apart from our old television and a few throw pillows, it had remained empty. There would be no grandmother to stay with us this time while Mom and Dad spent long days in the city with Dana. What would we do? Would they leave us on our own? The very thought troubled me. How could *I* take care of Corey alone?

"They may do another series of chemo. They may move on to stem cell transplantation. They've had some good results with that. They may use autologous blood stem cell transplantation, or they may seek a donor. But whatever . . ."

But I had tuned Dad out. I didn't want to hear about it. All of those big words that I didn't understand. I didn't *want* to understand them. It wasn't fair that we had to be thinking of things like cells and transplantations. It wasn't even fair that we had to be hearing words like leukemia and cancer. What had we done to deserve this? What? Why was God so angry with us? Or if not angry . . . uncaring? I thought He had answered our prayers, but He hadn't. He hadn't done anything at all. Just . . . just given us false hope. We all thought that Dana was better. That things were as they should be, but they weren't. I'd prayed often, thanking God for giving Dana back to us. Now I was so mixed-up. I just wanted to run away and cry.

Mom was speaking. "Erin," she said softly. "I think Dana needs you right now. This is very difficult for her. You've always been able to bring her some comfort. She's up in your room and she—"

Without even thinking about it, I was off my chair. I headed for the same door Brett had. I heard my name, but I didn't turn around. I just kept running. I had to get away. Somewhere alone. Here I was with the whole world collapsing in on me, and Mom was expecting me to be of comfort to Dana.

Blindly I ran from the house, slamming the door behind me. I wished I had the luxury of a car. Then I'd drive and drive and drive until I was far away from all of the pain and suffering of my household. But I was stuck. There was really no way to escape. I headed for the tree fort and groped for the nailed-on ladder rungs. Up I went. It was hardly big enough for me to lie facedown without legs and arms dangling over the sides, but I sprawled right where I dropped. I buried my face in my arms and cried and cried until there were no more tears.

At first all I could think of was my own suffering. My life had already been torn apart because of Dana's illness. Now—just when things were beginning to be normal—we were to go through it all over again. It didn't seem fair. I didn't think I could do it.

Then suddenly I thought of Dana.

How could she stand it? How could she go through all the sickness . . . the pain . . . the loss of her hair . . . everything that was wrong? It wasn't fair.

My tears changed to tears for my sister. For one moment I was almost ready to sacrifice for her. To take her place if that could be arranged. And then I got real. I would never be able to stand the suffering as silently—as sweetly—as Dana. I would rage and storm against the disease. I would scream at God for letting it happen. I would be so angry. So bitter.

But not Dana. She had spent her days of suffering reaching out to others with similar pain. Through her little notes of encouragement and her e-mail messages, she had managed to find a way to bring comfort to others who were also struggling. I couldn't help but admire

Dana—even when I wished to escape from the presence of her illness.

Once my thoughts were transferred to Dana, I began to remember other things. She had spent the year trying to catch up with her class. Dad had hired a tutor for her math course. She had almost completed her freshman year of high school. I still vividly remembered the first day she returned in the fall. It had been an exciting day for both of us. And Dana had fit right in again. Her hair, not quite the same color that it had once been, had grown long enough to cap her head in a cute, curly 'do. It was now a softer shade, just a hint of red highlighting the soft brown. But it was long enough and thick enough for her to visit the hairdresser and have it shaped into a style that was becoming. I almost envied her. I'd never yet been to a stylist, and I recognized that her haircut was much more *in* than mine. She had put on some pounds too, so her clothes were actually fitting—not just hanging, as they had when she'd been so thin. In fact, Dana was turning a few heads. I'd seen it happen when she walked down the school hallways. Guys would stop what they were doing and turn to get another look at her.

But now . . . it was all to be lost again. Dana would undoubtedly lose those pounds and that curly hair—again. She would lose the hours of classroom study that would propel her toward the coveted diploma. She would lose her strength, her bright eyes, and sense of humor. She would lose her dreams and plans and even more of her teenage years.

And I would be a loser too. I knew that. Everyone in our house would. Dana's illness was robbing us all. Not just Dana. Cancer was a spoiler, a taker of life even while one still lived. It was a dream robber . . . a home wrecker . . . a plan changer . . . a peace stealer . . . and, for some, it was a grave filler. I started to cry again. How could one disease have such power to destroy?

And then I thought of something Mom had said when Dana had been so sick before. She said that cancer was a faith builder. A magnet to draw one closer to God. Well, maybe for Mom—but not for me. I didn't feel close to God at all. He seemed to be a long, long way off, if He really existed.

But my own deeper self denied that I doubted His existence. If He didn't exist, how could I be so angry with Him? How could I feel bitter that He had not answered my prayers if He was just a figment of people's imagination? No, I was sure that God was real. He just wasn't keeping His part of the bargain, that was all. He was supposed to look after His children.

My thoughts jumped forward. If God wasn't upholding His end, how could He expect me to carry mine? At that moment my decision was made. I wasn't going to pray to Him anymore. I wasn't going to have anything to do with Him at all. I'd make Him suffer—just as He made me.

I heard my name being called, but I didn't answer. I didn't even move. I still wasn't ready to talk. I hadn't sorted through everything that I had to process. How this new illness would affect us all. What Dana, my sister who had become my best friend all over again, was going to have to endure before another remission. Why this had happened to us now. I needed a little more time on my own.

Eventually I rubbed my eyes and climbed stiffly down from the tree fort. Already the evening sky was darkening. I had spent a couple of hours in seclusion.

Corey was outside with Max. He was trying to teach her how to retrieve a ball. She was quite willing to chase after it whenever he threw it, but she had no idea she was to bring it back to him again. Each time she grabbed it, she raced off, prancing and jumping and feeling very pleased with herself for managing to catch it.

"Where were ya?" Corey asked when he saw me.

At first I wasn't going to answer, and then I decided I would. "The tree fort."

"I woulda went too."

I did not correct his grammar. Nor did I tell him that at the moment he would not have been welcomed. I just ruffled his hair a bit and passed on into the kitchen. I hadn't done any of my afternoon chores. I wondered if Mom would be upset.

But when I entered the kitchen there was no scolding. In fact, Mom didn't say anything. She did come to me and put her arms around my shoulders and drew me close for just a minute. I didn't want to start crying again, which I was afraid I would, so I pushed back rather quickly. She didn't say anything even then. Just let me go.

"I'll be right back to set the table," I managed to tell her. "I need to see Dana first."

As I climbed the stairs to our room I tried hard to think. I wasn't sure what I could say to Dana. I couldn't say, as I'd said so often in the past, "I'm praying for you." I knew better than to lie right in the face of God.

When I opened the door, Dana was not lying on her bed crying into her pillows, as I guess I had expected. She was sitting at her computer, no doubt sending out another e-mail message. When she heard me enter, she half turned.

I didn't speak. So she did. "I guess you heard."

I could only nod.

"I need to start chemo again."

"I know."

"They want to start right away, so I can't even finish the school year. And I nearly made it all the way through too." Her words seemed conversational—almost natural. Her face was expressionless.

I understood her words, but I couldn't find the heart to answer.

"I'll lose my hair again."

I could only stare.

Then Dana swung back around to the computer. "I saw Matt at the hospital today. Remember him? I told you about him before. He's only seven. His cancer is worse than mine. They're taking him to Disneyland—if he gets well enough after this treatment series."

I still didn't respond. The tears had begun to gather in my eyes again.

"I'm writing him a story. It's the story of the boy with his lunch—only in my own words. I'm telling him where to find it in the Bible too. I hope he reads it."

Dana began to type again.

I just stood, fidgeting. Mom had said that Dana needed me. She didn't. She was doing just fine. To look at her, you'd never know she'd just received word that she was headed for more of those awful treatments.

"Well—I've gotta set the table," I mumbled. I turned to go.

I was almost to the door when Dana stopped me. "Erin . . . do you mind if we still share our room? I feel so much better when you're here with me."

I swallowed hard. It was a few moments before I could manage, "Sure. That's fine."

❧ ❧ ❧

The youth pastor called a special meeting for all the church youth. There would be an all-night prayer gathering on behalf of Dana. I knew it would be pretty awkward to try to get out of—but I dreaded it. I had made up my mind not to pray anymore. Wouldn't I be a hypocrite if I went? Yet how could I possibly refuse to go? Dana was my sister. What would Dad and Mom think?

I almost caught myself praying that I'd catch a bad cold—or something. *Praying* had been such a normal response to all my problems that it was hard to break the habit. The first few words were already forming in my mind before I jerked myself to a mental halt.

The night arrived, and Dad said he'd drive me in. Mom had already fixed up a bagged snack to take along and made sure my Bible was handy on the kitchen table. Dana was taking a nap, so Mom had brought it from our room the last time she'd checked on Dana.

It was with a heavy heart and a heavier conscience that I climbed into the car. Dad didn't ask any questions. I guess he just assumed Dana was on my mind again.

"Give me a call in the morning if you want to come home earlier than seven," he said as he dropped me off. Seven was the time that the prayer meeting was to disband.

I nodded. I wished I could crawl right back into the car and go home with Dad then and there.

The youth were already gathering. They seemed excited and challenged about being called to pray. I wasn't feeling that way at all. I guess I got off easier than I should have, though. Everyone seemed to think that my

long face and slumped shoulders were because of Dana.
And they were, in a way, but my resolve not to believe that
God loved me or sought to do anything on my behalf was
what really made me sullen.

We started off by singing several praise choruses. Normally I liked to sing, but the words didn't come easily
now. Interspersed among the songs were little sermon-
ettes and reminders from our youth pastor—things about
the greatness of God and the power of prayer and all that.
I tried not to listen, but I couldn't help but hear. After
about half an hour we went to a prayer time. One after
the other of the youth group prayed for Dana—that she
would be healed, that it would happen quickly. That she
wouldn't have as much sickness with the chemo as she'd
had before. That she would continue to have her faith
strengthened, even in the midst of her pain and suffering. They prayed for the rest of the family too. Even for
Brett. Maybe *especially* for Brett. The youth pastor even
dared to wonder if God may have allowed Dana's illness
to bring Brett back to Him. It made me angry with God
all over again. Why take it out on Dana just because Brett
was being dumb? Besides, I reasoned, if it hadn't been
for Dana's illness, Brett would still be fine.

Yet deep in my heart I was glad they were praying.
Surely—surely God would listen with so many people
bringing sincere requests. Maybe He wouldn't even notice that I was stubbornly refusing to join in.

After the prayer session, in which I had not said one
word, we took a break. We went down to the church
kitchen, where Mrs. Fallon had snacks set out for us.
Then it was back upstairs. We started with singing again.
Then we switched to giving testimonies. That went on for
some time. I sat numbly and listened to the voices bounce

around me. I purposely tried not to understand the words. Then the pastor was speaking directly to me.

"Erin." I think he had to say my name a second time before he caught my attention.

"Erin, would you like to share your feelings with us?" I didn't.

The words that I wanted to say, I would never have dared. I could have said, *Yes, I feel like I'd like to go home. Put an end to this farce.*

"How can we better pray for you?" our youth pastor persisted.

I didn't think I cared *how* they prayed. But just as I looked up, I saw Graham. He was looking directly at me, and there was such care and pain in his eyes. I lowered my head and tried hard to sort out my confusion. Our friendship had become very special to me. I couldn't let Graham know what I was thinking. How I was feeling. How angry I was with God. I just couldn't—Graham would never speak to me again.

The whole group seemed to interpret my struggle as being part of my grieving over Dana. It made me feel even more of a hypocrite. But I used it. I looked up and brushed away at make-believe tears. I let my voice drop low and broken and said, "It's . . . it's so hard to explain. I can't even put it into words."

The words were true. The message was not. Girls started to cry and boys shifted uneasily. Graham even crossed over beside me and put his arm around my shoulder. It wasn't really a boy-girl hug—just the comfort of a friend. Still, it was heady. I was very conscious of the fact that he was pulling me up close against his side while the whole youth group looked on in silent sympathy. They started to pray again, and this time *I* was mentioned in their prayers just as much as Dana. I took a deep breath. It was going to be one long, long night.

❧ ❧ ❧

Mom and Dad left for the cancer treatment center with Dana. Grandma Walsh—no, Grandma Paulsen, I needed to remember—came to stay with us. Of course she brought her new husband with her. They were staying in my parents' room. He was very nice to us—but mostly he just sort of stayed out of the way.

Dad kept us in touch through phone calls. Mom even talked with us a few times. Dana was not doing well. The scans and probes and all the stuff they were doing to her already had her sick. I didn't ask any questions. I really didn't want to know.

The only thing that really kept me going was the fact that school was almost over and summer break was ahead. I knew Mom would be busy and that my summer activities would have to be accomplished without her available to drive me anywhere. I also knew that Brett would virtually disappear again, especially once he'd graduated from high school. But Corey and I could enjoy each other. I determined in my heart not to think about the cancer treatments this time.

On the day of Brett's eighteenth birthday, Dana, Mom, and Dad were all away. I quizzed Corey about what Brett might like to do, and we decided to take him miniature golfing. We secretly invited Travis and Graham to meet us at the little golf course at seven in the evening. I had to tell Brett part of our plans to be sure he'd be there. In fact, I reminded him twice. His reply was barely audible.

We waited for him for half an hour before accepting the fact that he hadn't bothered to come. Corey wanted to wait longer, but I knew in my heart the whole idea had flopped. Travis and Graham gamely tried to cover the awkwardness and offered to do a round anyway, but my heart wasn't in it. I tried to imagine whether or not I'd have done the same thing in his place. But I don't think I would have been able to disappoint Corey. His tears nearly broke my heart.

※ ※ ※

I listened only halfheartedly when Dad called to update us about Dana's condition. She had stayed longer at the treatment center this time—there being some kind of complications. Mom had quit trying to explain it all to me, and Dad seemed resigned to let me back away.

Just before Dana's expected arrival home, Dad rearranged some of the rooms. Her bed was placed in the bedroom of Grandma's former suite and a futon was purchased for the sitting room. I presumed that this was for Mom to use on the nights she was needed near Dana. I wondered if anyone knew that Dana requested to stay with me. I chose not to offer the information. Even though I felt bad about reneging on my promise, I was grateful that another arrangement had been made.

Brett helped Dad move the furniture, but he didn't talk much. I figured he had hoped the suite would be given to him. They were huffing and puffing to get the futon frame through the doorway when it occurred to me that I could make an offer.

"Dad, what if Corey moved in with me, and then Brett could have his old room back."

The furniture paused midair, but Brett's answer came immediately from where he was hidden behind it. "No."

"But then you wouldn't have to be in the basement anymore. Why not . . . ?"

"No." The frame lurched a little as Brett gave it another tug.

I turned to Dad. "Don't you think . . . ?"

My words were cut short by Dad's voice. "The decision is Brett's to make." I could read the uncertainty in his eyes. "Thanks for offering, Erin." Dad picked up his end of the futon and continued to heave it forward.

So I went back upstairs to gather the bedding. Dana's pretty blue comforter would now be separated from mine. I tried not to let it matter to me, but it didn't work. Something about the move didn't feel right.

When Dana finally returned home in July, she was emaciated and slow. Even her bones seemed to have shriveled. I tried not to show any outward emotion, but I'm afraid I cringed more than I wanted to as Dad helped her into the house. She smiled when she saw her new room and didn't mention the fact that we wouldn't be sharing. I hoped she didn't read between the lines and know I felt relieved.

In August, just before school was to begin again, Brett moved out. We'd come home from church, and I'd decided to take care of the stacks of clean laundry from the laundry room. There were only a few items of Brett's, but the trip downstairs revealed that everything else he owned had been cleared out—and he was gone.

I stared for some time and then put the socks and change of underwear on the empty dresser. My heart sank. I couldn't pretend I hadn't noticed. I would have to go back upstairs and give the news to Mom. Brett wouldn't be the one to see the hurt in her eyes that his leaving would cause. No, it would be me. So many things fell to me. It wasn't fair. I wondered where he would live. And then I just didn't care.

I tried to hide that fact when I brought the news to Mom. She was seated at the kitchen table thumbing through a recipe book, but she didn't look as though she were really studying the recipes. She had a far-off look in her eyes and a tired slump to her shoulders. I just hated to add to the burden she already carried.

"Mom," I said, trying hard to keep my voice even. "Brett's gone."

By the panic that came quickly to Mom's eyes, I knew I hadn't chosen my words too well. "What do you mean?"

"All his stuff is gone."

She was up off her chair and down to the basement before I could even turn around. I didn't know whether to follow or to stay put. Before I could make up my mind, Dad came in, the newspaper in his hand.

"Where's Mom?" he asked, noticing the open recipe book on the table. I'm sure he thought it must be something to do with Dana again.

"In the basement." I wondered if I should say more. At length I did. I figured Dad could handle it. "Brett's gone."

"Gone? Gone where?" For just a second Dad's face reminded me of Corey when he came to our room in a thunderstorm.

I shrugged my shoulders, but I don't think he saw it.

He was already heading for the stairs.

As I stood alone in the kitchen, I labored through all the ways Brett's leaving would affect us. Then I found myself thinking of Corey. He would be devastated. He would take it as personal rejection. I allowed myself to loathe Brett for his selfishness, even while I knew I was becoming increasingly tempted to follow him away from the gloom and chaos and pain of our home.

They were gone for a long time. When they did reappear, I could tell that Mom had been crying and Dad didn't look much better. It made my anger at Brett even more intense. Why did he do this to them? Why *now*?

I was about to blurt out something about Brett's selfishness, which I'm sure would not have helped the situation, when I noticed Mom was carrying a rather crumpled bit of paper. She lowered herself slowly into the kitchen chair again and pushed the recipe book aside. "He left a note," she said, seeming to imply that it was terribly considerate of him. "He's found a little apartment in town. Closer to his work."

I wondered momentarily if my parents were buying that excuse. I certainly wasn't.

"It's on Maple Street—in that little apartment block."

I knew the building. It wasn't the fanciest place in town. But I sensed that Mom was pleased Brett had chosen to go back to our old neighborhood.

"Number 112," Mom went on. All the time she talked, her fingers kept smoothing out the piece of paper. "He doesn't have a phone yet, but he'll let us know. . . ."

"You gonna let him stay?"

Dad had just been sitting in the chair beside Mom rubbing his two palms together. He was staring at his hands, but his eyes weren't really focused on them. His head came up when I spoke. He just nodded. It was Mom who answered me.

"Brett is going through a tough time right now. Maybe it's best that he has a bit of space. At any rate, it might only make him more . . ." Mom hesitated, probably searching for a word that would describe Brett's attitude without branding him a rebel. ". . . more upset," she finally continued, "if we put pressure on him to come back right now. He's having a difficult time growing up and dealing with a sick sister—all at once."

"But his friends," I interrupted. "He sure hasn't picked . . ." I choose a different tack. "They aren't that good for him. They might—"

Mom stopped me. Her shoulders fell, then lifted, but when she looked up she looked assured, even though fresh tears glistened in the corners of her eyes.

"Erin . . . there comes a time when as parents we have done all we can do. The Bible says to train up a child in the way he should go. We've done that . . . to the best of our ability. God knows that. Now . . . now we have to trust. Just trust. We don't like what is happening in Brett's life right now, but we can't force him to make good choices. We can just continue to pray that he will know how much we love him . . . how much God loves him and . . . and decide . . . to make the right choices himself. We need to have faith. In God. In our teaching. And in our son."

Dad reached out and clasped Mom's hand. "Brett's a good kid at heart. He has so many qualities we're proud of. And remember, he still has much of God's Word hidden in his heart, Erin. That's powerful stuff. And, as your mother said, God still loves him. Satan hasn't won yet. Not by a long way."

I think, by their words, they were encouraging each other. Mom sort of leaned up against Dad's shoulder and even managed a bit of a smile. I just shook my head. I guess at the moment I would have been happy to see Brett suffer a bit. That wasn't the way they seemed to feel. Way down deep inside I guess I felt good about it. Unconditional love was something to really hang on to.

CHAPTER
SIXTEEN

WITH DANA AT HOME AGAIN, the only time I could really forget her suffering and just be a teenager was at school. And as classes began, I threw myself into my studies. It was a chance to get out of the house and feel alive. My grades soared, and I became more involved in other activities besides basketball. Now that I knew many of my classmates well, it was easy to make arrangements for someone else to stop by and pick me up for school events. It made me feel independent and in control. Things that I hadn't felt for a very long time. And Corey was back in Mom's care. That gave me mixed feelings because, in addition to this energetic third grader, she had Dana to nurse. But I tried hard to set those feelings aside. I was more and more repelled by the morbidity that seemed to hang over our home, and I had twinges of guilt for leaving Corey there.

One of my ninth-grade teachers took me aside one day and suggested that I get involved in the school newspaper. He said I might even try running for an office in our student government. He had nice things to say about my being a *leader*. I liked that. It was great to be looked at as special in some way.

But near the end of September, Dana went back to the cancer center due to more complications she'd experienced, and I let the whole idea of student government go. I let all the other extra things go too. How could I be a leader at school when I never knew when I'd be needed at home to help with Corey, or keep up with laundry, or cook our meals, or other responsibilities? With Mom gone and Grandma not there, I knew enough not to bother to ask if I could be absent as well.

Basketball, though, was something I couldn't possibly give up. The season started again, and Graham came to all the games. I guess I was more conscious of the fact that he was there than I would have liked to be. Occasionally I could hear his voice over the noise of the crowd, cheering me on. Sometimes, if the game didn't go too late, we went out for a Coke with a group of other kids before I caught my ride home. It sort of made up for the fact that Dad and Mom were hardly ever able to be there. I didn't miss them nearly as much anymore. Maybe I had just gotten used to it.

The team had a special meeting after one of our practices, and the school principal came down to talk to us. We couldn't believe what he had to say. Since our junior varsity team had been doing so well, the school had decided to enter us in an out-of-state tournament in two months' time. We would all be required to have our own spending money for meals and snacks and whatever else. The school would pay for transportation and lodging.

We were ecstatic. Never had we dreamed of such an opportunity. But even as we celebrated, I knew I'd never be able to ask Dad for the money. With everything that was going on with Dana, there would never be money for a basketball tournament. For a moment I felt really down . . . and angry. Too much was disappearing in my life. Too many things I'd had to give up.

And then a new idea dawned on me. I'd earn my own way. Surely Mom and Dad couldn't object to that. I'd take babysitting jobs, and I'd save every penny and still be able to go on that trip. At least it was something to look forward to.

But it was more difficult to manage both school and work than I had thought. True, Brett had managed a job, but he'd made little effort to keep up his grades. I wouldn't allow myself the same casual attitude. But it wasn't to be worked out easily. I couldn't begin my class assignments until after my charges were settled for the night, so many nights I found myself still up at midnight completing homework assignments.

The extra advantage of work was that it kept me away from home even more. Many nights when I was dropped off after sitting, I dreaded opening the door and going inside. I didn't want to hear the report of Dana's problems as relayed by Dad, and I didn't want to see Mom ragged and tired. The sleepless nights that Dana and Mom spent together were far enough away that it didn't waken the rest of us. I hated to admit such selfishness, but I had grown weary of all the nighttime noises and bustle.

I was aware, too, that I had become very distant. Dana was behind closed doors now, and it was far easier to shut her out of my life. True, I still, though at times reluctantly, gave up many of the privileges I could have experienced if she hadn't been ill, but that was no reason to withdraw from her. She was my sister, so I tried to visit her at least once a day when she was home, but I just couldn't bring myself to ask about how she was feeling.

Instead, I talked about school and games—even Graham. She asked a steady stream of questions when she was feeling well enough to talk with me, and I hoped it wasn't dreadfully wrong to be so self-centered in our conversations. It had become easier and easier for me to cover up my true feelings—the conflicted, desperate ones—and pretend that I was happy. The truth was, I cried often when I was alone in my bedroom.

I hated the feeling of being deceitful, but it seemed to be the only merciful thing to do. I couldn't be honest. That would only cause everyone more pain. So I feigned cheerfulness and helped out whenever I could. That made me feel a little better. But I wondered if Brett's road to decline had started out in the same way that I was allowing myself to go—bending the truth by pretending, and shutting out my family.

During the winter months Dana had begun to look far worse than she ever had before. Though I tried not to absorb the details of her situation, I did realize that her medical problems had escalated. She was experiencing almost constant fevers, sores, and nausea. She had also developed a horrid lung infection. I could hear her rattling cough from downstairs throughout the night, and I pressed my pillow over my head in an attempt to block it out. It never seemed to bother Corey—he slept soundly—at least he never came into my room during the night.

My meager bank account began to grow. I scrimped on all my expenditures, saving every little bit I could toward the trip with the basketball team. If only I would be able to save enough.

One night, long after he had been put to bed, Corey

appeared at my elbow as I sat doing homework at the kitchen table. I passed him some of the potato chips I'd been eating and chided him gently for getting up.

"I couldn't sleep. I just got thinking."

I stood to get him a glass of water, and he followed me to the sink. "What were you thinking about?" I asked.

"Misty told my class that her grandma got cancer. I wish she didn't. It made me feel really bad for her."

"We know about cancer. Don't we, Corey?"

He nodded, not looking up. A moment passed and then he spoke again. "Is Dana gonna die?"

The glass I was holding slipped into the sink and shattered. I left it where it lay and dropped down to eye level with Corey. "Why would you ask that?" My words sounded harsher than I had intended.

"Misty said her grandma is dying."

I swallowed the lump that was rising in my throat. "She probably has a different kind of cancer. I don't think it could be like Dana's." Tears were already welling in my eyes. It must have been obvious even to Corey that my words were shallow and empty.

"But she's sicker this time. I hear her. She coughs a lot. And she doesn't breathe good. I think she might be dying too." There were tears running down his cheeks.

I pulled him close and held him as tightly as I dared. All my thoughts were churning, wondering when it would ever end. How much longer would we have to face this disease? How many more of our growing-up years would be spoiled?

At last he pushed away from me. "Can I sit with you, Erin? I'll be real quiet."

"Of course. You can even get your pillow and a blanket, and I'll move my books into the living room. Then you can lie on the sofa. Okay?"

He nodded and headed back to his room. I was numb as I turned to clean up the broken glass from the sink.

❀ ❀ ❀

My parents were visibly pleased when I finally had enough money for the trip. Dad even slipped me a ten—"a little something extra." Our team had continued to have a winning season, and we seemed primed to sweep the finals. This invitational tournament would arrive just before we headed to the last games, and our coach had lectured us over and over again on the importance of taking it seriously, even though it wouldn't count for or against us on the season's record. Psychologically, he insisted, it was important that we win.

We were also told that we were to get extra sleep during the week before the tournament. I tried, but between my studies and my jobs, I found myself coming up short. On Thursday night, the last night before we were to leave, I had finally been able to get to bed early. I was hoping to make up for the time I'd lost during the week. Dana had been doing better. Mom was even back in her own bed, attempting to get some much needed rest.

In the middle of the night, I was startled awake. There had been a noise. A sound that had registered to my unconscious mind as being wrong—*terribly wrong*. I rushed to the door and pulled it open, searching the hallway in one direction and then another. But there was no one there. By now my adrenaline was pumping. I was certain I'd heard a sound. I moved softly toward the stairs.

Then I heard the sound again. It had come from

below—from Dana's rooms. Without pausing to wonder further, I called out to Dad and Mom and raced down the carpeted steps. For some reason, I knew without a doubt there was a problem. And I was afraid.

She was there, seated on the bathroom floor of the little suite, her arm bent at an odd angle and tucked against her. Her face was contorted in pain. I dropped down beside her and called to Dad again. He appeared in the doorway.

"What happened? Erin, what's wrong?"

"It's Dana's arm. It's bent wrong. I think it's broken. She must have fallen—but she won't talk to me."

Dad squeezed past me and bent down where he could see for himself. Dana still couldn't answer us. Her pain was too great. But we could both see clearly that her arm had been badly injured.

Mom arrived and then Corey. I stepped out of their way and back into the bedroom, trying to draw Corey away from the scene. Then Dad shouted out to me that I should call the ambulance, so I grabbed Corey's hand and dragged him along.

"My name is Erin Walsh. I live at 1441 Walnut Lane. My sister fell in the bathroom and broke her arm. Please hurry."

The emergency operator did not understand. "Are your parents home with you?"

"Yes, they're with Dana, but they need help."

"Are they able to drive her to a medical clinic?"

"No. Please! You've got to send an ambulance. My sister has cancer—leukemia. She's very sick. You need to send someone right away. She doesn't even breathe well—and now with her arm, I'm not sure—"

The woman on the phone cut me off. "We'll send

someone right away. I'm already sending the call through our system. Try to calm down so you can talk to me. Can you repeat your address please?"

I was grateful to hear that they'd come. "1441 Walnut Lane." I said it as slowly and clearly as my labored breathing would allow. "It's the house right at the end. You can't see it through the trees. Just follow the paved driveway. I can even stand on the road if you think it would help."

"No. No, wait in the house with your parents. What was your name again?"

"My name is Erin."

"Erin, how old are you, dear?"

"I'm fourteen."

"Listen carefully. Don't hang up the phone, but go to your parents and ask them if your sister is breathing okay. If she is, then have them check the skin around the break to see if the bone came through, and make sure they cover her so that she doesn't get chilled. Can you do all that?"

"Yes." I dropped the phone on the counter and charged back into Dana's rooms.

After repeating the instructions to Mom and Dad, I ran back and picked up the receiver. "She's breathing okay. She's been having trouble with a lung infection, but she's breathing pretty good right now. The skin isn't broken. But the arm . . . her arm is bent in the middle of the bone, and it's just hanging there."

"How is she handling the pain? Is she calm?" The voice remained so controlled it was eerie.

I struggled to speak without gasping. "I think so. But they can't get her to say anything. She's just staring now."

"Okay, Erin. She might be going into shock. Is she sitting down?"

"Yes. She's on the bathroom floor. Oh, please hurry."

"They're on the way. They've already left for your house. Listen. Make sure she's covered well. And if they can lay her down without moving the arm much, tell them to do it now."

I ran back and delivered the additional instructions. Daddy had already laid Dana back, and Mom ran to grab the comforter off Dana's bed. Dana's face was deathly white. I scurried back to the phone.

"She's lying down. But her face is white, and Daddy says her hands are cold." My throat was tightening, and I could feel sobs shaking my voice.

"Okay, you covered her well?"

"Yes. Yes!"

"Erin, dear. Listen. I need to ask you some more questions. Listen to me. Can you listen?"

"Yes." I looked toward Corey. He was crouched on the kitchen floor clutching Max.

"How old is your sister?"

I couldn't see why she needed to know that. Or the numerous other questions that followed, but I answered each as best I could. Then, at last, I heard the sound of a siren approaching.

"They're here!"

"Okay, honey. You hear them coming?"

"Yes! Yes. They're pulling into the driveway. I've got to go let them in." I didn't even stop to hear her answer. I dropped the phone and rushed to open the front door. "Through the kitchen—to the right—in the bathroom."

Max began barking. A fearsome, growling bark. I grabbed for her collar as three men hurried past us and into Dana's suite. The lights on the ambulance were still flashing. It made the living room pulse with a reddish glow. We could hear them questioning Dad; then two of them came back and headed out to their vehicle.

"Max! Hush."

Corey was crying, and the dog was still barking. I moved them both to the sofa and pulled them up beside me. "Hush!"

The two men came back, carrying a stretcher between them. In no time they had Dana strapped in and were speeding away from the house. Dad and Mom had gone upstairs to their room and were scrambling around. I could hear their footsteps and the sound of drawers opening and closing. They were dressing. They would be following Dana.

At last, Max fell silent.

Mom flew past. "Erin, can you watch Corey? We'll call as soon as we know anything."

"Okay."

Dad stopped to hug me—hard—and then hurried to follow Mom to the car. Corey and I were left alone, and neither of us wanted to go back upstairs. Not alone. Not after what had just happened. The house had a sinister silence.

Instead, we curled up on the couch together and turned on the television. Corey fell asleep quickly. I threw the afghan over him, then stared at the screen in silence.

At three o'clock in the morning we finally received a call from Mom and Dad. Dana had been going into shock, but the ambulance drivers had managed to get her through it. Mom and Dad were waiting for the doctor to arrive for further word. They would call again later.

I didn't wait for any more news. I dialed the number for my school and then my coach's extension number. I left a message on his answering machine. I wouldn't be on the bus that was to leave at 6:30 sharp. I wouldn't be able to make it to the tournament. Then I hung up the phone and cried until I fell asleep, lying on the floor beside Corey. The television was still droning on in the corner when I woke in the morning.

A while later Dad came home to gather a few clothes and to shower. I hadn't bothered to get Corey and myself dressed and off to school, but he didn't scold me for it. He just answered our questions and then headed back out, taking a change of clothes for Mom too. He had said that with the injury, Dana probably would be in the hospital for a lengthy stay.

I wondered, as the door closed behind him, if he would ever remember what the night's events had cost me. My team would play without me, and all the special memories that could have been mine were forever lost. The endless hours of babysitting and the late nights studying no longer mattered.

Corey was occupied with a video, so I knew he wouldn't notice me leaving the room. I went upstairs and dumped the contents of my purse on the dresser. The ten-dollar bill from Dad I had folded alone and placed at the bottom. It seemed to mock me as it lay on the top of the little stash. I grabbed it up and headed for Dad's office. I would return it. It was of no use to me now.

But as I drew near to his desk with tears of anger and disappointment spilling down my cheeks, my eyes fell on a framed picture placed beside his pencil holder. It showed me bundled in the warmth of a fur-trimmed parka, and my Daddy was holding me tightly in his arms as he prepared to give me a ride down the hillside on a sled.

Such love welled up within me, I couldn't hurt him. I just couldn't.

I wiped at my cheeks. My anger now turned into genuine sorrow. Not for me but for him. In my heart I hoped he'd never ever remember that this was to have been my tournament weekend.

❧ ❧ ❧

It was several weeks until Dana had begun to heal, and so she'd been transported to the cancer treatment center. Her progress reports had begun to sound very good, and Corey and I spoke often about what we'd do when Dana came home. We were surprised when Mom and Dad called us together again to explain Dana's prognosis. Even Brett was in on it. We learned that it was time for a bone-marrow transplant. Dana was showing signs of responding to the most recent treatments, and her body might be able to stand the stresses of the procedure. I cringed at the grizzly picture it brought to my mind.

I wondered if a bone-marrow transplant was similar to a heart transplant. But how could it be the same? Bone marrow, according to my biology classes, was in the center of a body's bones. I tried to imagine how it could be cut out and replaced, but I couldn't bear to think it through. I could imagine no reasonable way of doing such a thing.

The next information in this discussion was that Dana would need a donor. This came as an even greater shock. Were the rest of us to be subjected to some type of surgery? And how could this donor afford to part with his bone marrow? Wasn't it fairly necessary for health?

Dad tried to explain, but his words were halting, and he failed to express himself in his usual clear, forthright manner. It must have been very difficult for him to tell three of his children that they might have to sacrifice from their own healthy bodies in order to save the life of a sibling. We each agreed to be tested to see if we could donate the marrow, but it was a very frightening commitment to make.

The medical tests we faced brought firsthand knowledge of Dana's world. It was scary to be the one to sit in a small waiting room and wonder what might happen once I was asked to step into the next room. I could see my hands trembling. I wondered if I might faint. Corey didn't look much better. I had rarely seen him sit so still.

Brett was called first. He rose stiffly and followed the nurse away. It seemed to be forever before they came back and asked for me. Brett hadn't returned. I guessed he had needed some time to recover. And I thought about Corey. How could anyone put him through all this? He was so very young.

When it was my turn, I cast a glance back at Mom and Dad and followed the white-clad attendant into an examination room. The room was bright with steel and white. I dutifully took a seat on the chair I'd been instructed to use. Soon there came a rap on the door and a nurse entered.

"I'm Carol," she said, smiling.

I tried to respond with a casual "hello," but the words caught in my throat. I wished I could have a drink.

"So you're Erin. It's nice to meet you. I just met your brother, and I understand there's one more to come."

I swallowed hard and hoped she didn't expect me to

pick up my end of this conversation. I could see she was reaching toward a tray of shiny implements and sterile packages that sat on the counter beside her. I forced myself to look down at the floor.

"Okay, Erin. We're ready to start. If you can just relax. All we're going to do today is take a little blood. Do you want me to explain anything—answer any of your questions?"

I shook my head vigorously that I did not.

"Well, okay. Try to relax. This won't take long." I could see the nurse was preparing the needle. I felt queasy as she pushed it into my arm and drew it back so that my blood filled the little container she had attached. I thought of Corey going through the same thing, and I felt even sicker as the nurse reached for another cylinder to fill.

❧ ❧ ❧

I was not a compatible donor. I couldn't help feeling a great relief when the results of the testing were phoned to our home. As Dad continued listening to the report, my next thought was for Corey. Surely he wouldn't be the one. But we soon could tell the tests had shown he also was not a good match for Dana.

My eyes turned to Brett, whose face had taken on an ashen color. Without Dad even saying it, I knew Brett was the only one of the three of us who was acceptably compatible. I held my breath and watched him rise from his chair in our living room. He moved to the window, his fists clenched tightly. I could tell that he was laboring over this news. How would he respond? For one moment I was sure he would refuse. It seemed like forever before he turned to face us.

"When do we start?"

Mom had begun to cry. Dad moved toward Brett, hesitantly placing a hand on his shoulder. I watched to see how my brother would react. Brett turned toward Dad, his face contorting as he fought for control of his emotions. Then Dad drew him close, holding him tightly, and they both began to weep.

I didn't see anything else that happened. I just sat and cried.

The following morning Brett visited Dana in her room before she left for another trip to the center. She had requested that he come to her before they left. Brett had squared his shoulders before he went in. I could imagine what a difficult thing it was for him to face her. It had been quite some time since he'd seen Dana.

When he came back out, his head hung low and his eyes were red. I tried to guess what she had said to him. I was certain that a great deal of it must have been her attempts to thank him, but he had been with her for some time. She must have said a number of other things as well. But whatever it was, it seemed to have had an overwhelming effect on Brett.

Corey and I stood with Max at the window and watched them all leave. Then they disappeared down the driveway, and I was left alone. It was some time before I could rouse myself. I felt listless and ashamed. I had hoped that it wouldn't be me, and I had gotten my wish. It was an empty feeling to know I had not even wanted to help my sister in the only way that any of us could.

CHAPTER
SEVENTEEN

MORE THAN EVER it seemed that all the conversations in our house were concerning Dana's illness, the treatments she'd had or was due to have, and plans for her upcoming marrow transplant. Mom was in Dana's room constantly, checking her temp, giving her medicine, making sure she was drinking enough, and on and on.

There wasn't such a thing as family mealtime anymore. We heated soup, popped something in the microwave, or Dad picked up something at a fast-food place on his way home from work. Then we ate whenever we could fit it in, often one at a time. We didn't even bother to set the table anymore.

Corey didn't seem to be suffering as far as growth was concerned. Every now and then, I looked at him and realized with a bit of sadness that he was no longer my baby brother. It almost seemed that I was losing him too. I never had time to really enjoy him anymore, mostly just making sure he was dressed properly and fed and fairly clean.

There was constant contact with the center. Either Dad was on the phone with some doctor or Mom was receiving new instructions from a nurse. I hardly ever had a chance to even call Marcy. But then, I had rather grown away from Marcy anyway. She didn't play basketball, and I no longer went to the youth group regularly. I still saw Graham quite often, but I tried to avoid all discussion of Dana's illness with him. It was easier than trying to carefully say things so I wasn't expressing something I didn't really feel or believe. Still, my conscience suffered sometimes at the deceitful impression that was left by what I *didn't* say.

Dana was taken in for some more tests and analysis. Mom looked a little brighter when they returned home. The report was that unless something happened to set her back, they could go ahead with the transplant. We were all anxious for this procedure to actually take place—all, maybe, except Brett. I wondered if he was dreading it as much as I would be. It was scary to think of doctors invading your body, removing something vital for life and health.

The date was set, and Grandma promised that she'd come to be with us. And then, as usual it seemed, Dana messed it up again.

I guess it wasn't Dana's fault. She didn't get sick on purpose or anything, but all of a sudden her temperature shot way up and she began to shake and cough and nearly choked. When she started to turn blue, Mom screamed for Dad. It was utter chaos. The ambulance was called again. They took her to the city hospital after they attached her to tubes and oxygen and all that. I didn't hang around to watch. It was too dreadful and frightening. I was sure she was going to die before they even got her to the hospital. I think Mom thought so too. Even with all

Dana had already been through, I had never seen her so frantic.

This time Dana spent almost two weeks in the hospital, too sick for them to even dare try to transport her to the cancer treatment center. Every time the phone rang, we expected it to be bad news. Mom stayed right at the hospital, and Dad might as well have. He was scarcely ever at home. So Corey and I were pretty much on our own. I had to miss a few school activities. Corey needed someone to be there for him. It was okay when we were both at school. But he couldn't be alone once the school day was finished—he wasn't even nine yet.

Brett was dropping in fairly often. He didn't really say so, but I think he was a bit worried about us. Just brought things to eat and checked out things like Corey's Cub Scout schedule and the like.

Finally Mom came home, more to make sure we were okay and to catch her breath than anything. She looked hollow eyed and bone weary. I had never seen her look so tired.

"I think she's going to make it," she informed us quietly, sitting at the kitchen table resting her head against her hand. "She is gradually getting back some strength again."

And Dana did. But it was a long, difficult haul. And then the doctors had to increase or change her medication or something in order to try to build her up again for the transplant procedure. She was back and forth to the treatment center, and I wondered if Brett appreciated the delay. I guessed he was rather anxious to get it over with so he could stop dreading the unknowns of the whole thing.

Finally a new date was set. I knew that Mom and Dad

were praying fervently that nothing would happen to postpone the operation again. I would have been too, had I still been praying. And I guess I would have been praying—if I had really believed that prayer did any good.

Corey made up for it. It was really strange, but I was glad. I guess, way down deep inside, I still had the impression that prayer *did* make a difference, because even in my cynicism I made sure Corey said his prayers each night. And I listened carefully to make sure he covered everything concerning Dana. I thought *if* God could hear and *if* He cared to answer, it just might be that He would listen to Corey.

I suppose I was sort of waiting to see what disaster would strike to prevent the treatment. But none did. Dana was not at all well, but she was no worse than she had been for weeks. The doctors said to bring her in. So Mom and Dad phoned Brett to be at the house by ten the next morning and packed up the car.

❧   ❧   ❧

Grandma was away on a cruise with Mr. Paulsen when the date for Dana's treatment was finalized. So Dad had to quickly arrange for someone else to stay with us. The woman who was coming was from some home-care facility. I was really nervous about it. We didn't even know her.

I had looked in on Dana that morning before leaving for school. She was pale and still struggling to breathe properly, but she looked as if she was sleeping. Knowing how little sleep she actually got, I didn't waken her. I felt a knot in my stomach as I turned to go. I wasn't sure I'd ever see Dana again. She was so desperately sick. If only she could get the treatment she needed—then she'd have a chance to get well again.

I was awfully tempted to pray. I needed something. Someone. I felt so all alone and helpless. But I swallowed the lump in my throat and went down to see if Corey was ready for the school bus.

We had to leave for school before the new "sitter" arrived, and I knew Mom wouldn't have much time to acquaint her with the house and fill her in on what was expected. I supposed there'd be much I would need to explain later.

I hated coming home that night. I think if Brett had still been in his little apartment, I would have taken Corey by the hand and gone there. But Brett wasn't there. He was at the cancer center too. Fleetingly I wondered if people who were giving their bone marrow ever died doing it. Then I pushed the thought aside. I wouldn't even let myself think about that.

When the bus brought us home at the end of the school day, I grabbed my own backpack of books with one hand and Corey's with the other and headed for the exit. Corey was still trying to finish a story he'd been telling his friend Blake. I guess it was about Max. He tried to hang back even as I pushed him forward. "And she did," he called back. "She dug a hole and put it right down in it."

I knew the bus driver didn't like dawdlers, so I tried to hurry Corey along. He was still walking backward, yelling back to Blake. "Next time I'm gonna give her my old fuzzy slippers to bury. I want new ones. Leather. Like Brett's."

I wasn't looking forward to arriving home. I had no

idea who it would be who'd welcome us. Was she strict or lenient? Sweet or sour? She could be anything.

"Erin," asked Corey, "who's the lady who'll take care of us? Is she nice?"

"She'll be nice," I muttered to try to ease Corey's mind. I figured she wouldn't be able to keep the kind of job she had if she wasn't at least decent.

"Why didn't Grandma come?"

"She's on a trip."

"With Grandpa?"

Corey was the only one who could manage calling Grandma's second husband "Grandpa."

"Yes."

"Why?"

"Why? Because they needed a little vacation."

"Why didn't they go on vacation after Dana got better?"

"Corey, I've already explained. This is the third time they've scheduled this vacation. Dana's treatment dates keep being changed."

"Will they change them again?"

"No . . . I don't think so. They're at the center now. This time it should work out okay."

"Good," said Corey, "'cause I asked God to make her better—really fast. I don't like it when she's so sick."

I didn't like it either . . . but I didn't say so.

Corey changed the subject. "What's her name again?"

"Whose name?"

"The lady who's taking care of us." Corey sounded rather impatient that I wasn't following his train of thought.

"I don't know. Mrs. Lewis or Leon—or something."

"Leo—that's it. Leo." Corey was pleased to have the

name in place. I had no idea if he was right, but I really didn't care.

It was very unnerving to open our door and feel like an intruder. This strange woman was already there in our kitchen. She looked like a pleasant-enough sort, nothing unusual. She was working on a casserole or something. Ingredients were scattered about on the counter. She turned and smiled. "Hi," she greeted us.

I guess we answered. But Corey turned suddenly shy. I felt him push back against me.

"Would you like some cookies and milk? I baked chocolate chip. I hope that's your favorite."

That caught Corey's attention. He loved chocolate chip cookies.

"Just toss your jacket and pull up," she continued. "My name's Meg."

Meg? Mom and Dad never allowed us to address grown-ups by their first name. But Corey, who suddenly seemed perfectly at ease, threw his backpack and his jacket on the bench just like he had been invited to do and moved toward a chair at the table.

"Can I have three, Meg? I'm really hungry."

She added another cookie to the two that had been placed beside Corey's milk glass.

"I don't think I'll have any," I said hesitantly. "I have lots of homework."

It just didn't seem right to be having cookies and milk with some stranger named Meg in Mom's kitchen. She just nodded and let me go.

* * *

The first phone call came that night. They had arrived safely. Dana was tucked in at the center, and so was Brett. He was going through a few more preliminary tests in preparation for the surgery. The doctors were hoping to proceed the next day.

We were all a bit anxious the next evening. Even Meg seemed to have an ear tipped toward the phone. The call finally came. The transplant surgeries were over. Things had gone reasonably well. The doctors were pleased so far. Brett was just fine, and Dana seemed to be resting well.

Now it was a time for *wait and see.*

CHAPTER
EIGHTEEN

THE BONE-MARROW TRANSPLANT seemed to
work for a while without Dana's body reacting against the
new cells. We had hoped that things were going to be
okay. However, she'd needed so much of various medications to fight off any possible reaction that her body
seemed unable to cope with anything new. She really was
not doing very well.

She was kept in the hospital so they could monitor her
closely and also so she wouldn't be at risk for infections.
Mom and Dad were back and forth so much I figured
they'd wear out the road.

Meg came and went with regularity. Corey and I got
quite used to her. Grandma came a couple of times too,
but it wasn't always easy to make the necessary plans ahead
of time.

In a weird kind of way, it became almost routine at
our house to live with interruptions. I think we got used
to it, and we assumed that whatever plans were made were
sure to be rearranged in some fashion. Or discarded entirely. It got so it was pretty hard to schedule anything at
all. You just knew they wouldn't work out. Graham was

always so understanding whenever I had to call and cancel an outing with the youth group at the last minute. It made me realize what a special person he was. Our *first date*—if you could call it that—had been over a year before. Mom and Dad didn't really view it as dating, since we always went with the church group or with one family or another. But for me, in a teenage way, I thought of Graham as my special friend. My "steady." In fact, Graham was about the only truly steady thing in my life.

But even though I was used to the chaos, I was not prepared for Dad's next announcement to the family. He had gathered us together on one of those rare occasions when we were all home at the same time—all except Dana, who was still in the hospital.

I noticed again how weary he looked. But there was something else. His shoulders sort of sagged, and his eyes had a troubled look. He reminded me of our team after we'd just lost an important game. That defeated look. I was sure it was going to be more bad news about Dana.

But after looking over at Mom as though to gain some strength from her support, he let his eyes travel over us one by one, then took a deep breath. "Your mom and I have been doing a lot of thinking—and praying—and we've finally decided what will be best for us all is to . . ." He hesitated for a moment. I think that it was hard for him to continue. ". . . to sell the house."

I was totally confused. What did he mean? What house?

"We really don't need a place this big," he went on. "Grandma isn't with us anymore, and Brett is on his own. So this house is really more than we need."

Corey caught on first. "You mean *this* house?" he burst out.

Dad nodded.

"But we can't. All my stuff is *here*."

"We'll move your stuff."

"Not my tree. Or the fort. And Max likes it here."

"We all like it here," put in Mom. Her voice sounded weak.

"Then why are we gonna move?"

I think Corey expressed the feelings of all of us. Dad ran his fingers through his hair and looked over at Mom.

"It's not that we don't like it here," he said. "But this place is more than we need now, and the monthly payments . . ." He paused, then must have decided on another approach. "There have been a lot of extra expenses with Dana's illness. We're getting deeper and deeper into debt. Selling the house is one way we could ease some of our monthly bills. We could find a nice smaller house in a good neighborhood and—"

"But I still couldn't move my tree." Corey seemed to be the only one able to respond.

"No," Dad agreed. "You couldn't move your tree. It's too big now. But you might be able to plant a new one. Watch it grow."

Corey didn't look convinced. In the meantime, my thoughts were swirling one way and another. I had a tree too, though I certainly wasn't as attached as Corey. It would be far tougher for me to leave Dana's little weeping willow or Corey's mountain ash. Though it would certainly be a relief to leave behind all the reminders of Dana's illness and crisis moments. But I did like it here. It was home. It had been home now for almost three years. I liked the space. The view. The feeling of having room to grow. I'd hate to lose this house. I'd really hate it.

Brett sat and said nothing. He didn't even look up. I didn't suppose he'd care much one way or the other because he had his little apartment in town. I felt a bit peeved that he wasn't willing to fight for the rest of us. Wasn't that what big brothers were for?

To my surprise he did speak up. "What if I moved back home and helped with the house payments?"

I was as surprised as Dad looked. Independence had been Brett's chief goal for a very long time. But after the initial shock, Dad shook his head slowly. "I appreciate that, Brett. More than I can say . . . but no. Even that wouldn't be enough. With what we have invested here, we hope to be able to purchase another house outright so we won't have a monthly house payment to worry about. It's very important that we not put our home in jeopardy with a second mortgage. With a house paid for, we can start to work on some of the other bills. See if we can get them whittled down."

I hadn't realized that our finances were so bad. That there were so many bills to pay.

"We're sorry to have to ask you to . . . to give up your home," Dad went on. "But if we don't make a move—work it out voluntarily—we might be forced to sell eventually. Then . . . we'd have no control."

I felt sick inside.

"When?" It was the first word I'd uttered.

"Well . . . we expect to talk to a Realtor soon. The home could go up for sale by the end of the week."

"Max won't like it," Corey insisted, but his tone indicated that he'd given up his fight.

Brett said nothing. Just sat there leaning forward, his elbows on his knees and his fists tucked under his chin. His eyes looked dark. Brooding. I wondered what he was thinking. For the first time in many months I felt sorry for Brett. Really sorry. I wished there were some way I could reach out to him. I could see that he was in as much pain as the rest of us.

"When do we hafta move?" This question from Corey.

"That's hard to say. Sometimes a house sells quickly. Sometimes it takes a very long time. Sometimes—on rare occasion—it doesn't sell at all."

I saw a glimmer of hope lighten Corey's eyes.

"But we are hoping—praying—that this one will sell quickly," Dad explained. "We really do need the money."

I shrugged and fidgeted to let my folks know as far as I was concerned the meeting was adjourned. There was nothing we could do about it anyway. But Dad straightened in his chair, looked around the room, and cleared his throat. I knew even before he said it that he was going to suggest we have prayer together. When I bowed my head I clenched my jaw. *Why in the world do we always go through this familiar ritual?* I wondered. *It never seems to do us any good.*

❊ ❊ ❊

On Friday morning a man in a bright jacket pounded a sign into the lawn at the end of our drive. Corey said the jacket was yellow, but I thought it was more of a gold color. But the jacket wasn't what really drew our attention. The sign did. It said our home was for sale.

I thought about it all day at school. I guess I expected to arrive home that afternoon and find packed boxes sitting throughout the house. Or maybe empty rooms with the furniture all gone. But when I walked into the kitchen, nothing had changed. I felt momentary relief. Maybe the house wouldn't sell.

But the sign did not go away. And on the next Monday when I came home from school, I was informed that the real estate agent was bringing someone to look at the house after dinner. Would I please check to make sure my room was presentable?

From then on my room always had to be presentable. Possible buyers tramped through our house on a regular basis. I didn't want to be there. I hated to see them come and go and exclaim about *this* or explain how they would change *that*. One woman even said Corey's tree was too close. She'd have it removed. *Removed*. Without any idea of what the tree was all about, how special it was to all of us.

So I stayed away as much as I could. Mom was often away too. I don't know if she orchestrated it that way or if she really was needed at Dana's hospital. Corey and I, with the help of Meg, managed to keep the house reasonably ready for these intruders. Dad came and went—looking wearier than ever.

During the time people were looking at our house, Mom and Dad were busy looking at other people's houses. It seemed to be a long process without much headway. I wondered if there were really so few house possibilities out there, or if it was just hard to pick one of them after having designed a house for our family and lived in it so long.

At any rate, my parents usually came home discouraged. Then one day they looked a bit more hopeful. They had found one with *promise*. I wasn't too sure what that meant and was hesitant when they wanted to take Corey and me to see it.

I didn't like it. But then I hadn't expected to.

It was a small ranch, pushed up almost to the sidewalk, with dark gray walls and ugly green shutters. The roof came sloping down until you felt you'd need to duck to enter the door. That wasn't the case, of course. It just made you feel that way.

Inside it wasn't much better. Mom walked me through, exclaiming how this could be changed and that could be opened up to let in more light and the bathroom could be enlarged by robbing from the bedroom closet. After where we'd lived, this was not a pleasant house. But I didn't say so. Mom and Dad had suffered enough without my adding to it. I nodded. Even tried to smile. But all the time I was still wishing our home wouldn't sell. That we could stay right where we were. I fervently hoped that Corey was faithfully doing his praying. This was one change in our life we didn't need.

If we did have to move, at least I wouldn't need to be there for long. Like Brett, I'd get my own place. Once I was eighteen I could legally be on my own. Come summer I'd be fifteen and have my driver's permit. Though it did me little good with neither parent available to accompany me on practice sessions.

I was beginning to hope our house really wouldn't sell. I answered the door one night, and there stood the man in the gold jacket. He grinned and extended his hand. I wasn't used to shaking hands with adults—except at church. It made me feel funny.

"Your folks in?" he asked. His voice sounded a bit too cheery. I wasn't used to that either, at least lately.

"My father is."

"May I see him? I've got some good news."

Even as I nodded, I had a sinking feeling. I was sure

that what this man would consider *good news* wouldn't be good news to me. Or Brett. And especially not to Corey. I silently hoped the buyer was not the woman who was going to rip out Corey's tree.

I nodded again and stepped back so the man could come in. Dad was in his office. I went to get him, leaving the man standing in the entry, his jacket looking very yellow in the light of the hallway.

"The Realtor wants to see you," I said to Dad as I poked my head in the door. Then I went on to my room. Later I would look Corey up and maybe read to him for a while. Right now I needed a bit of time alone.

CHAPTER
NINETEEN

IT'S ONE THING TO PACK for a move when you're excited about a new home. It is another matter entirely when nobody wants to leave. This was the case with us. Mom worked for days systematically emptying closets and cupboards and labeling packing boxes. She was getting close to completing the task when the cancer center called again. Dana had taken another bad turn. Mom tossed a suitcase in the car and left, her expression grim, her eyes weary, and her shoulders bent. That left us to finish the last of the packing and make the move.

A sense of mourning fell over our house as we gathered together the last of our belongings and stuffed them into boxes to be whisked out the door and into the borrowed truck. Our nearest neighbor, Rayna's father, had graciously offered his vehicle, and Dad was glad we wouldn't have to rent a moving van. But the modest-sized truck required many trips and certainly made the whole procedure drag out.

The furniture went last, spread over the course of three days. Brett, Travis, and Graham did much of the heavy lifting and transporting. Dad's time was used up

between trips to the center and the job that he was dog-
gedly trying to fit in. Travis had completed his first year
of college but hadn't started his summer job yet. I think
he enjoyed being back with Brett again. As they worked
together, Travis was telling Brett stories about his classes
and the dorm life. I think, in his own way, he was hoping
to convince Brett that college wasn't so bad. He knew Dad
and Mom were both really disappointed when Brett had
decided to continue his job with UPS instead of leaving
for college after graduating from high school.

The guys huffed and struggled with the heavier pieces,
but little by little our spacious home was emptied of its
contents. I hated the feel of the stark rooms. It made *me*
feel empty inside too. *What an awful way to begin a new
summer,* I mourned inwardly.

Graham was the one who drove Corey and me away
from our home for the last time. Graham reached for my
hand as I struggled not to cry. Then Corey crawled up
from the backseat to sit between us in the front and I
cuddled him close. We didn't look back. It was far too
painful.

The new house was a jumble of furniture and boxes.
Brett had tried to decide where Mom would want things
to be placed, but he had very little knack for it. We rearranged as many of the furnishings as Graham and I
could manage and then tried to stack boxes so they would
be out of the way before he needed to leave for home.
The church had offered to send a group of men to help
with the moving, but with only one truck, it had not
seemed reasonable.

Now I surveyed the disaster area that we were to call
home and dragged myself off to the kitchen to begin
placing dishes into cupboards. It was a time-consuming

task. I was pretty sure Mom would have done a good deal more cleaning first, but I was too tired to care.

It took me another full day before I had unpacked almost all the kitchen things—leaving in boxes what wouldn't fit inside the cupboards. Then during the next day I arranged the bedrooms as best I could, and Dad found time to set up the washer and dryer. We worked together late into the night on the rest of the house. It had begun to take shape, but we worried that Mom would feel compelled to pick up where we'd left off the minute she got home. We both knew what she needed—rest. So we hid as many of the remaining boxes in the basement as we could manage.

When she finally was able to come home and see how we were doing, she seemed greatly relieved. I don't think she had expected us to have accomplished so much of the moving in and arranging.

"Oh, Erin. It's very nice. I like the sofa there, and you've even hung some pictures. Thank you." She reached to hug me close. "Thank you so much. I know it must have taken a lot of time and work."

I thought about asking how Dana was doing, but I decided against it. Mom would let me know when she was ready to talk about it. For now I just followed her to the kitchen while she took her first look around. She exclaimed over the cupboards as she opened each one.

Later Graham and I drove to the corner store to pick up a few groceries. He seemed to welcome the opportunity for us to be alone to talk. As much as I enjoyed his company, I felt just a bit awkward during moments like these when he tried to coax my inner thoughts from me. I knew our closeness was crippled by my disillusionment about God. Graham was a good friend—a best friend—

and I was sure he hoped we could come to mean even
more to each other. But I had presented such a false picture of myself to him. He was the pastor's son. And more
than that, I knew he really believed that God was *God*. I
wondered if he'd even look at me if he actually knew my
heart.

❧ ❧ ❧

Dad did his best to make our new place seem like
home. I think he was particularly concerned for Corey,
who was still mourning the loss of his mountain ash. *"It
was just getting big enough to make berries to feed the
birds,"* Corey had lamented as he'd told it a tearful
good-bye.

As soon as we were functional in the new house, Dad
proposed that he and Corey make a trip to the nursery. I
had no idea where they'd put trees. The small backyard
was crowded as it was. But Corey fairly danced through
the kitchen where I was trying to heat some spaghetti for
lunch.

"We're gonna get some more trees. They'll grow up
fast." I wondered if the last statement was his attempt to
console me.

But Dad checked his enthusiasm. "Just one," he said.
"Only one."

Corey spun on his heel and looked at Dad, his eyes
wide.

"There's only room for one." Dad was quite firm
about it.

I could tell by Corey's face that he was dreadfully disappointed. His chin dropped and his eyes looked so sad.

Then he swallowed and nodded.

We ate our lunch in relative silence. Then Dad and Corey left and I cleaned up. When they returned, a small spruce tree rode in the back of the van.

"Have you decided where you want to put it?" I heard Dad ask as he wrestled the tree through the van's back door.

Corey had no hesitation. He ran on ahead and stood firmly on the spot he had chosen. He must have already given it careful thought.

"Right here."

Dad rested the tree on the ground. A frown creased his forehead. "You can't see the tree out of your window from there."

"I know."

"I thought you wanted to be able to watch it. You said you picked the spruce because the robins like the branches to build in."

"I know," said Corey. "They do. I watched them build in Brett's tree at our other house."

"But you don't want to watch them build here at this house?" Dad seemed puzzled.

It took a moment for Corey to answer.

"It's for Dana," he finally said. "She can lay right in her bed and watch the robins."

I turned away. I didn't want to cry, but the tears were already stinging my eyes. Maybe Dad was bothered by tears too. It was a few moments before I heard the shovel start digging the hole for the new tree.

❧　❧　❧

Mom called every night with a summary of the day. But the news about Dana continued to worsen. Things had come to the point where she asked us to keep the pastor updated. I wasn't quite sure why she wanted him to be the first to know. It probably had something to do with the prayer thing again. It seemed to give her comfort to know that our pastor was aware of the situation on a daily basis. When Dad was home, he was the one to make the call. But often, Dad was with Mom and Dana, so I was forced to pass along the information. I hated the job.

Pastor Dawson was a friendly, likeable man. I had always appreciated his jovial way of putting everyone at ease, but I wished with all my heart that he were someone other than Graham's father. It made me twice as uncomfortable making the calls.

It was a difficult balancing act for me, giving coherent summaries of Dana's progress and trying not to immerse myself in the medical jargon. Even worse, it was hard for me to express normal concern for my sister without stating definite prayer requests. It seemed so hypocritical to ask others to pray when I wasn't praying myself. I wished I could have remained out of it entirely, but I couldn't tell my parents I wouldn't help. So I went along with everything they asked me to say.

"Hello, Pastor Dawson."

"Erin, it's good to hear from you. I've been wondering if the new antibiotic has been effective."

I recited the details as best I could. "I guess it is helping. Mom says Dana's fever has dropped a little and that her potassium level has risen slightly. But she was only able to walk a few steps and is extremely nauseous. They're concerned about her blood count, which is still the biggest problem because they're not seeing the improvements they feel they should have by now."

I could tell he was making notes as I spoke. "Oh, I'm so sorry. How are your parents holding up?"

"Well, they had a visit today from a family whose son had leukemia. When they bring him back now to get his testing done to make sure he's still in remission, they visit throughout the ward. I guess Mom was very encouraged to talk with them. And she was very touched that someone would go to that trouble to encourage others."

"I'm glad to hear it, Erin. And how are you and Corey?"

"We're all right. Thanks."

"Well, I'll pass this through our prayer chain. Thank you for calling."

"Thanks. Bye." I laid the phone back in its cradle and put my head in my arms on the counter beside it. How much longer could this possibly go on?

I jolted when Corey tapped my elbow. "Erin, are Mom and Dad coming home?"

"Not tomorrow. They're going to stay with Dana."

His eyes clouded. "I made a tower with my Legos. It's the biggest I ever made. I wanted Mom to see it."

"Save it. They might be home in a few days."

His face set in a stubborn frown. "You always say that."

"Say what?"

" 'In a few days.' That's what *everybody* always says. But I don't think they mean it. I think it's just a lie." He spun on a heel and went back to his room. Suddenly I heard a crashing sound, and I hurried to follow him.

"Corey, stop. Don't knock it down. You worked so hard."

"But I wanted Mom to see it. And she won't." He

kicked the pile of tumbled bricks again. Then his anger dissolved into tears. "I just want to see her, Erin. I just want Mom."

"I know, Corey." I reached for him, but he pushed me away.

"Don't. Leave me alone."

He had never spoken that way to me. I wasn't sure how to react. "Do you really want me to leave?"

"Yes." His chin came out, and he kicked the Legos again. "Just leave me alone."

I closed the door quietly and went back to the kitchen. I had done everything in my power to be what Corey needed me to be. Over the last few years I had mothered him, cooked for him, read to him, and taught him to read. He deserved to have his mom home—some of the time. Resolutely I picked up the phone and dialed the emergency number I'd been given to leave messages.

"Dad, it's Erin. Corey's really upset. I think Mom needs to come home. If you get this message, please call me back. It doesn't matter how late it is. Bye."

❧ ❧ ❧

Mom arrived home the next day. Dad had stayed behind. I left the house soon to give Mom time alone with Corey. Besides, I was afraid she would start telling me about the treatments and what Dana was going through. I didn't want to hear it. I called Graham from the nearby gas station, and he invited me to join him at the church, where he was going to make updates on the church web page. He was soon there to pick me up. The long drive didn't help. I was still angry by the time we arrived at the church office. It wasn't fair. Everyone had already suffered so much. And Dana hadn't improved at all.

I thought I could hide my anger. I planned to just keep the feelings bottled up again, but I wasn't successful this time.

I'd been silently watching the screen as Graham clicked away at the keyboard, updating the posted information. But my thoughts had been drifting far beyond the computer screen.

"What's wrong?" I hadn't noticed that Graham had stopped what he was doing and was studying me instead. "You haven't said a word for an hour. Please, Erin," he pressed. "Tell me what you're thinking about. Is it Dana?"

"It's always Dana." I let the words fly with more force than I'd expected.

Graham pushed away from the desk and took my hand. "You'd feel better if you just talked about it once in a while."

He had no idea what he was saying. I drew my hand back and stood up. "I need to walk."

"I'll come."

"But you've got more to do."

"It can keep." He seemed to have decided not to let me outmaneuver him this time.

I headed down the empty hallway, and he followed close behind. Suddenly I was angry with him too, and I turned to face him. "You don't understand, Graham. You don't know what it's like. You just don't understand."

"*Make* me understand."

"You can't!" My hands began to shake a little. "Please, leave me alone. I just need to be alone." It sounded like

Corey's words echoing in my mind.

"But, Erin, you're my best friend. You're more than a friend. Let me help."

The words exploded from me with pent-up emotion. "How can you say that? You don't even know me."

Graham recoiled, his face full of confusion.

"This . . . this idea you have of me . . . it's not what you think it is." The words burst from me, and there was no going back now. "It's not even real. It's like a game. I pretend to be what I think you want me to be. But I'm not that. I'm not like you . . . and I can't pretend anymore. I don't believe that . . . that God is what He's supposed to be."

I could see he was hurt and bewildered, but I couldn't stop. "And I don't care anymore. I don't even care what happens to Dana." Once the words were out, I knew they weren't true. I cared very much. "I mean, I don't think I can . . . I don't think I have the ability to care anymore."

At Graham's stunned look, I hurried on. "You don't know. . . . You can't understand. You've never had anything bad happen to you, so you can just go on believing that God is . . . is like a . . . a Santa Claus or something." Tears by now were pouring down my cheeks as I looked up at him. Graham stared back at me for a long time. I finally spoke again. "I lost my sister a long time ago. Don't you understand? *My* Dana is not the body that's lying in that hospital. She was . . . she *was* my friend. She was my *best* friend." I could hardly go on, but I forced myself to be truthful. "I don't pray about her anymore, Graham. I don't pray about anything. I don't think God listens. I don't think He cares about me, and I sure don't think He cares about her." My last words were nearly drowned out by my sobs.

Graham stepped back. I covered my face with my hands so I wouldn't actually see him walk away. I turned to lean against the cold concrete wall and gave myself to weeping.

It was some time before I gained enough control to begin wiping away the tears. When I finally gathered myself together and pushed away from the wall, I was shocked to find that Graham was still there.

He was silent, still confused, and even looked scared. But he hadn't walked away as I'd expected. And now that my outburst had passed, I was too embarrassed to say anything more.

Graham eventually seemed to find courage to speak. "I know you're angry. And I know you're hurt. It's true that I can't feel what you feel. I can only imagine. But, Erin"—his eyebrows knitted together and he searched my face closely—"don't say God doesn't care. Because He does. And someday this will be over, and you'll be facing Him. You can either be ashamed of the way you respond now, or you can use this as a time to show your faith. To grow."

"But I don't *have* faith anymore," I insisted, the tears threatening again. He clearly hadn't heard a word I'd spoken.

"I don't believe you, Erin. You're being lied to. Satan is using this to try to tear you down. But God won't let him. I know that is true."

Satan? I wondered why we needed to include him in this conversation. It was God. Wasn't it God's decision that Dana be sick and God's choice that we watch her suffer? But Graham sounded absolutely certain that my confusion was from another source. An evil one. Could I have been wrong in blaming God?

After a heavy silence, Graham offered, "Do you want me to drive you home?"

I just nodded.

The ride was a silent one. It wasn't until Graham walked me to the door that he spoke again. "I'm going to pray for you, Erin. I'm going to pray that you face up to God. If we can't see each other anymore, that's okay. I don't want you to have to pretend. Not to me or to anybody. But I do care about you. Very much. Like a sister, if that's all you want. The most important thing is that you get your view of God lined up with the truth. That you don't lose your faith in Him. That's what matters most. I'll be praying for you. Every day."

Graham took a deep breath, tried for a smile, and walked away then. I stood and watched him go. I was astonished that his faith was so unshakable.

❧ ❧ ❧

I saw very little of Graham for the remainder of the summer. I wasn't sure if he was angry with me, but I tried to tell myself that it didn't matter all that much. And I was so truly relieved to feel like I could stop living a lie all the time. But I missed him deeply—most of all his ability to make me laugh. But at least I felt like I could be honest again.

Dana came home near the beginning of August, just as we were gearing up for school. This would be my sophomore year, and I wondered how much of it would be used up in emergency calls during the middle of the night, lengthy conversations with inquisitive friends about Dana's health, and taking care of all the things

Mom was too tired or too busy with Dana to do. But I was glad they were home again. Even with Dana requiring so much care. It was better for Corey this way. I supposed it was better for me too.

I missed our other house more than ever. Cramped closets, close quarters, and no place to go to get away from the situation made me feel boxed in.

Corey was starting fourth grade, and it seemed easier for him to be back in school. It filled his days. There were friends to see and challenges for him to conquer. Summer had been hard for him. He'd spent far too much time alone.

Brett, of all things, had started to come around to visit or to stop for supper. I wondered where he stood, and if he was still angry about taking second place to Dana's disease. He never said anything to me. And I didn't ask.

But Dana was still not really improving. She stayed in her room all day, though she was able to sit at her computer some of the time. I think it was her way of reaching outside her limitations, gaining some measure of freedom. I was glad she'd found *something* she could do to pass the time.

No matter how late it was when I finally entered our room to retire, Dana was still awake. Still restless. We talked then. I couldn't avoid it. It seemed strange at first. It had been so long since we'd really talked. At first it was just polite little snatches of conversation. I didn't ask her how she was feeling. I guess I was afraid she might tell me. I didn't want to discuss her illness. I didn't want to hear of more complicated medical procedures that weren't working.

Instead, I told her little things about my day. About friends we had in common. Just little bits of news that I heard at school or in the town.

Gradually the conversations grew longer, more complex, until I found myself actually looking forward to them. It was *almost* like it had been before Dana became so ill. But then I'd look over at her as she grimaced with a sudden pain, or closed her eyes tightly while she struggled to take a deep breath, and all the joy would go from the exchange. Pretending didn't change things. Dana was very sick. Then I'd suggest that she needed her sleep and turn over with my back to her so I wouldn't need to watch her. It was hard to block it all out. I found myself wishing the house were bigger. That I didn't have to share a room with Dana. I even thought that I couldn't wait until I'd be able to move out of the house. Anything to block out the glimpses of a sister who was so sick, who needed so much.

CHAPTER
TWENTY

WE HAD VERY LITTLE TIME to readjust to Dana's being at home. Her frequent visits back to the cancer treatment center revealed that the marrow transplant had not been effective. She would need to be readmitted, and the prognosis was quite grim. Dad said the cancer had spread to some of her other organs. I shuddered when I thought about the patchwork of disease that her body had become.

And it had been given a new name—*acute myeloid leukemia*. It sounded much worse to me. I didn't know if they'd misdiagnosed her in the first place, if this had developed in addition to what she'd already had, or if it had been that all along and they'd just put the real name to it. But it was very sobering.

Dana's attitude had changed along with the new diagnosis. She seemed resigned to the fact that she would not get well again. She had not seemed surprised by her worsening condition. She had not tried to fight against it in any way. Almost as if she had expected it.

We packed her things and carried them back out to the car. She had hardly gotten back to us, though it had been over a month. I wished I could feel numb as I so often had before. I tried to put the emotions aside, but it was as if the calloused wounds around my heart had broken open again. I loved her so much. And yet—I could hardly admit it even to myself—I almost hated her too. I tried in my mind to separate her from the disease, but it had so completely consumed her. And the fact that she seemed to accept the additional diagnosis so easily only increased my anger about it all.

With no outward trace of my turmoil, I gingerly hugged my sister good-bye. She was sixteen. She was bald, frail, emaciated, and sick. And she had already wasted three long years of her life fighting leukemia. I turned away and walked toward our little house.

※ ※ ※

I had never before been to visit Dana at the treatment center, but Dad and Mom had sent word for us to come. That in itself was a little scary, though they tried to assure us that there was no immediate crisis. "It's time" was all Mom said.

Brett drove. He and Corey and I rode together. We even had to take a map along to make sure we could find our way. Brett had paid little attention when Dad had done the driving. Mom or Dad could probably have driven there in their sleep—and it was likely they had come very close to it on occasion.

We asked at the front desk to be given directions to Dana Walsh's room. The receptionist smiled broadly and called an attendant to show us the way.

"We all love Dana," she informed us. "She's a favorite here."

I cringed. Who would want to be a *favorite* at a cancer treatment center? But I followed along behind the young woman in white. The walk from the nurses' station to Dana's room took us down several long hallways. And of course there was evidence of the sick all along the way. There was the hospital odor hanging in the air, and wheeled carts carrying medications, and gleaming medical equipment stored here and there. Snatches of conversations reached us as we passed each open door, carried on by low, respectful voices. Nurses worked behind their counters at almost every turn. Most of the patients who walked toward us down the hall or rested in the small sitting areas were old. Here and there was someone who looked to be the age of Mom or Dad. I thought about Dana, here among the elderly, dying alongside them. It just wasn't fair.

God must not care about fairness, I thought fleetingly.

Then the attendant pushed through a double set of doors, and I realized that I had been wrong about this being the domain of the aged. Here were the children. All ages. All descriptions. Many of them had bald shiny heads or else hats that betrayed their attempt to hide the fact. I noticed some with missing limbs. Those who were lying in the rooms we passed were hooked to tubes for medications and nutrition. Yet many of them were smiling, as if they were not in a hospital being poked and cut and forced to endure all manner of sickness in the name of healing. I choked back my tears and turned my head away.

I could hear Mom's voice, and I knew we were approaching Dana's room. I braced myself for the whiteness, the starkness, the smell of disinfectant.

Dana's room was nothing like I expected. There were balloons on the window ledge, waving brightly with each gust of air, and stuffed animals on the little table by the door. The walls were covered with cards and letters—many of them e-mails that had been printed and saved. And there were pictures everywhere.

"Hi, guys." Dana sounded weak, but she managed a smile.

Corey moved toward her first. He grasped her hand and returned the smile. "I like your room. It's got neat stuff."

She swallowed hard before she could speak again. "I'm glad you're here."

"Hi, Dana. Hi, Mom." Brett walked to where Mom was seated and leaned down to hug her.

"Did you have any trouble finding the place?"

Corey spoke for us. "No, Brett only turned wrong once."

"Hi, Erin."

My eyes met Dana's as she spoke my name, and I forced my legs to carry me to her bedside. She had gadgets all around her and several tubes coming from somewhere beneath her covers. Her face was pale. She made no effort to rise up. I supposed she was too weak for that now. "Hi," I managed.

"I'm glad you came."

I smiled in response. I wasn't glad to be there.

Mom pulled up three chairs, and we took seats around the bed.

"We were working on a scrapbook. Would you like to help?"

"Maybe later." I was glad Brett bowed out of the activity on behalf of us all. I had no interest in an album just then. But Brett cleared his throat like Dad did before beginning a family conference and said, "I'd like to talk to Dana. And Erin."

What was this? I couldn't believe I had heard him say the words.

Before I could react, Mom smiled and took Corey's hand to direct him out of the room. She pulled on the oversized door and let it swing itself shut behind her.

I turned to Brett, wondering what on earth he planned to say.

He began with resolve. "Dana, I asked Mom if I could talk to you. I think she told you that I asked to have some time with you and Erin."

Dana nodded a response.

"I wanted Erin to be here too, because I wanted her to hear what I came to say."

Dana smiled at him silently.

"I want—no, I *need* to say I'm sorry. I'm sorry for the way I've acted since you've been sick. And I'm sorry it made you feel unloved."

I wanted to bolt from the room. It was far too much. To be in Dana's hospital, in Dana's room, and to be hearing Brett coming clean for years of anger, of self-centeredness. I couldn't imagine why he had wanted me to be present.

Tears began to trickle down his cheeks. Here he was, my grown-up brother, crying. Repenting. "I know it's not your fault that you got sick. I knew all along it wasn't right to blame you, but I couldn't seem to stop myself. I hope . . ." His voice cracked, but he went on. "I hope you can forgive me. And I want you to know how much I love you."

"I love you too." Dana could not speak aloud, but she mouthed the words to Brett.

He scooted his chair a little closer to Dana and glanced over at me, as if to include me in what he was saying. I could barely see through my own tears. "I keep wishing we could go back. I hate growing older. We've got so many good memories together as kids. Do you remember the times we spent with Mom and Corey by the creek? Or catching fireflies under the trees at our old house? And the costume party at Carli's?"

Dana pointed up at her collage of pictures. We were all there together—the old lady, the teddy bear, and the butterfly.

"I remember it all—that's how I keep going." She swallowed again. "I just think about all the good times."

Brett managed a crooked smile, and then choked a little. "You always made me feel better than anybody else could. It hurt so much to see you suffer and not to be able to stop it. I couldn't seem to do anything but walk away. I wish I could go back. I wish I could do it all over again—differently."

"It's okay," she whispered. "I understand."

Brett grabbed for a tissue from Dana's bedside table and blew his nose hard. Then he handed one to me. Dana's eyes were teary too. She turned them on me.

"I love you too, Erin."

I pushed my face into the tissue and pretended I too needed to blow. The truth was I just couldn't face Dana's eyes.

"Erin." Brett spoke my name with the same resoluteness he had used to address Dana. "I want to apologize to you too. I've already had a long talk with Mom and Dad, and I talked with Corey last night. I waited to talk to you here because I wanted it to be the three of us again."

I couldn't speak yet, so I blew my nose.

"I've missed a lot of your life too. And I'm sorry. Can you forgive me?"

He stood to hug me and I reached up to hug him back. If only the clock *could* be turned back. I'd give every material possession I'd ever held dear. We embraced for several moments, and then he reached carefully for Dana's hand.

Brett spoke again. "I'm going to go get Mom. Okay?"

"Okay," she answered. "I love you."

"I love you too."

He left us alone, and I turned my face to the floor, trying to gather my composure.

"Erin."

I looked up again. Her gaze was impossible to ignore.

"You're still angry."

My lip began to quiver.

"You'll get past it too. I know you."

A breathy gasp escaped me. "Oh, Dana. You have no idea."

"Yes. I do." Our eyes met again. "Graham came to see me—he told me you were in such pain. That you thought you'd given up on God. But you know what, Erin, He hasn't given up on you. I've been praying for you."

There it was again. I couldn't believe my ears. My sister—my dying sister—had been burdened by a request to pray for *me*. I needed to get out of there. I needed to walk.

"There might not . . . be much time." I could tell the words were coming more slowly. She was laboring to speak. "I wanted . . . you to have a chance . . . while I'm still here."

That was enough. I could take no more. I rose quickly, slipped out the door, and nearly ran down the hallway. It was difficult to find a place to be alone. I stepped into the stairwell and shoved the heavy door closed behind me. I was sobbing and shaking. I couldn't see my way to go farther, so I sank down on the top stair.

Mom found me and took a seat beside me. I had not yet regained control of my emotions, but I decided to talk to her anyway. "I can't do this. I just can't do it."

"Erin, what are we asking you to do?"

"Dana wants me to stop being angry. She says she wants me to do it while she's still alive. Alive! I have to hurry and deal with this while my sister's still alive?" My voice cracked.

Mom sat for a moment before speaking. "It's not for her sake, you know. It's for yours."

"But how can I, Mom? How can I just turn off my feelings so I can clean up all this mess in the time we have left? I don't know how. I don't know where to begin."

"Well, Erin, we need to pray—"

I didn't let her finish. "I can't. I won't do it. How can you even *ask*?"

"I don't . . . I don't know what you mean." Mom seemed to be caught entirely off guard by my outburst.

"We've *been* praying. We've all been praying. It hasn't worked. How can you even suggest that we pray anymore?"

Mom rose stiffly, and I saw the fire in her eyes. "What do you *mean*, it hasn't worked?" Her voice had risen, and it echoed through the open staircase.

"Dana. She's in there. She's dying. God didn't do *anything* for us," I cried.

"Is that what you see? Is that as much as you've understood? Why, Erin, how can you be so blind?" Her passion had not been what I'd expected. "I watched my daughter fall ill to a devastating disease and I prayed like I've never prayed before that I would have the courage and strength to help her. Only God could have carried me through in the way that I needed in order to minister to Dana. I could *never* have managed it on my own. Never."

"But, we asked God to—"

"Let me finish. And your dad, watching the finances as closely as he has. He says over and over again that there's only one answer for the fact that we've been able to stay afloat. God did it, Erin. God made it work. Everything timed perfectly so we could make ends meet. Save a home. Meet expenses. Only God could have helped us manage things that well.

"And all the other timing worked out too—can't you see the *timing*? I had all those special years at home with you—loving you and nurturing you. Even with Corey. If God hadn't held off Dana's illness until Corey was in school, I don't know how I could have managed."

I dropped my eyes in silence.

"And, then, think about the fact that we had Grandma just when we needed her. Not selfishly keeping her, but just at the times when we had so few options. Can't you see it, Erin? It was God." Her voice was pleading with me now. "And Dana's remission. It was a gift. It was the breath of strength that carried us through the painful times that followed. How much more could God have done for us? I've seen His hands holding us up every step of the way."

"But, Mom, she's still dying."

Mom pushed back my hair and cupped my face in her hands, drawing close to me so that her eyes looked directly into mine. "We're all dying, Erin. Life is not what we're trying to hold on to for Dana. It was never about *keeping* her, even though it hurts so to lose her. We're praying to release her . . . whenever it's God's will that she go. And we pray the same for you . . . and for Brett . . . and for Corey. We don't waste our prayers on salvaging life here—we're asking that God call you to the life that's eternal. And that's what God has given to Dana. Life that won't end. She's almost made it through all the pain and arrived at the *beginning*. God has answered *every* prayer."

I leaned against Mom and cried.

❦   ❦   ❦

Mom and Dad spoke with the doctors later that afternoon. More test results had come in. The medical team was ready to admit there was nothing more that could be done for Dana. More treatments would only make her more ill. And so there was not much left to discuss. In keeping with her request, Dana was coming home.

I've no idea why I hadn't realized the inevitable—but I hadn't. Surely in my heart I knew, but my head refused to accept it. Or maybe my head knew, but my heart denied it. I don't know. Anyway, all this time I was thinking that Dana was battling an illness and would eventually win.

I'd been angry with God for not acting. For not short-ening the days to a *speedy* recovery. I guess I was still ex-pecting Him to intervene in spite of all my raging against Him. It didn't seem fair that Dana should have to be sick and weak for such a long, long time just so God could prove to all of us that He was in control. But maybe I had a different idea of how He controls things. . . .

Even my talk with Mom didn't jar me to the realiza-tion that this was a losing battle. Even when I myself had said the words, *Dana's dying.* I guess I hoped if I said them right out someone would step in to deny them. No one did.

It was an e-mail that did it. I walked into our room after an exhausting basketball game. I was feeling up . . . yet I was down. I had played a good game. Coach had been most complimentary . . . but we'd still lost. By one measly point. It might as well have been a hundred. A loss was a loss. It really stung.

I thought at first that Dana was asleep, but she stirred. I hoped I hadn't disturbed her. I heard a little sigh. Then she spoke softly. "Katie's gone. Her mom sent a note."

"Who's Katie?" Even as I asked the question, I knew the answer. I wished I hadn't asked.

"From the cancer center. She was a real sweet kid."

I didn't want to hear any more. I began to gather my things to prepare for bed and headed for the hall bath-room.

"It won't be long until we'll all be there. All in our special little Going Home Club."

Dana's words brought me up short. She spoke with such finality. Such acceptance. I wanted to lash out at her. Deny what she was saying. I swung to face her.

"You're not gonna . . ." Suddenly I couldn't say the word.

But she understood. She looked directly at me, her eyes not wavering. "I am, Erin. I am going to die. Maybe not tonight. Maybe not tomorrow . . . but soon."

She was silent for a moment and then continued, softly. "Remember way back when I said I was afraid I was going to die? Well, I'm not afraid anymore, Erin. Jesus has promised He'll be there waiting for me. Some days I can hardly wait."

I wanted to deny her words. She had said them with a wistfulness. With *longing*. And suddenly it hit me like a blow. It was true. *My sister was going to die*. Die. A teenager. And there was nothing that I could do to stop it. Nothing anyone could do.

I rushed from the room and down the hall to the bathroom. I was sure I was going to be sick. My stomach knotted until I felt nauseated. My legs felt as if they could no longer support me.

How could this happen? To us? What had we done? Why? Why? We had prayed. We had fought. We had even sacrificed—so much—and Dana was still going to die. Die! My sister. My sister.

I felt myself going down and didn't even try to stop it. My body slumped forward. It was much later, after all my tears of anger and pain were spent, that I found myself squeezed into the small space between the tub and the toilet, my face buried in the soft plush of the pink seat cover.

Why haven't I known all along? I chided myself when rational thoughts returned. *Everyone else did. Why have I refused to believe it? Dana. My sister, Dana, is going to die.*

I suppose it was partly because this all had gone on for such a long, long time. We had learned to take one day at a time. Just living and making it through seemed to take all our energy and attention. It had begun to seem that this was life. This day-to-day caring for an ill family member. Now I was forced to realize that there would be an end. An end I didn't want, but couldn't prevent.

A fresh burst of tears bent my head again. I hardly noticed the dampness of the pink plush from my former tears. The pain was almost too intense to bear.

But for some reason I didn't lash out at God again. Maybe I had at last lost all hope that He really did exist.

I had never felt so all alone in my entire life.

CHAPTER
TWENTY-ONE

A SIREN WOKE ME in the middle of the night. It had become a familiar-enough sound that at first I just rolled over to go back to sleep. Then full consciousness jerked me upright. The siren was pulling into our driveway again. That meant Dana was in trouble.

I heard hurried movements and hushed, worried voices. I didn't hesitate longer but fumbled in the dark for my robe. I had retired on the family room couch so Mom could have my bed. Even before I had thrown the robe about my shoulders, I was through the arched doorway.

I was just in time to see Dad's back as he ran toward the front door. "What is it?" I called out after him, my voice husky with fear.

He half turned, but only for a minute, and called back over his shoulder, "Dana's stopped breathing."

A chill passed through my body. I didn't know whether to follow Dad, hurry to where Dana was, or run back to the couch. Then I heard myself saying, "Oh, God. Please . . . help us."

The words came very naturally from the anguish of my

heart. They should have surprised me after what I had been feeling . . . and saying. But they didn't. And in that brief moment, I knew I meant the words. That I believed God *could* help us. And perhaps, even more importantly, I believed that He *would*. He'd been my mother's strength through all this pain. He could do something for me. For all of us.

Already two paramedics, equipment in hand, were dashing up our front walk. They knew the way to the room where Dana lay. They'd been there before.

I wanted to follow. And I wanted to flee. I did neither. I just stood rooted to the spot and continued to pray. Tears ran down my cheeks, and they were not all for Dana. My sorrow and my joy were all so intermingled. Even as my spirit felt the stirrings of renewed life, Dana might be fighting for her last breath. I knew that. But for the first time since her illness I was actually ready to let her go. "Lord . . . your will," I managed to pray. At the same time, I hoped with all of my heart that God would still give us some time together. "I know you can heal her," I whispered. "But if you don't, I know you love her a lot more even than we do. . . ."

By the time the stretcher was pushed rapidly out the doorway toward the waiting ambulance, Dana was breathing again. Raspy, catchy little breaths—but she was breathing. I stood and cried some more as I watched her go. Then I followed outside into the chill of the night, my robe inadequate against the sharp wind. Just before they pushed the stretcher inside, I managed to slip up beside Dana. I didn't know if she could hear me, but I took her cold hand. "Dana," I said. "Dana . . . come back. Come home again . . . okay? And I'm praying for you. . . ."

And then I was being nudged aside by paramedics in a hurry to get her to emergency.

Mom and Dad were already climbing into the car to follow. I watched until the blinking red light turned the corner at the end of the block, and then I returned to the house. But I didn't go right to sleep. I couldn't. I had a lot more praying to do. I fell on my knees by Dana's now-empty bed and confessed to God all the anger and bitterness. I asked Him to forgive me and to cleanse my heart of all its selfishness and sin. By the time I was ready to try to reclaim sleep, I was feeling clean and free from the bondages of bitterness and anger. I was at peace.

❧ ❧ ❧

Dana did come home again. After three days in the hospital, she begged to be allowed to return to her own room. I was waiting for her. Mom and I tucked her in and made her as comfortable as we could. She managed a weak smile. "It's good to be home," she said. She looked at me. "I heard what you said before they put me in the ambulance," she said. "Thank you, Erin. I'm so glad."

I could only squeeze her hand in response.

"Would you like me to read to you?" I eventually offered. Dana had been asking for her Bible to be read to her because she no longer had the strength to hold it and turn the pages.

"Later. Right now I just want to rest."

I saw Mom bite her lip as she started to leave the room. Dana called to her, and Mom turned back, coming over to sit on Dana's bed.

"Momma. One of these times the paramedics aren't going to be able to help me." It was a forthright statement made with no emotion. Mom just nodded.

"Please, Momma . . . let me go. I'm ready to go Home. I'm really . . . really tired of all this fighting for life . . . all the pain. Please . . . next time, don't call them."

I couldn't tell if the intensity in Dana's eyes was stronger than the sorrow in Mom's. I saw her lip tremble. She reached out and took Dana's hand. "Oh, honey," she said, and she was crying now. "You don't know what you're asking of me."

But Dana was persistent. "Momma . . . you know it's going to happen. There's nothing you can do to stop it. The oxygen . . . the medicines . . . they just prolong the pain. I . . . I'd much rather just go to see Jesus."

Her voice was little more than a whisper. Yet we both heard her clearly. For a long moment Mom could not respond. She just sat there holding Dana's limp little hand in her own, rubbing it gently with the tips of her fingers. At last she spoke. "I'll try."

I could see how much the two words cost her. I put my arm around her shoulders and cried along with her. Then Dana looked up at us with the most beautiful smile. "Thank you," she said softly. "I'd like to be Home for Christmas. That will be your gift to me."

❧ ❧ ❧

Mom and Dad talked about it. They concluded that if Dana was to be allowed to die at home, they wanted a medical person on hand to make sure she didn't suffer needlessly. It was going to be another expense, but now we were not thinking of money. A little lady by the name of Miss Williams was found. She was used to in-home care and had sat at the bedside of many terminally ill patients. I liked her immediately. She was so kind and gentle with Dana, seeming to understand exactly what to do to ease her pain.

We were not required to employ her for long. Dana slipped away peacefully just as a full moon was casting its last shadows over the little evergreen Corey had planted outside Dana's window. Miss Williams, who had been sitting by her side, had barely enough time to summon the family. I was always thankful that Brett had decided to stay with us that night. He was there too, his muscled arm tight about Corey's shoulders. And there would not have been time for the ambulance to arrive before Miss Williams whispered, "She's gone."

I looked at her . . . my sister. It seemed that she had been dying forever. At times it had even felt like a bad dream that would just go on and on . . . and now it had actually happened. So quietly. So gently. She was gone. She had made it to heaven . . . Home, in time for Christmas . . . and with days to spare.

I heard muffled sobs around me, but my eyes were so blurred with tears I couldn't see clearly. I pressed up against Dana's bed and took her hand. It was still soft and warm to my touch. "I'll miss you so," I was able to whisper, and I knew it was true. In my heart I knew that in years to come when I thought of Dana, it would not be of the wasted, pain-wracked Dana. No, it would be the vivacious, caring sister with whom I had shared a room. A room where we often snuggled together, telling secrets and stifling giggles under a faded Barbie quilt.

❧ ❧ ❧

The days before the funeral are only a collection of fragmented memories. I was there . . . yet I wasn't. I was still functioning, but my brain didn't seem to be connecting with what was taking place around me. It was an eerie feeling. Or it would have been, had I not had this new understanding of a Presence with me. This wonderful sense of deep peace underlying the sense of loss.

I was in the kitchen making sandwiches for a simple noon meal on the day before the service was to take place at our church. Brett came in and flipped a kitchen chair around to straddle it. "Hi," I said, continuing to spread butter on thick slices of wheat bread.

He just nodded.

I didn't say any more, and he just sat and watched me. Finally he shifted slightly, and the look in his eyes intensified. "How you doin'?"

I knew by the tone of his voice and the look on his face that it was much more than social chitchat. I took a deep breath at the same time I felt the tears pushing behind my eyes. I did manage to say, "Okay."

He nodded. "Good."

We were silent for several minutes again. I guess we were both too emotional to speak. "And you?" I asked at last.

He nodded. But it wasn't an indication that he was also okay. It was just an acknowledgment that he'd heard my question. "I've been better."

My hands slowed in their activity. I stole a peek at Brett. He looked as if he'd "been better."

"Anything I can do?"

He shook his head. "I don't suppose. Guess I'm the only one who can do it. But I think it's too late."

His tone was so full of anguish that I stopped spreading the butter altogether. "What . . . what do you mean?"

"She's gone now," he said, his lip trembling. "I wasn't much of a big brother. I wasn't there for her like I shoulda been."

"You were," I quickly defended him. "You came—"

"That's just it. *I came*—now an' then. I came. I should have been here, Erin."

"*I was here*—at least most of the time—and I couldn't do anything for her."

"You did. Maybe more than you'll ever know. She told me so herself. She said she didn't know what she'd ever have done without you over the last tough years. She said you were the only part of a sane world she could still hold on to. She said that, through you, she at least got to live some of the experiences of being a teenager. All the things she missed."

"She said that?"

He nodded.

Now it was my turn to feel regret. "But she didn't, Brett," I confessed. "I really didn't share a lot with her. I missed those years myself. Almost all of my teen years. They're gone. I never got to do most of the . . . the normal things. I missed . . . so much. Her cancer did that. I hated her illness. I was mean about it. I didn't spend nearly enough time with her. I mean . . . I know cancer took her life . . . but it took so much from all of us. I hated it . . . the constant worry. Mom and Dad always gone. Trying to take care of Corey. Missing all the fun. I hated it." I took a deep breath. "I even thought I . . . I hated God. *Honest.* I was so angry. I'm very ashamed."

"*You* were angry at God?" He sounded surprised.

"And I was worried about you too," I confessed further. "I was so afraid you'd get into really deep trouble and something bad would happen to you. And I couldn't even pray anymore. Only Corey . . . he kept praying . . . for all of us."

"I'm sorry, Erin. I really let you down." Brett sounded so sad.

"It wasn't your fault," I quickly assured him.

"It was. I mean . . . I didn't intend to get in with those guys. It was just . . . I was so . . . so mixed up and they . . . they seemed cool. Before I knew it I was in deeper than I intended to be. I didn't know how to get back out. I wanted to come home . . . truly I did. But every time I came, things were just so . . . so different. It didn't seem like home anymore. I didn't know how to fit."

"None of us knew how to fit. It *wasn't like* home anymore. Not for any of us."

He nodded. I think he was beginning to understand.

"You know what," I continued after a few minutes of silence. "I think it *can* be home again. Oh, not like it used to be . . . but home. We owe that to Corey, Brett. The poor little guy. Do you realize he's spent almost half of his life living this nightmare? Maybe . . . maybe we can still turn that around. He had faith when the rest of us copped out. He's . . . he's a pretty neat little brother."

Brett looked up at me and nodded. I knew he was willing to try.

❧ ❧ ❧

The day was cold and windy when we left for the church to say our good-bye to Dana. The service was to be one of celebration. A celebration of Dana's life and also a celebration that she was now safely at home with her heavenly Father. But at the moment it was hard for me to think of it that way.

We had all shared in the plans for the service. Even Brett had helped. Her favorite songs would be sung by the congregation. The youth pastor would read her favorite Scriptures. Several of the young people would give a tribute—if they could control their tears. Corey had written his own little tribute that he had given to the pastor, and Mom and Dad had agreed that it could be read, though they didn't yet know what Corey had said.

Both sets of grandparents were able to join us, even the ones from Bolivia.

Dana wore her favorite hat—the one with the animals all traveling around it. She hadn't bothered much with hats lately, so it was almost startling to see her in one now.

She lay as if asleep against the frilly white pillow. I couldn't get over how peaceful she looked. There was no more pain-crease pinching in her face. She looked perfectly relaxed. Almost happy. And beautiful. In her hand she held a sprig from Corey's spruce tree, a red Christmas ribbon brightening up the green.

The service went pretty much according to plan. I was proud of the members of the youth group. In spite of their deep emotions, they did a great job of sharing what Dana had meant to them. How her faith grew as she traveled through her dark valley of cancer. Graham said it best. "I prayed for her often. And each time I did, it was as if my prayer came back as a blessing for me. At first I wondered why, and then one day when I talked with her she explained it. Every day she prayed for each member of the youth group by name. She asked God to strengthen our faith. To help us to grow in Him. To use the energies that we were given to honor Him with our lives. I knew then that Dana's prayers of faith were being answered." Graham's voice broke during that last sentence.

We sang the final hymn together. It was an old, old one that Dana loved. Grandpa Tyler's voice was rich with emotion and sang out clearly from where he stood next to Grandma. "When we all get to heaven, what a day of rejoicing that will be. When we all see Jesus, we'll sing and shout the victory." I knew in my heart that Dana would be there waiting when I arrived.

After the pastor led in the last prayer, he pulled out the sheet of paper that Corey had given him. I wondered if he was going to be able to read it, but after a few moments he found his voice.

Dear Dana,

You were a good sister. I remember when you used to read to me and play games before you got so sick. You even let me win sometimes.

I know that you wanted to go to heaven because you hurt so bad, but I really am going to miss you here. Max will miss you too. When you see Jesus, tell him that He needs a big house for our family because we are all going to come.

I love you very much.
Corey

❧   ❧   ❧

Grandma and Grandpa Tyler came back to the house with us after the funeral was over. Grandma and Mr. Paulsen came too. I guess the conversation that took place in our kitchen surprised us all.

"I never thought much about religion," I heard Mr. Paulsen say while I was setting the table. "I didn't care if other people wanted it, but I didn't figure it was for me. But what I have seen over the past months—what I have heard today—there's got to be something to it."

I saw Grandma reach over and take his hand, her eyes shining with tears.

Grandpa Tyler said, "Believe me, my friend, there is. I don't know how we would have made it through the last months without our faith. There is nothing harder on parents than seeing their children suffer. We know how much Dave and Angela—and their children—have gone through over the past years. Such a long, long time to walk through the valley.

"Just as they read in Dana's favorite psalm today, we all need to face that dark valley of death, but the important thing to hang on to is the fact that is first mentioned there. 'The Lord is my Shepherd.' That about says it all. We need Him—so much. First of all as our Savior. Then as our Shepherd to lead us through all of life—especially in the tough times.

"And to know for a fact that the last words are real as well. 'I will dwell in the house of the Lord—forever.' That is priceless. But we can only claim that promise when we have accepted His way. We are sinners. We need to admit that, and seek His forgiveness. 'For God so loved the world that He gave His only begotten son, that whosoever believeth in Him should not perish but have everlasting life.' "

Silently I quoted the well-known words with Grandpa Tyler. For a time I had almost let their truth slip away from me. I clung to them now.

I looked up in time to see Grandpa Paulsen nod his head, a thoughtful look in his eyes. I noticed that Grandma Paulsen, too, was nodding. Inwardly I breathed a prayer. Was this one way God might use our dark valley for good? Dana would have thought it was worth the suffering.

CHAPTER
TWENTY-TWO

OUR HOME WAS ODDLY QUIET and still. There was nothing more that had to be done, yet there was so much that could have been taken care of had there just been the interest or the desire to move forward again. It seemed unnatural to be at rest and together after all our compressed responsibilities and our disjointedness. I think Mom and Dad felt it too. The inactivity. The lack of requirements. It was unsettling.

I tried to think of something I could do to shake the sensation. Surely a project would help, like getting ready for Christmas—or perhaps finding someplace interesting to go. But I had neither the inclination nor the energy to pursue anything, so I did nothing.

One evening Dad tried to read his newspaper, but he soon set it aside. "I think we all need to load up the van and go somewhere."

Mom looked across at him from where she reclined on the sofa, pretending to be watching a TV game show. "What did you have in mind, dear?"

"I don't know. But surely we can think of something. What haven't we done in a while?"

"Bowling," Corey was quick to respond. "I want to go bowling."

I wondered how long it had been since we'd done anything as ordinary as bowling. Probably a very long time, because Corey had never done it.

"Okay," Dad chuckled. "Let's go bowling."

I followed rather halfheartedly as we gathered coats and headed for the van. Mom ran back inside to make a quick phone call. Then we set out. The bowling alley wasn't far from our home. It was crowded and noisy—just the opposite of where we'd been. I supposed if we were trying to shake away the strangeness that we'd felt at home, this was as good a place as any. I sat down and began to put on the bowling shoes.

"Hi, Erin." A familiar voice from behind made my heart skip a beat.

I did manage to respond. "Hi, Graham. I didn't expect—I had no idea you'd be here."

He smiled, broad and pleasant. "Your mom called. She said you might like some company."

I tossed Mom a smile of thanks and moved toward Graham. "I'm glad you came. Are you planning to bowl?"

"I sure am. I've already got my shoes on and everything." He shook a foot where I could see it to prove that it was true, then he winked at me. "I intend to win tonight." He pumped an arm, and we laughed.

We divided ourselves between two lanes. Dad and Mom and Corey played on one. Brett and Graham and I played on the other. None of us were particularly talented, so there was plenty of opportunity for laughs and good-natured teasing. And we all enjoyed watching Corey most of all.

After talking ourselves into a third game, we finally had to admit it was time to call it a night. Graham asked to drive me home, and Dad nodded. I think he was even pleased. It was kind of neat that my parents liked him so much.

We walked to Graham's car in silence, and I climbed inside while he held my door. It felt awfully good to be with him again. Familiar and safe. I leaned back against the seat and waited for him to slide in beside me.

We had already pulled out of the parking lot before he spoke. "I've been thinking about you a lot. How are you doing?" The gentle sincerity was still in his voice. I had missed it so very much.

"Pretty well. Christmas will be hard for us—and good all at the same time. I think we all feel listless, but tonight helped. And it's kind of nice to be with you again." I smiled at my little quip, and he smiled back in the dim lights. I knew there was more he wanted to know, but I wasn't sure where to begin.

"I do see it now . . . the answers to all those prayers," I started slowly as he began driving. "It took some very painful conversations—with Dana and Mom—and God. Now I see so much more of the big picture. The ways God really was taking care of us." I paused to collect my thoughts. "You were right. And Dana said pretty much the same thing. In a way, this *was* an opportunity for us to be faithful. Dana came through with flying colors. She was inspiring. I'm afraid I failed pretty miserably. But I learned a lot too."

The traffic light ahead turned red, and we slowed to a stop. "I owe you an apology, Graham. I said some awful things. I wish I could take it all back."

"Erin," he whispered, "I forgave you for that a long

time ago." His hand reached across and grasped mine. "I only hope there's still time to start over. You know, I meant it when I said that you're my best friend."

My face flushed with the warmth of the joy bubbling up inside me. And I whispered back, "I'm so glad you can still say that."

❀   ❀   ❀

Christmas was fast approaching, though our family felt little in the way of the usual "holiday spirit." Shortly after Thanksgiving we had managed to put up a tree, mostly for Dana's sake, since she was then still with us and Mom thought it might bring her some pleasure. Now it was well into December, and there was little other evidence of Christmas in our home. Even Corey was fairly ambivalent to the fact that his favorite time of the year was almost upon us.

I was doing homework at the kitchen table one afternoon, and Dad came in with the mail and dropped a number of envelopes at the other end. He pulled out a chair and sat down to go through them. "That's interesting," he murmured.

Mom hung her dish towel and moved to take a look. "What is, dear?"

"There are several Christmas cards here from people I don't know. Four addressed to *The Family of Dana Walsh.*"

Mom thumbed through and opened one. She read it aloud. " 'Dear Dana's famly, My name is Matt. I am Dana's frend and I have cancer too. I am 8 years old. My mom said I could have a Christmas card to send you. I want to say I am sorry that Dana died. I miss her. She use to write me alot. Espeshly on the computer. She told me Bible stories. I asked for a Bible for Christmas. Dana said she liked to reed hers, it made her feel better. I hope it helps me too because I will probly die soon too. I hope you have a grate Christmas. Love, Matt Sanders.' " There was a drawing, too, that Matt had made of the children's ward with Dana in the center.

Dad looked a little shaken. Mom laid the letter slowly on the table and dropped into a chair beside him.

"I met him," she said almost tenderly. "It would make Dana so happy to know Matt wants a Bible. I think he was extra special to her."

Dad squeezed Mom's hand and reached for another envelope. " 'Dear Walsh Family, Merry Christmas from Dana's nurses. Angela, we were very surprised by the Christmas gifts. It was so thoughtful of you to send them. It means a great deal that Dana had wanted us to have them. We miss her deeply. She touched so many here. Best Wishes, Joyce, Karen, Gail, Beth and Rita.' "

Dad placed the card back on the table, and Mom began to explain. "We did a little shopping in our last days together. Dana was certain she wouldn't be with us this Christmas, but she wanted to give presents anyway. So she did her shopping early with the help of the Internet." Mom smiled at Dad. "It made her happy knowing she wouldn't really miss out on gift giving."

Dad's eyes dropped. He fingered the card as Mom read another.

" 'Dear Dave, Angela and family, We're the parents of Sondra Fleetwood. We wanted to express to you our thanks for sharing Dana with us. Sondra thought the world of Dana, and we've been so thankful that she could have a friend at the clinic who was so outgoing and caring—and such an example of grace under fire. Few of us can accept suffering the way that Dana did and still be so focused on others. The thought of seeing Dana always gave Sondra something to look forward to on our visits to the cancer treatment center. And I looked forward to the times when we prayed together, Angela. I find it's so much harder to pray when I'm alone. We'll all miss Dana deeply. May God bless your Christmas, Ed and Lisa Fleetwood.' "

By then, we all had tears in our eyes. It was painful to read the cards—and wonderful too. Each one represented another person or family that Dana had impacted. I had not thought much about her world at the center or the friends she'd made. We read another card, and then another. Then we pinned them carefully in a row along one wall in the kitchen. It would be a little easier to celebrate Christmas with the cards as a reminder of Dana.

The next day, four more cards arrived. And on the next, we received a flower arrangement from our church and six more Christmas cards. The kitchen wall was beginning to fill, and with it a warm feeling of Christmas, in its truest sense, grew in our little house. We were enveloped in the wonder of love and hope. The lingering oppressiveness of death was being swept away in the victory of life.

❧　❧　❧

Corey woke early on Christmas morning and came directly to my room. "Erin. Psst, Erin. It's morning. Are you awake?"

I moaned. "I'm awake now. Is anybody else up?"

"Nope, but I think if we make a little noise, they'll come." His eyes twinkled.

"Okay. I'll get up."

I struggled into my robe and walked with Corey to the living room and our Christmas tree. We turned on the Christmas lights, then headed out to the kitchen. I talked him into letting me fix the coffee and a little breakfast for the family before I set him loose to start making his "noise." He worked beside me in the kitchen and then scurried out to bang around near Dad's office door, where Brett was sleeping, stretched out on a cot.

"What'd you let him do *that* for?" Brett's hair was disheveled and his eyes were still nearly shut when he shuffled into the kitchen. I laughed. He still seemed to have trouble getting his motor running in the mornings.

"Merry Christmas, big brother."

"Yah, whatever." But he didn't look as Scrooge-like as his words sounded.

Mom and Dad arrived shortly after Brett. They were pleased to see breakfast already prepared and were glad I'd been able to stall Corey off a little while. It was still very early.

We took our seats and paused to pray. "Heavenly Father," Dad began, "we have so much to thank you for. For each person around this table, and for Dana who is already in your hands. Thank you that because you allowed your own Son to leave your side and come to us so long ago, Dana can be with you now when her life with us is over. Thank you that you are sovereign over life and death."

I sneaked a peek at my family. At Corey, who was nine and still, somehow, our baby. At Brett, who was now a man, and whose heart had returned at last to our family. At Mom, whose eyes looked almost completely rested again from the long struggle that Dana's illness had brought. And at Dad, who had never wavered from his role as leader of our home. I loved them all so deeply. It was so wonderful to feel, though we were not *all* present, that we were whole as a family again.

Dana had selected gifts for each of us. I didn't know what she'd tucked into the other Christmas presents before she had wrapped them, but I was overwhelmed with what she'd placed in mine. Laid on top, in a new frame, was her picture of the costume party—the one she'd placed so conspicuously near her in the hospital room. I studied her joyful, carefree face and the beautiful butterfly wings she'd labored so long to create. I wondered, as I had once read in a children's story, did one really receive wings as a reward upon arrival in heaven? If it were true, then Dana had spent her short lifetime crafting them—just right.

And underneath the picture, wrapped in tissue, were her journals, with a note thanking me for allowing her to share the joys and adventures of my teen years. The years she'd missed.

In my heart I knew that someday I would read through the journals and know from Dana's own heart exactly what her valley of shadow had been like. For now, it was enough just to hold the notebooks against me and smile through my tears.

Children's Books by Janette Oke

Making Memories
Spunky's Camping Adventure
Spunky's Circus Adventure
Spunky's First Christmas

JANETTE OKE'S ANIMAL FRIENDS
(full-color for young readers)

Spunky's Diary
The Prodigal Cat
The Impatient Turtle
This Little Pig
New Kid in Town
Ducktails

CLASSIC CHILDREN'S STORIES
(for older readers)

Spunky's Diary
The Prodigal Cat
The Impatient Turtle
This Little Pig
New Kid in Town
Ducktails
A Cote of Many Colors
A Prairie Dog Town
Maury Had a Little Lamb
Trouble in a Fur Coat
Pordy's Prickly Problem
Who's New at the Zoo?